VAMPIRE UNDONE

KEEPERS OF THE CHALICE 3

TAMAR SLOAN

IVY LANE

CONTENTS

CHAPTER 1

MADELEINE

S hadows and wind. Maddy knows nothing else as she falls. A scream rips from her lungs and tears up her throat, raw as if she's been yelling for hours. Her arms flail around, trying to catch hold of something, anything, which will stop her rapid descent into the dark nothingness that presses around her. The wings she'd sprouted during the battle with Malcolm and his men have disappeared. They faded away as soon as she'd leaped into the Grave.

Suddenly, her back hits something solid and the air is shoved out with a whoosh. She groans, closing her eyes and rolling to the side, gasping for breath. The landing had been rough, but while she struggles to pull air into her lungs, she realizes she doesn't seem to be injured from the impact. When she's finally able to breathe again, she settles onto her back and opens her eyes.

Gray clouds swirl in the sky, twisting and roiling as if on the verge of unleashing a terrible storm. There's no thunder, however, or any other sound for that matter. Maddy braces her hands beside her, grit pressing into her palms, and pushes herself to a seated position. Goosebumps pebble on her arms and she brushes her wind-tangled hair out of her face. Her pulse pounds in her ears, deafening in the utter silence of the world around her. Her lips part and her eyes widen.

This is her world, or at least, some semblance of it.

She's sitting on the ground amid headstones cracked or worn with age. The cemetery. With shaking knees, Maddy rises to her feet and peers around. This has to be the same cemetery, but everything is dark, void of all color except shades of gray and darkest black. She pulls in a breath, noting the complete lack of scent.

Purgatory.

"I did it," she whispers. Her voice seems to be swallowed up, as if Purgatory itself absorbs every sign of life, even a person's voice.

Quinn. Maddy turns, trying to find the woman she'd leapt into Purgatory to follow. There's no sign of her. A voice echoes through the dark and she whirls, but she's still alone.

"Hello?"

Again, the voice continues but Maddy can't pinpoint the source. Then, she catches the sound of her name and realizes Caleb is calling for her.

"Caleb?" For a moment, her heart beats wildly. He didn't try to follow her, did he? Vampires aren't allowed in Purgatory. Her eyes lift skyward again, eyebrows scrunching at the twisting, whirling clouds. Caleb isn't here, or Galina. Maddy's hearing their voices calling from the living realm.

The reality of what she's done begins to sink in. She jumped into Purgatory. She's a living person, and she willingly entered a place only meant for the souls of the deceased. She rubs her arms as her hair raises on the back of her neck. Quinn had jumped in, as well, but while she's technically a soul from Purgatory, she'd worn the mortal shell of a young woman. If Quinn can be here and survive, then so can Maddy.

She props her hands on her hips, peering around. She looks nonchalant, but in her chest her heart races. A sense of wrongness settles on her like a second skin. She shouldn't be here. Jumping into Purgatory was impulsive and foolish. What made her think she'd even get back out? She swallows the bile rising up her throat at the thought.

There had been no choice. An evil entity has taken up residence in Purgatory and is controlling the souls within. Quinn is going to take the obsidian to him whether she wants to or not, and Maddy has to capture her before it's too late.

Caleb's voice still echoes through the cemetery, and though his frantic tones tug at Maddy's heart, she heads toward the road leading back into Mercy City. She has no idea where Quinn's gone, but she's clearly no longer in the cemetery and the city is her best bet. Maddy tries not to think about Caleb's fading yells as she steps onto the road.

Or how it may be the last time she ever hears his voice.

She folds her arms and holds them tight to her body. Purgatory is cold and desolate. She can't imagine spending any length of time here and pities the souls who are trapped in this place, unable to move on to the next phase in whatever afterlife they'll have in their future. Her footsteps are nearly silent, the scuff of her boots swallowed into the pavement. At the edges of her vision, the landscape is nothing more than a blur of gray until she turns her head. Then, it sharpens into focus but everything holds far more shadows than is natural. Maddy tries her best to ignore those shadows, and what may be lurking inside.

Where has Quinn gone? Maddy squints at Mercy City ahead, finding the total lack of any lights or noise extremely disconcerting. If the evil entity Quinn had told them about was truly waiting for her to return with the obsidian, would he have had the chance to get his hands on it already? Maddy quickens her pace, praying she isn't already too late to stop Quinn from giving him the obsidian.

She passes houses and small businesses. Every building seems to be nothing more than an empty shell, a reflection of the real world. She frowns at a swing set in a front yard. One of the swings moves slightly but doesn't make a sound. The sight creeps her out enough to quicken her pace.

The first sign of life drifts across the pavement as the tall buildings of Mercy City rise before her. She halts, heartbeats pounding, and watches what can only be a spirit crossing the road. The man doesn't see her, but he mutters to himself. His eyes are vacant as he walks, zombie-like, around a corner. Maddy loosens her breath. She isn't certain what will happen if she tries to interact with the souls trapped in Purgatory, but she's hesitant to find out.

As she passes the first of the buildings, a few more spirits walk toward her. These, too, are muttering. She presses her back against the glass front of a clothing store, watching as the souls pass.

"The reapers," one says. "When will the reapers come?"

Beside the woman who spoke, a man shakes his head slowly, his eyebrows pinched together. He looks like he's having trouble stringing together a thought. He doesn't answer the woman as the small group passes by.

Hadn't Quinn said something about the souls being unable to pass on? Perhaps the entity was somehow blocking the reapers from entering Purgatory to claim the souls. A dark thought comes to Maddy's mind. Perhaps the reapers are working for the entity. She knows nothing about reapers, but it didn't seem beyond the scope of reality that beings who harvested souls would join up with an entity that thirsted for something as dark and dangerous as the obsidian.

Another spirit passes by. This time, the soul looks right at her, the man's eyes so empty she wonders if he can actually see her. Maddy's lips lift into a tentative smile. The spirit blinks slowly, then peers ahead once more. After several more encounters with the souls of Purgatory, she realizes they can likely see her, but none of them have spoken to her or acknowledged her existence in any way. A woman approaches, the spirit's feet shuffling as if she cannot be bothered to walk properly anymore.

Maddy bites her lip, hesitating as the spirit draws near. Then, she speaks. "Excuse me, I'm looking for a young woman. She's like...well, like me." In other words, not dead.

The soul lifts her eyes to Maddy, lets out a long sigh, then looks away. Muttering to herself, the spirit continues down the sidewalk. A shiver ripples through Maddy at the stale existence these souls are living. Then, out of nowhere, Maddy catches a scent. She can't describe it, exactly. It's almost like a blend of perfume and earth.

"Quinn," Maddy mutters. There could be no other explanation. Nothing else in Purgatory has a smell, so it has to be Quinn.

Like a hound on a scent, Maddy follows the trail. Now and then, she loses the scent and has to backtrack or explore the area. For the most part, though, she's able to keep on Quinn's trail. The excitement at finding evidence of her quickly fades away as Maddy walks on and on, though. Quinn has gone far, she realizes, in just the few second lead the spirit had gained when she leaped into the Grave.

The buildings seem to flash by Maddy one second, then crawl past her the next. She continues walking, but each minute drags on and on until the hours begin to feel like days. She stops, her pulse quickening. It hasn't really been days, has it? She shakes her head. No, it can't possibly be taking so long. She starts to walk again and studies her reflection in a window as she walks. Her pace is normal, a bit quick, even. A part of her had been afraid she was doing nothing more than zombie-shuffling like the souls in the city.

She peers down alleys and into windows. She pokes her head into what was supposed to be a bakery, as the sign on the door indicates, but the chairs remain empty and no freshly baked goods sit inside the glass cases. The scent she had been following to find Quinn fades the farther Maddy travels. Quinn, wherever she is, seems to be traveling faster. Again, Maddy picks up the pace, half-jogging down the sidewalk, but the quickened gait doesn't seem to be getting her anywhere any faster.

A frustrated cry tumbles past Maddy's lips when she turns a corner, certain Quinn had gone that way, and finds nothing but more dark streets, gray skies above, and a lone soul wandering past a computer store. By the time Maddy reaches the next block, she's almost certain she's been wandering for at least a day. Though the sky hasn't changed in color or light to indicate the fall or rise of the sun, she can feel time slipping away in her bones.

Stopping, she leans against the edge of a building and braces her hands on her knees. Her hair slips over her shoulder as she hangs her head, pulling in steadying breaths. She wishes Caleb were with her. It seems strange to miss him already, but he feels so far away and who really knows how long she's been truly gone. God, what if she's been down here for a mere day, but weeks or months have passed in the living world? She straightens, rubbing her chest at the echo of heartache the terrible thought brings. What if Caleb has been waiting for her, day after day, week after week? She can't imagine the pain and frustration she's causing and wishes she could tell him she's okay. More than anything, she wishes she were with him again. Her thoughts tumble back to the moments before the battle, the tender words and the press of his lips on hers so vivid she can nearly feel him with her.

She has to find Quinn. It's the only way to get back to Caleb. If she finds Quinn, they can return to the Grave, and hopefully end up back in the living world.

Turning back toward the sidewalk, Maddy takes one step, then halts. An image of her and Cora, younger, maybe a few years ago, flashes by her. They were laughing, walking through a park, heads close together. It was near the end of high school. Maddy blinks and another image rushes by, scattering through her. Her mom had brought home her favorite ice cream and they were on the couch together, watching a movie. Then, she's in a café on campus, poring over a textbook while Cora sets down a steaming cup of coffee. Over and over again, images of Maddy's life flicker by.

A squeezing sensation clutches her chest. Longing, she realizes. For a moment, she doesn't dwell on where the images had come from, but instead lets herself sink into those memories. She clings to each and every facet of that normal life she'd once had. She misses those days. She misses studying with Cora at their favorite café, sipping lattes and munching on bagels. She yearns to be able to go inside after a day of classes, toe off her tennis shoes, and flop on her bed to read a book. How long has it been since she sat down and had a meal with her mom? When was the last time she drove her car to pick up Cora for a day of window shopping and gossip?

Laughter breaks through the silence of Purgatory and nearly makes Maddy jump out of her skin. She instinctively reaches for her stakes, the only weapon on her, then realizes she must have dropped them back in the living world.

A man watches her, a pleasant smile spread across his equally pleasant face. He isn't extraordinarily handsome or tall. Indeed, everything about the man seems extraordinarily ordinary. His hair is a soft brown, cut short and neat. He wears faded jeans and a T-shirt. Something about him seems off, however. It isn't until he speaks that Maddy realizes this man isn't a soul. He seems every bit as alive as Maddy herself.

"Hello, Madeleine," the man says. "My name is Orion."

CHAPTER 2

CALEB

C louds drift over the moon, scattering shadows over the carnage still fresh in the cemetery. Caleb doesn't look at the bodies Malcolm and the sorcerers re-animated to do their bidding. He doesn't look at the witch or the pretty angel or his vampire companions.

He stares into the Grave with his heart in his throat and fear burning through his veins.

"Maddy!" His voice echoes into the night and is answered with silence. Shock makes him still, the kind of stillness only vampires are truly capable of achieving. His chest doesn't rise with a breath and his eyes don't turn away from the hole in the ground.

Quinn jumped into the Grave and instead of waiting to discuss their next move, Maddy leaped right in after her. Caleb had been too slow to make a grab for her. He calls out her name again, knowing he won't hear a reply. He can't decide if he wants to throttle her or pull her into his arms when he sees her again. The possibility Maddy may not make it out of Purgatory is slammed into oblivion before it can take root in his mind.

His fingers tighten and loosen, the only outward reflection

of the turmoil churning inside of him. He should have gone after Maddy instead of standing here with his mouth gaping in surprise. She could be in danger or hurt. He needs to be at her side. Bits of loose dirt tumble into the Grave as Galina steps up beside him.

"I hope you're not entertaining foolish thoughts," the witch says. "You cannot follow her in there. You know this."

Scowling, Caleb angles his face toward her. "So I've heard. Do we really know if that's the truth, though? Maybe Quinn was trying to warn me, or maybe she just didn't want me to follow her into Purgatory."

Galina crosses her arms and glances down into the Grave. "Are you willing to risk leaping in there to find out?"

After a beat of silence, Caleb shakes his head. "No, I'm not." He runs a hand through his hair and huffs out a sharp breath. "But we have to do something."

"I agree. Give us a moment, and we'll make a plan. We can't rush this."

Caleb's nostrils flare. "Can't rush this? What about Maddy?" He throws a hand toward the Grave. "She could be trapped down there. She could be lost and unable to find her way back. What if the spirits are attacking her?"

The witch clicks her tongue. "Spirits cannot physically harm the living in Purgatory."

"And the evil entity Quinn was talking about, the one she's been forced to serve, what about him?" Caleb glances toward the Grave. "You can't expect Maddy to go up against someone we don't know anything about. She fought well against Malcolm and the rest, but we don't know what this entity is capable of doing. We don't even know who it is."

"I know." Gabby comes to stand beside Caleb with Colt at her side, and Cora and Mason behind them. The angel crosses her slender arms and narrows her gaze toward the Grave. "Let me guess, this entity is in Purgatory causing trouble with the souls there?"

Caleb eyes her. She was the one he spoke to when he'd overheard Malcolm talking to the sorcerers about raising an army of revenants. Without her and Colt, Malcolm and his ilk may have defeated them. "That's right. You think you know who the entity may be?"

Gabby exchanges a glance with Colt, then nods. Blonde waves spill over her shoulder and she impatiently tosses the locks behind her with a sweep of her hand. "Yes, I know who the entity skulking around Purgatory is. He goes by the name Orion."

"Orion?" Galina purses her lips, as if trying to remember where she may have heard the name before.

Caleb angles his head to the side and narrows his eyes. He tries to recall if he's ever heard the name but if he has, it's slipped through his memory. "I don't think I've ever heard of anyone named Orion. Who is he?"

"We've faced him before," Gabby said. "We killed him, too, but for some reason, it appears the reapers never took his soul. He's since been dwelling in Purgatory instead of moving on to hell where he belongs. He was evil in the living world, and it seems he hasn't improved upon death."

A sense of urgency speeds up Caleb's pulse. He can't leave Maddy in there with this Orion person. He peers over at the angel, who is frowning down at the Grave again. "You said you've faced him before?"

"Yes. And, as I said, we had hoped his death would be the end of him. I'm not sure why the reapers left him in Purgatory. We've tried to question them about it, but they are silent about their actions. They operate outside of the scope of this world, follow their own rules, and do things for their own reasons."

Caleb knows this. Reapers are neither evil nor good, but live a gray existence in between the lines. It wouldn't be beyond them to serve or obey this evil entity if it somehow favored them. Judging by the grimace on Colt's face, he's thinking similar thoughts.

Gabby sweeps away a few flecks of dirt and ash that cling to the ridiculously short skirt she's wearing. "Orion is a major pain in the ass. He almost brought the world close to extinction once already."

"And if he is trying to get back into this dimension..." Galina says.

"Exactly." Colt leans forward, looking past Gabby's shoulder at the Grave, a trickle of hellfire dancing around his fingertips as if he expects Orion to pop out of Purgatory any second. "If Orion is attempting to get back to this world, it will prove disastrous."

"Especially if he ends up possessing the obsidian *and* Maddy's powers."

Cora and Mason draw closer. Caleb nearly forgot they're still in the cemetery. "We can't let that happen," Cora says. "Maddy is strong, but she's out of her element in there. If this Orion guy is as bad as you say, then every second we spend here chatting only gives him more of a chance to get a hold of Maddy and the obsidian. She may be able to stop Quinn, but how long will she be able to hold Orion off?"

Caleb's skin feels tight as he starts pacing. Every facet of his being wants to fling himself into the Grave and find Maddy. She needs his help and he's trapped in this place.

The sudden blare of a rock song breaks the silence which had settled over the dark cemetery. Gabby pulls a slim cell phone out of a pocket in her skirt. She curses quietly then walks several paces away, answering the call.

"We'll get her back." Cora glances up at Caleb, a grim determination in her gaze.

Caleb stares back at Maddy's best friend for a long moment. There's no denying the strange connection he feels with her, almost as if an invisible string ties them together. He has no romantic feelings for Cora, but he still feels protective and responsible for her. He'd made her, after all.

"I never really got the chance to apologize," Caleb murmurs to her. "For turning you into this."

Cora lets out a small laugh. "For making me a nearly unstoppable being? Yes, I'm so put out over it." Still, beneath the light-hearted words, Caleb can sense the turmoil within her.

"It gets easier, you know, being a vampire. People will eventually forget you. Once those anchors fall away, you won't have them holding you back."

"Yeah." Cora's lips twist to the side in thought. "I'll also lose my humanity."

Caleb grows silent for a moment. How many vampires had he met who ring true to Cora's claim? Countless. He's seen too many vampires who have given in to their predatory nature with no regard whatsoever for human life. Blood, violence, and sex rule many of his kind.

Taking Cora's shoulder, he gives her a light shake. "I won't let that happen to you. Things will be different." He is the new vampire king, after all. He could change things and make them better. First, however, they have to solve the problem with the obsidian and this Orion person.

Cora returns his stare for a long moment. Then, quietly, she says, "I trust you."

Caleb clears his throat and nods. He can't put into words how much her trust means to him, especially after everything he's done to Cora. He pretended interest in her so he could get closer to Maddy, then to save her life he changed her into what many perceive to be nothing more than blood-sucking monsters. He doesn't love Cora, but he cares for her enough to want her safe and happy. The fact she trusts him to do so makes him want her life to be fulfilling all the more.

"Well, we need to hustle out of here." Gabby joins them once again by the Grave, slipping her phone into her pocket. "Lucifer and Michael aren't seeing eye-to-eye, which is quite possibly as equally disastrous as what is happening here. We're off to mediate."

"Hang on." Caleb steps quickly over to Gabby and makes to grab her arm. Colt's wings fan out and he glares at Caleb, eyes sparking with warning. Caleb bares his fangs at him but doesn't move another inch. He turns his attention back to the blonde angel. "What about Maddy? We need your help to get her back. You can't just abandon her to Orion. You said yourself he's dangerous."

Gabby taps her foot, eyes narrowing toward the Grave. Then, her stare sweeps to Galina. "How educated are you in astral projection?"

The witch's eyebrows rise and she glances between the Grave and Caleb. "I'm a bit out of practice, but I know how it is done."

"What's astral projection?" Mason's been silent for the most part, but Caleb watches his friend glance uneasily toward the Grave, then at the witch.

Galina lifts her chin. "Astral projection is similar to an out-of-body experience. The consciousness of a person can travel physically into another place or dimension. In this case, it would mean traveling to Purgatory."

"You mean to do this to Caleb?" Mason shakes his head. "And what if you can't get his consciousness back from Purgatory?"

"Then he will live the rest of his life as a vegetable," Gabby says brightly. Her smile fades as she stares at the vampire king.

"No spirit will ever give a vampire access to Purgatory. The only way he's going to get in there to save Maddy is through astral projection."

Colt touches the back of Gabby's arm and murmurs something in her ear.

The angel nods. "I'm very sorry, but I have to go." She smiles over at Cora. "Don't worry, you'll have our friend back in no time. Be sure to give her a tongue-lashing for me when she returns."

Cora grins back. "Oh, I plan on it."

Gabby grabs Colt's hand, then locks her gaze with Caleb. "Get Maddy out of Orion's clutches and don't let him follow you back through." With that, the two flap their great wings and leap into the sky.

"Let me speak with Galina alone," Caleb says. Mason and Cora hesitate a moment, but neither of them argue as they drift off deeper into the cemetery. With a sigh, he turns back to Galina. "Do you really think this astral projection thing is something you can do?"

"No, I'm not entirely certain. Like I told the angel, it isn't something I've done for a long time, and certainly not on behalf of anyone else. I've astral projected myself but never another person. But I know the logistics and I'm willing to give it a try." She cocks her head to the side, studying him. "If you agree to do this, there are rules you will need to follow."

Caleb frowns. "What rules?"

The witch pulls her braid over her shoulder, her fingers playing with the frayed end. "Once you're inside Purgatory, you cannot touch anything. You will be little more than a spirit yourself. No matter what happens, you cannot try to interfere with the souls in there. If Maddy is attacked, you won't be able to physically help."

Caleb grinds his teeth. He cannot even imagine watching

someone try to hurt Maddy and be unable to do anything to protect her. Still, he supposes the astral projection is better than nothing. At least he'll still be able to be with her.

"Also, Orion will have the power to send you back into this plane of existence on Earth if he so wishes," Galina says. "Purgatory is now his dominion."

Caleb doesn't care. It's a risk he's willing to take. "I'll do it."

"Good." Galina nods. "Give me a moment to get my thoughts together, then we'll send your consciousness into Purgatory."

Caleb turns his gaze to the Grave. He's nearly certain a chill escapes the entry to Purgatory and sends goosebumps breaking out over his arms.

"Hang on, Maddy," Caleb murmurs. "I'm coming to get you."

CHAPTER 3

MADELEINE

The very air around Maddy seems to cool in the presence of the man who calls himself Orion. He still smiles at her, a pleasant curve of his lips that barely meets his eyes. Orion is so unassuming and yet something like dread crawls up inside of Maddy, a deep-rooted instinct that tells her she needs to keep her guard up around the stranger.

"Who are you?" Maddy asks.

Orion tilts his head back and laughs, sticking his hands in his pockets. It's a gesture so utterly human that Maddy narrows her eyes in suspicion. Amusement dances in the man's gaze as he settles it back onto her. "I think you mean 'what are you?', do you not? I can see it in your eyes, the doubt. I can't say I blame you. This is Purgatory, after all. Who else would be wandering around here, speaking to you, unless such a person had bad ideas?"

"I never said anything of the sort." Maddy notes the distance between them. The man is much closer than she realized, and she isn't all too comfortable with the fact. She tilts her head, studying him, but also notes places she can run for a quick escape if need be. "You didn't answer my question."

"You mean your question behind the question?" Orion shrugs a shoulder. "I am a spirit here, like so many others."

Maddy shakes her head. "You're not like the others." She glances around, but there are no souls in sight. It's not unusual, there had been spans on her walk so far where she was utterly alone, but their absence now feels different, almost as if the souls in Purgatory are hiding. "They never said anything to me. They barely even glanced in my direction."

Orion eases down onto a nearby bench that looks out on what would be a busy street in the business district in the living world. Here, in Purgatory, not even a bit of trash blows across the empty road. "Most of them have been trapped here for a long time, or what seems to be a long time. They have lost all sense of their former humanity. They no longer know how to live, so they wander around, subconsciously seeking anything to fill the void that's grown inside of them."

Well, that's certainly depressing. Maddy glances around the dark, gray world of Purgatory. She can't even imagine what sort of dreary, dead existence the souls here are suffering. "Why are you so different from them?" Again, in her mind, she wonders what Orion is that he's able to be here and talk with her like this.

He tilts his head up, staring at her. He pats the empty space on the bench beside him. "You can sit down. I promise I don't bite." His lips stretch in a big grin, showing his perfect, white teeth.

Maddy's had her moments tangling with beings with much sharper teeth so she sits on the bench, still leaving as much space as possible between the two of them. The perfectly normal seeming man makes her skin itch and it's an effort not to squirm beside him.

"I was like you once," Orion says.

Maddy quirks an eyebrow. She seriously doubts that. "In what way?"

"I wanted to be normal." Orion props his ankle on his knee and leans into the back of the bench. "I wanted a normal life, and yet I wanted great things."

"I don't want great things," Maddy says. She props her arm on the bench's metal armrest, but her fingers curl tightly around the end.

Orion chuckles. "Says the young woman, a very much alive young woman, poking about in Purgatory."

Maddy grinds her teeth. She can't let this Orion fellow know why she jumped into the Grave.

"I was normal," Orion repeats. "I wanted great things. And, like you, I inherited a great legacy."

The hairs on the back of Maddy's neck rise. How does Orion know anything about her? Does he know about her ties to Dracula or that she's a hunter? "You don't know anything about me."

Orion's eyes dance, the only sign of bright life in the horrid realm of the waiting dead. "To the contrary, I know much about you. I saw through your mind moments before you saw me."

Maddy's eyes widen slightly. The memories which had flashed by her...that had been Orion seeing into her mind? Her back stiffens and her mind begins to think of a way to get out of her current situation. She has to, quickly, before Quinn gets even farther away.

Orion lifts a hand and she shifts her feet, ready to bolt, but the man merely rests his arm on the back of the bench. "I didn't mean to frighten you. It is merely a gift I possess, and much of the time it is unintentional. I only wanted you to understand I know you. I was great and gifted until the powers that be took everything away from me and locked me in here."

"Why?" Maddy bites out the word sharper than she means, but something about this man has her on edge.

"Jealousy," Orion says. "Plain and simple. The same will happen to you if you're not careful. I know you want a normal life. I saw what it was like for you before it became infested with vampires and all of their dangerous entanglements. I saw your life before you learned about the Order."

God, how much does this man know about her? Has he seen her growing up? Training with the Order? Has he seen her making out with past boyfriends, or does he know about...

"I can help you be with him," Orion said.

"Who?"

Orion gives Maddy a knowing grin. "Your vampire, Caleb. I know what he means to you. I *saw* what he means to you, despite the rocky terrain the pair of you have tread."

Maddy feels a sense of violation at the intrusion into her thoughts, her life, and her relationship with Caleb. She crosses her arms as the back of her neck heats, thinking of the last kiss she'd shared with the vampire king. "I don't see what my relationship with Caleb has to do with anything."

"Because I know what you truly want, Madeleine." Orion drops his leg, only to prop his ankle on his opposite knee. "You want a normal life. You want to finish college, hang out at the café with your friends, and go out on Friday nights with Caleb. It's quite difficult to do such things when you are both entangled in the Order and every other supernatural problem cropping up."

"It's awfully presumptuous of you to think you could possibly know what I want in my life." Admittedly, Maddy has thought about it on occasion. What would it be like to live a normal, happy life with her friends, and with Caleb?

Impossible. That's the reality of it. Cora is a vampire. Caleb is the newly appointed vampire king. No matter how much

Maddy would love to have a normal life, that ship had not only sailed the moment her mother told her about the Order, but the ship's been struck and sunk to the bottom of the ocean, forever out of reach. Maddy doesn't point out any of this, however. She can't help but be curious how Orion thinks she could have any sense of normalcy in her life.

She purses her lips in a show of weighing his words. "How can it be possible?"

He studies her for a moment, peering at her with such scrutiny Maddy edges away from him a bit. Then, he turns, lifts his arm, and points. "There is your solution, Madeleine."

Maddy follows his line of sight to a tall building. The shape is familiar, along with the countless windows and the sharp, modern angles. There is no light gleaming on the sleek surface of the building, or people moving in and out of the doors, or climbing out of cars beside the wide, stone steps. Caleb has been inside that building not long before, hours, maybe days, depending on how long she's been in Purgatory. She, herself, has been inside that building.

She returns her attention to Orion. "What does the Merrick Group of Industries have to do with me and Caleb leading a normal life?"

"Did you know they have developed a supposed cure for vampirism?"

"Yes, I...hang on," Maddy says. "What do you mean, a supposed cure?"

Orion glances back up at the building. "Do you really think such an industry would want to help vampires?" He shakes his head and leans forward with a sigh. "The cure they're speaking of currently is not really a cure at all. At least, it's not a cure the vampires would want."

Maddy's heartbeats quicken. She has a feeling she knows where this is going, but she has to be certain. "Tell me."

The stranger's eyes pin on hers. "The cure created by the Merrick Group is nothing more than a death sentence in a pretty, promising package. Once it is administered to a vampire, it will kill them."

Maddy swallows. She feared as much. "How does that help me, though? If the cure actually doesn't save vampires like they claim, how can it help me and Caleb?"

"You could still have someone to make the actual cure, of course. You'll need something that will modify the vampire strain and remove it from them. All of the studies are with the Merrick Group of Industries. You simply need to find them and alter them to your needs."

The thought of not only sneaking into that building again, but also managing to find the exact material they need, plus someone knowledgeable enough to create an actual cure makes Maddy's head spin.

But the cure for vampirism is another problem for another day. She isn't even entirely sure Caleb wants to be human again. Instead, Maddy switches focus to the present, and the strange man sitting beside her. Most people don't simply help someone, and to such an extent, out of the goodness of their hearts. Orion knows about her, Caleb, and even the apparent cure held by the Merrick Group. She wishes to know what Orion's true motive is for helping her, and what the benefit of such help will be to him.

"You seem like you want to help me, but what's the catch?"

The corner of Orion's mouth twitches up into a crooked smile. "I knew you were clever." He taps his temple. "I've seen it." He twists toward her, facing her fully. "I think it's best if we're both up front, don't you? I want you to find Quinn for me."

A chill scatters up the back of Maddy's neck. Orion knows about Quinn, a spirit put into another body by a necromancer.

To her knowledge, the only other people who know Quinn was taken from Purgatory would be her friends and the person who was pulling Quinn's strings.

The evil entity.

She should have known from the start that Orion's presence was suspicious. None of the other spirits in Purgatory gave her more than a glance, let alone utter a single syllable to her. The man seated on the bench beside her is the same one who has been torturing and controlling the souls in this place. Maddy doesn't let the surprise and fear show in her features.

"Why do you want me to find Quinn?" She tilts her head, a show of curiosity scrunching her eyebrows together.

"For the same reason you are down here, I'd imagine," Orion says. "The obsidian."

Maddy's pulse quickens but she doesn't bat an eyelash. "You want to use the obsidian?"

"No." The word growls up Orion's throat, the only sound of unpleasantness Maddy has heard from him. "I want to destroy it. Why do you think I was thrown into Purgatory? I know how to end the evil that is the obsidian, but those who wanted it for themselves cast me into this place. The obsidian is much too dangerous and volatile for anyone in this world to possess."

Maddy isn't completely certain if Orion is truly the evil entity Quinn had spoken about in the cemetery, but until she can prove otherwise, she'll keep her back up and go along. "Quinn won't exactly be the easiest person to catch," she says. "I wasn't even certain what I was going to do when I found her." It was a true enough statement, though she'd been thinking of certain ideas.

Orion reaches beside him. "Use these." He holds out a pair of what appear to be thin metal bracelets. They are not adorned with jewels or charms, but Maddy can just make out strange markings etched on their gleaming surfaces.

"What are they?"

"They are enchanted," Orion says. "They will cut off any magic or spells Quinn wishes to use. It will also put her spirit at your mercy, since you will be the one to put them around her wrists."

Maddy doesn't like the idea of having another person in her control, but she doesn't see another way out of this mess at the moment and she does need to catch Quinn. She reaches out and takes the bracelets, certain she can feel the power thrumming in the metal bands.

Orion points down the dark street. "I believe our mutual friend ran off in that direction."

He's helping her. Which means she needs to decide whether she does the same for him.

"I'll find her." Maddy stands, nods at Orion, and starts off once again.

She isn't certain how long Orion watches her as she makes her way down the empty street, but it feels like hours later she can still feel his gaze on the back of her neck.

Jumping into Purgatory had been easy enough, but escaping this place, escaping *him*, may just prove to be the biggest challenge of her life.

CHAPTER 4

CALEB

Caleb paces back and forth, earning a glare from Galina who's sitting cross-legged at the edge of the cemetery.

"I really need to concentrate," she says. An array of little bottles and stones are spread out before her. "And I cannot focus with you wearing a path into the earth."

Scowling, Caleb stops. He's anxious to get into Purgatory. Or, at least, a part of himself. His consciousness would travel into that place of souls, though Galina promised he would have a nearly physical form there.

"This is taking too long," he complains.

Galina doesn't look up from examining the contents of the bottles. "Do you want me to make a mistake and send your awareness elsewhere? How about into someone else's mind, or out into the cosmos itself?" She rolls her eyes up to him. "Be patient."

"Caleb." Mason points to a figure quickly approaching from the road.

After a moment Elias, the vampire who works directly with the council, halts several feet away. He quickly takes in the cemetery, noting Galina's presence as well as Mason's and Cora's.

"Where is your Madeleine?"

Something tightens in Caleb's chest at the way Elias spoke of Maddy. Your Madeleine, he'd said. Caleb likes the sound of it, not in a possessive way, but as if she's his to cherish and protect. He swallows, unable to admit he's let her slip through his fingers into a dangerous place on her own.

Cora scoffs. "Maddy took a nosedive straight into Purgatory."

Elias lifts an eyebrow and glances at Caleb, who nods in confirmation. He lets out a low whistle. "She sounds like a handful." He glances at Galina. "I'm assuming the witch is up to something to get her back."

"She is," Caleb says.

"Why did she go into Purgatory?"

Caleb hesitates for a moment, knowing whatever he tells Elias will be repeated to the council. He reminds himself he is the king, and it's his duty to inform the council of any recent developments. In all honesty, with everything going on, he'd nearly forgotten his own responsibilities. For a brief moment, he wishes he'd never agreed to become the king of the vampires. If he didn't, however, then someone else could be pulling his strings.

"We came here to find the necromancer but it turns out Quinn, the spirit who managed to get a hold of the obsidian, is much more slippery than we gave her credit for. She leapt into Purgatory. Maddy took it upon herself to jump after her. Galina is working on a spell that will allow me to get into Purgatory through astral projection."

After hearing a brief description of what exactly astral projection entails, Elias shakes his head. "The council will not take kindly to you losing the obsidian."

"I didn't lose it," Caleb says. He jerks his head toward the Grave a dozen feet away. "It's in there. It just isn't in my hands at the moment."

Elias simply stares at Caleb, deadpan.

"I'm going to get it back. Maddy is hot on Quinn's trail. I'll go in and get her out. Then, we'll have the obsidian."

"You are the king," Elias says. "You are the one who gives orders, for the most part, but the council is the one who backs you. If you are not capable of getting the obsidian, other alternatives may need to be considered."

Caleb's nostrils flare. Beside him, Cora and Mason grow very still, sensing the tang of danger in the air. On the ground, the witch continues preparing for her spell. If she senses the tension between the vampires, she doesn't let on.

Slowly, Caleb steps closer to Elias. "Are you threatening your king?" He hasn't been in a position of power long, but steel authority wraps around his words.

Elias, as if realizing exactly who he's been speaking to, lowers his eyes. "No, I'm not threatening you." He lifts his gaze again. "I'm merely informing you that the council is getting antsy. They want the obsidian in vampire hands."

Not knowing whether the council wants to use the obsidian or destroy it, Caleb doesn't comment. Instead, he narrows his eyes. "Tell me what the council is up to. As king, I have just as much right to know their movements as they do mine." He notes the conflict quickly cross Elias's face before it fades. The vampire before him has served the council much longer than he's served Caleb, but he cannot deny a direct order from his new king.

Elias lowers his voice, eyes flicking warily toward Galina. Cora and Mason are pretending to be focused on something in the distance, though they can still likely hear Elias's quiet words. "The members of the council have been in touch with several well-known mediums and psychics. At first, I wasn't privy to what they were trying to learn, but I finally found out a couple hours ago when they told me to relay their findings to you."

"And what have they learned?"

"There is unrest in the spirit world," Mason says. "Apparently, there is some sort of evil entity who is attempting to return to the mortal world to wreak havoc. The spirits the mediums were able to talk to were afraid, and for entities that are already dead to feel fear, well, it can't be good."

Caleb lets out a humorless laugh. "It seems to me the council needs to catch up with the times. What in the hell do they do all day?"

Elias tilts his head, a silent question in his gaze.

"We already know about the entity," Caleb says. "He's the reason Quinn leaped into Purgatory. The entity is the one pulling her strings and controlling the other spirits. He's holding them in Purgatory instead of letting them move on."

Elias peers over toward the Grave. "How do you know this?"

"Quinn told us as much. She's been fighting against the entity, but he's too strong. He must want the obsidian so that he can use it to return to this world once more." Caleb watches Elias's face pinch into distaste. "That's not the worst part. Apparently, the entity has caused trouble in our world before."

The vampire swings his stare back to Caleb. "What do you mean?"

"There was an angel here, Gabby, who spoke of a man named Orion. He caused a lot of trouble and nearly tossed the world into chaos before he was hefted into Purgatory. The reapers, however, let him be for reasons we don't know. Now, Orion is seeking to re-enter the world of the living."

"And Quinn, who is under this Orion guy's control, is taking the obsidian straight to him."

Caleb nods. "Yeah, as far as we know. Maddy jumped in to try and stop her, but we have no idea what kind of sway Orion holds over Purgatory and those who enter. She's likely in danger, which is why I need to go in after her."

"Damn it," Elias hisses. "Do you really think you'll be able to find her? It's Purgatory. Who knows what kind of hell you may be jumping into?"

"It's not hell," Cora chimes in. She looks up from where Galina measures out a spoon of powder and places it into a bowl. "More like the doorstep to hell, or heaven." Her lips twitch slightly as she peers over. "Have you been a good boy, Caleb?"

He fights the urge to roll his eyes. He doesn't recall Cora being so mouthy. Apparently, becoming a nearly indestructible supernatural being gave her a bolder tongue.

"I'll inform the council of your plans," Elias says. "I think they'll agree that you pursuing Maddy into Purgatory is risky, but I don't see any other option at this point. You must get the obsidian."

Eyebrows lowering, Caleb glares at Elias. "I am well aware of what I must do."

He clears his throat, realizing once again he's overstepped his bounds as a subject of the vampire king. "I'll see you when you return." He gives a dip of his chin, whirls around, and flashes off down the street.

The witch breaks through the silence left in Elias's wake. "I'm ready."

Caleb hurries over to Galina, then sits on the ground beside her. Cradled in her lap is a bowl holding a sort of pale green paste. The color reminds Caleb of hospital walls and he tries not to think of the irony that the sickly green concoction that reminds him of illness is the same substance that will help take him into Purgatory.

"I'm not supposed to drink that, am I?" Caleb asks. He leans forward to sniff it, thankful it doesn't have a putrid odor. The paste smells like a mixture of fresh cut grass and cinnamon. An odd combination, but nothing that will send bile up his throat.

Galina takes four stones, each with a different symbol etched in its smooth surface, and places two on either side of Caleb and two on either side of herself. "No, you do not drink it."

"What are the stones for?" Mason asks. He and Cora have taken several steps away from the two sitting on the ground.

"The stones serve as an anchor, both so I can keep a hold of Caleb and so I remain grounded in this realm, as well. Astral projection is tricky and can go terribly wrong. It's important to keep a strong hold in the world of the living."

For the first time since deciding he wanted to follow Maddy into Purgatory, nerves begin to unfold in Caleb's stomach. "I'm not going to get stuck in there, am I?" He can't imagine the horror of knowing he's forever trapped in Purgatory while his physical body slowly rots away.

"Not if you listen to the advice I've already given you," Galina says. "Take care not to touch anything other than Maddy or Quinn, as they are there in the physical form. Leave the spirits alone. Try not to even make eye contact. The more you root yourself in Purgatory, the harder it will be to draw you back out again."

Caleb's eyes are drawn to Galina's finger as the witch swirls it in the green paste. "What about Orion?" he asks. "Am I allowed to confront him?"

The witch frowns. "I do not know. He was killed and his spirit sent to Purgatory, and yet the reapers let him be. Perhaps he is there in a different way, but it's better to be safe and keep your distance from him if you can." She stares across at Caleb, a bit of the paste dripping from her finger. "Are you ready?"

Caleb nods but glances over to his best friend. "If I don't make it out of this, take care of Cora." There hasn't been time to really help her adjust to her new life as a vampire. Mason is patient and thorough. He'll make sure Cora will be okay.

"I will." Mason's promise is firm, but unease tightens at the corner of his eyes.

Galina leans forward and smears the paste across Caleb's forehead. He grimaces and makes a noise of disgust in his throat. It feels like she smeared smashed peas across his face. After drawing the line, the witch dips her fingers in the paste again and dabs out a series of dots along the line.

"Once I begin the incantation, you will grow sleepy and then fall unconscious. Then, your mind will begin its journey to Purgatory. I will do my best to guide you there and will wait to pull you out. Picture where you want to go in your head. Picture Maddy in Purgatory and how much you want to be at her side. If everything goes smoothly, you should appear in Purgatory with her."

Caleb jerks a nod, and then Galina starts a low mutter. He doesn't understand what she's saying, but by the eighth word his eyelids grow heavy. His body starts to tip back, but he jerks, catching himself. God, he's so tired. He's barely aware of the witch anymore. Something begins to tug at his mind. He closes his eyes, trying to concentrate on the strange sensation. His back hits the ground and then he's up again, soaring toward the Grave, and down to Purgatory.

Caleb rushes into the Grave and plunges into darkness. He sees a light but as soon as he draws near, he collides with something. His astral self bounces backward from the force of the hit. He recovers and walks forward, hand outstretched, only to hit an invisible wall again.

What is going on?

Suddenly, as if a great hook has caught him around the

middle, he's yanked backward. In the next moment, his body twitches and then his eyes slowly open. Galina and the others are staring down at him.

With a groan, Caleb sits up. "What happened?"

Galina wipes the paste from her finger. "The spell failed. It would appear that your astral self faced some sort of block. Somehow, Purgatory has been closed."

Caleb launches to his feet with a curse. If Orion has managed to keep others from getting into Purgatory, does that mean Maddy is trapped in there?

CHAPTER 5
MADELEINE

Maddy's feet are sore. She dwells on the discomfort throbbing through her arches and into her heels. She's certain it's at least been over a day of walking, even though the distance she's traveled is skewed. A glance to the left shows another row of houses on the outskirts of Mercy City. She's barely made it into the suburbs when she should have reached this point in a matter of hours, not over a day.

"That damn bastard," Maddy grumbles. Orion had pointed out the direction Quinn had gone, but he'd neglected to tell her just how far she managed to travel. Maddy hates that she'd had no choice at the time but to agree to Orion's proposal. She hopes it doesn't turn back to bite her. She'll go along with it for the time being, but when it comes time to renege on their deal, she just has to put faith that she'll be able to follow through with her own plans fast enough.

Where on earth is Quinn going? Maddy can feel the slightest echo of her presence as she walks, like a tiny buzz left in the air in her wake. Is Quinn merely trying to keep moving, to keep hiding, in order to stay out of Orion's clutches? She doesn't blame the woman, of course. Maddy doesn't want to be anywhere near him ever again, especially if he really is the evil entity controlling the spirits.

A soul lingers at the corner of the sidewalk beside a mailbox. Maddy slows, watching the young man as he stares off across the street, seemingly at nothing. Had this been his home in the living world, or did he just happen to drift here unknowingly?

Biting her lip, she quietly approaches him. "Excuse me." The spirit doesn't even flinch. Maddy clears her throat. "I'm so sorry to bother you, but I'm looking for a friend and I wonder if you've seen her pass this way recently?"

The man continues to stare across the street. He doesn't move or blink. Maddy huffs out a breath. The spirits in Purgatory either are unable or unwilling to help her out. She skirts around the spirit and continues on her way.

After what feels like another day, Maddy finally leaves Mercy City and the surrounding homes behind. She stops and braces her hands on her knees, pulling in breaths of stale, odorless air. God, she's tired. She's hungry and thirsty. There's no water in Purgatory, and while there had been stores in the city, none of them held any actual goods. When was the last time she ate something or had a drink of water? How much longer can she go on before she falls over from exhaustion or dehydration?

Once she takes several breaths, Maddy straightens. She's on a curving country road surrounded by forests. Something about it seems familiar and it tickles at her memory. Has she been here before? The echo of Quinn's presence seems to be stronger and Maddy's heart jumps with hope that she's finally catching up to the fleeing soul.

The trail takes her off the road and into the forest. Maddy eyes the trees as she walks, the trunks rising up like dark, gray sentinels in the ghostly woods. The shadows are deeper here, and the back of her neck constantly prickles. She doesn't want to know if spirits linger in this place or if they're watching her. She continues through the trees, the lack of crunching leaves or birds chirping a disconcerting reminder she's still in Purgatory.

Maddy catches glimpses of something strange ahead and she quickens her pace. As she rounds a large oak tree, she finds massive stones rising from the ground. She blinks. She knew something had seemed familiar about that road and this forest. These are the ruins where Caleb had taken Quinn.

What's more, there, in the middle of the ring of stone pillars, *is* Quinn.

Relief and irritation flood through Maddy as she makes her way toward the young woman. "Do you mind telling me what the hell you're doing running through Purgatory like there's a fire on your tail?"

Quinn starts and looks up at Maddy, a hand flying to her chest. "You scared me."

Maddy rolls her eyes. "If you're really running from something, maybe you should be a bit more aware of your surroundings." She steps up beside Quinn. "What are you doing here?"

All sense of surprise falls from Quinn's face and she gives Maddy a soft smile. Her fingers trail over one of the stones, the one that Maddy had once seen with a hole dug at the base.

"He brought me here, you know," Quinn says. "Caleb. He flirted with me, well Ileana's body, anyway. He picked me up and drove me out here, all smiles and promises of adventure. Did he tell you that? Did Caleb tell you that while you were trying to help your friend Cora deal with the aftermath of becoming a monster, that he was in a bar giving all of his attention to me?"

Maddy knows Quinn is merely trying to rile her up but she can't stop the woman's barbed words from pricking her skin.

"How well do you know Caleb?" Quinn asks. "It's my understanding he used Cora just as much as he used me. Given his track record, I'd say he's using you, too."

"I'm not here to talk about Caleb." Maddy's voice is clipped as she stuffs her hands in her pockets. Her fingers touch the cool metal of the bracelets as she edges slightly closer to Quinn. "I want to know why you came to this spot."

Quinn tilts her head back and closes her eyes. "Can you feel it, the power, the darkness? I want to sink into it, let it fill my pores and stain my bones. It's amazing."

"What is?" Maddy's pulse quickens as she stares at Quinn, watching a manic sort of smile spread across the woman's face.

"The obsidian." Quinn peers at Maddy. "I can see why Caleb wanted to keep his claws in it. The strength it's given me is incredible. Having the obsidian dwelling inside of me gave me the power I needed to repel Orion's control over me."

Maddy's fingers tighten around the bracelets. "So Orion is the evil entity, then."

"Of course," Quinn says. "And now I am free of him. I'm free to do anything I want, thanks to the obsidian."

Unease sends Maddy's pulse thudding her in ears. "What, exactly, are you wanting to do?"

Quinn waves a hand. "Oh, Maddy, don't worry. You have nothing to fear. Neither does Caleb or any of your friends. I'm a spirit of my word, you know. The necromancer got me out of Purgatory, and away from Orion for a small time. I'll give the necromancer a shot of resurrecting his wife and then I'll deliver the Chalice to him so he can use it to control Orion. Once the necromancer dispels Orion, the spirits here in Purgatory will be out of his control. They'll be free to move on to whatever after-life awaits them next."

Maddy wants to let out a breath of relief, but something keeps a tight knot in her chest. A shiver shakes through her, the sensation she's known since childhood rising like a warning bell. While Quinn's plan seems genuine, the obsidian isn't something that would work toward a happy ending. There has to be more going on that Quinn isn't saying. She wants to save the spirits, but at what cost? What else does the obsidian-influenced woman have up her sleeve?

"So, that's it?" Maddy says. "You'll help the necromancer free the spirits of Purgatory and then, what, you'll move on with the rest of them?" If Quinn were doing this for the right reasons, that would be the only path she should take.

Quinn laughs, the sound echoing from the towering stones around them. "Oh, no. I can't just disappear from this place, and from the living world. I still have work to do."

"Like what?" The metal bracelets bite into Maddy's palms. As soon as the moment is right, she'll make her move. She'll have to be quick. She can't afford to let Quinn slip through her fingers again.

"Once the necromancer is finished taking out Orion, I'll kill him. He stole me from Purgatory and forced me into this body against my will. I cannot let such a thing go unpunished. He may have thought to use me to help bring back his dead wife, but in the end, I will be the one tugging the strings. It won't be just him, either. Every supernatural being will come under my dominion." A crazed light shines in Quinn's eyes. "Just wait and see, Maddy. My whole life, and my whole death, people have tried to use and manipulate me. Now, it's my turn to grind people to dust under my heel." Quinn's mouth spreads wide as she laughs.

Hairs rise on the back of Maddy's neck. Quinn is insane, either by being under Orion's control for so long or, most likely, the obsidian is already poisoning her mind.

"Is this really what *you* want, Quinn, or is this the obsidian's influence?" Maddy's throwing a lifeline out to her. If Quinn is still in there, fighting against the obsidian, maybe she can find a way to help.

Quinn's head tilted to the side, blonde hair spilling over her shoulder. Her eyes narrow as she stares at Maddy. "What are you talking about?"

Maddy's hopes deflate. Clearly, Quinn isn't even wholly aware the obsidian has taken over her mind. Or, maybe she does know, and simply doesn't care. The fact she's grown so power hungry in such a short amount of time puts Maddy on edge. She has to make her move before it is too late.

In a swiftness honed thanks to the training with Felix's Order, Maddy pulls the bracelets from her pockets, flips open their clasps, and latches them around Quinn's wrists in a manner of seconds. Then she steps back, heart pounding, waiting.

A groove etches in between Quinn's eyebrows as she peers down at the bracelets. "What are these?"

Maddy pulls in a breath, readying herself for the eruption she knows is heading her way. "Orion gave them to me. He told me they would hold you to me. I'm supposed to bring you back to him, Quinn."

Quinn's eyes widen and she throws her palms out towards Maddy. Nothing happens. She tries again then again. Whatever magic the woman is trying to summon doesn't answer. "No." Quinn's voice shakes. "No. What have you done?" Her voice rises into a scream that shakes through the trees. "What have you done?"

Maddy winces at the panic she sees in Quinn's eyes and reminds herself the obsidian is likely putting on a show. "I'm sorry, Quinn."

"I don't understand," she says. "Why would you do this? He'll torture me, Maddy. Don't give me back to him. He'll hurt me. He'll kill me."

Maddy doesn't remark on the fact that Quinn, technically, is already dead. "Orion told me he can help me have a normal life with Caleb. He knows that's all I truly want. If I give you back to him, he claims he can make it happen for me."

Baring her teeth, Quinn spits, "He's lying." She shakes her wrists, then tries to undo the bracelets. There's a spark and she yelps, drawing her hand back. The bracelets are stuck on her until Maddy takes them off. Quinn's nostrils flare. "He'll never help you. He'll never help anyone but himself."

"You were just spouting off about how the supernatural world will be bowing to you, Quinn, so spare me the lecture on morality."

Quinn suddenly drops to her knees and holds her wrists out toward Maddy. "Take them off. Please. I'll give you anything you want. I'll give you the Chalice. To hell with the necromancer. You still need to help Zariah, right? I'll hand over the dreamcatcher, too, and you can heal her."

The offer is tempting. Maddy was able to heal Zariah's body, but her connection to magic is still broken. Closing her eyes briefly, she reminds herself to stay the course. She has to see this through or they will all be doomed.

"I'm sorry, Quinn. I have to do this." Maddy reaches down, grips Quinn's arm, and hauls her up.

Quinn screams and fights but isn't strong enough to break free of Maddy's hold.

Maddy ignores her pleas and curses as she begins the long walk back toward Mercy City, dragging the captured spirit along with her.

CHAPTER 6

CALEB

C aleb is only vaguely aware that someone is speaking to him. A buzzing fills his ears as he stares at the Grave, fingers clenching into fists. He'd been so close to getting to Maddy. He yearns to reach her with every fiber of his being and can think of nothing else but getting her away from Orion. A hand clamps down on his shoulder and he whirls to find Mason staring at him.

"What?" Caleb asks.

Mason huffs out a sigh. "I said, we'll figure this out."

"Figure it out?" Caleb bares his teeth. "How, exactly, are we supposed to figure this out? Maddy is trapped in Purgatory. Orion could have his hands on her right now, stealing her magic before killing her. I need to go there, now."

Galina is putting her stones and bottles back inside the hidden pockets of her clothes. "Well, we can't get in there at the moment. You need to calm down a bit and think."

His nostrils flare, but he knows the witch is right. He won't make any progress rescuing Maddy if he keeps riding the wave of anger, fear, and panic trying to drown him. His jaw slides back and forth, crushing the retort he wants to spit at her. Mason and Cora watch him silently, tension tight on their faces.

The witch's features soften as she steps closer to Caleb. "I understand. You want to save her, we all do, but just because the astral projection didn't work does not mean there isn't another way."

Caleb takes a deep breath, doing his best to calm down, then nods. "Okay, so what now? Can you think of another way into Purgatory, or a way to break through Orion's block?"

After a moment of silence, Galina says, "Unfortunately, I don't. The realm of spirits is not my main point of study. It's a shame Gabby had to leave but even she may not know of another way. There is someone who may know, however."

Caleb's eyebrows rise, easily catching onto Galina's line of thought. "Nim," he says. He's already in motion when he speaks again. "Let's get back to the city and go to Veritas."

They make quick work of traveling back into the depths of Mercy City. More time has passed than he realizes and by the time they reach the ancient, massive library, the first light of morning is spilling across the steps. The door is locked and Caleb bangs his fist on it.

A moment later, a very annoyed Nim unlocks the door. "You couldn't have waited another ten minutes until we're open?" she mutters.

The group files in. "Sorry," Caleb says, even though he's not. "This is an emergency."

Nim glances at them, then locks the door again and leads them to a private room off the main floor. "Have a seat." She smiles at Galina. "Would you like some tea?"

Before the witch can speak, Caleb cuts in. "We don't have time for tea. Maddy jumped into the Grave and into Purgatory, going after Quinn and the obsidian."

The librarian angles her wheelchair closer to the table. "Yes, Gabby told me as much a little while ago." She pats her pocket, the rectangular outline of a cell phone showing. "That was a foolish risk for Maddy, obsidian to find or not. She has no idea what sort of peril she's in if she remains inside of Purgatory. It is a place for spirits, not for the living."

Cora leans against the wall with a small smile. "That's Maddy for you, trying to do what's right and surging full speed ahead."

"I tried to go after her by way of astral projection," Caleb says. "Gabby suggested it since the spirits won't let vampires into Purgatory. Galina's spell didn't work, though. My consciousness was nearly at Purgatory when I ran into a block and couldn't get through. I had no choice but to return to my body and find another alternative." He waves his hands, indicating that's why they're here.

Nim frowns. "It sounds to me like Purgatory is now being fully controlled by the evil spirit, as he has done before." She shakes her head, her dark hair brushing her chin. "This isn't good, not at all."

"The entity's name is Orion," Caleb says.

Nim glares pointedly up at him and then a chair. She doesn't speak again until Caleb stops hovering, sinking down onto the cushion. "Yes, I am aware of who he is."

"You are?" Mason asks. He stands near Cora, arms crossed.

"Of course." Nim's chin tips upward. "He does have quite the reputation, though I suppose many of his dire deeds were silenced before the general public could learn of what he had done."

Unease begins to spread through Caleb. "Gabby says he was killed and tossed into Purgatory, but apparently the reapers left him there."

"That's right. Nobody knows what happened when his soul was initially taken by the reapers. They left him in Purgatory, but to what end?" Nim speaks softly, as if to herself. "It is unknown what happened when Arielle stabbed Orion. She used the dark ash retrieved from the faeries, you know. He's obviously much more powerful than he was when he was cast into Purgatory. Perhaps the dark ash didn't nullify his powers, but somehow magnified them over time?"

A dark thought flits through Caleb's mind. "Or maybe he was able to make the block into Purgatory because he's managed to capture Quinn and has taken the obsidian from her."

Galina's fingers drum on the armrest of her chair. "Let's hope that isn't the case. If it were, I fear he will already be readying to break free of Purgatory."

"I doubt he has the obsidian," Nim says. "At least, not yet. If he did, there is no doubt in my mind he'd already be wreaking havoc in the living world. He must have cast a powerful block with whatever magic he possesses after Maddy entered Purgatory through the Grave."

It was a small sense of relief that Orion likely doesn't have the obsidian yet, but Caleb is still anxious to get into Purgatory and help Maddy. "Is there another way into Purgatory?" he asks. "A way that would allow me to get inside physically."

Nim purses her lips in thought. "There is a secret way, a path only a few people in existence know about."

"Such a place exists?" Galina asks.

Caleb waits with bated breath. If there's another way into Purgatory, he's ready to take it, no matter the cost.

"The ancient gods made Purgatory to trap Orion the first time, and when they did so, they made a secret entrance not known by any but themselves."

"Hang on." Cora holds up a hand. "Purgatory was created for Orion? Like a prison?" Her tone is filled with awe and a bit of disbelief. "I didn't know Orion was such an old supernatural being."

Nim nods. "Yes, he is."

"If the entrance is only known to the gods, then how is it that you are aware of its existence?" Galina asks, settling a scrutinizing stare on Nim.

The librarian chuckles. "If you are asking if I'm an ancient god, no I'm not. I'm simply well-educated." She shifts in her wheelchair and clears her throat, adopting a tone similar to a lecturer on a college campus. "Back in the 1500s, an Archivist by the name of Afonso Dos Saritos served under the famous Ferdinand Magellan. You know Ferdinand was part of the Magellan-Elcano expedition?" Everyone looks blankly back at her. "Anyway, Afonso found reports of the entrance inscribed on a volcanic rock somewhere on an island in the Pacific."

Caleb leans forward, pulse quickening. "Do you know of the entrance or where its exact location is?"

"I have the information. It's somewhere in the library but I know for a fact the notes of Afonso are within these walls." Nim wheels backwards. "Give me a bit and I'll find it." She swiftly leaves the room.

In Nim's absence, Caleb turns his attention to Cora and Mason. "I want you both to go to the council and keep an eye on them. Help them out with the vampires in the city and make sure they are ready to fight in case Orion breaks free of Purgatory. Remember, we already have other enemies on the loose." Felix's rebel Order would still be causing problems.

The pair nod and Cora pauses in the doorway. "Get my friend back for me, okay?"

"I will, Cora. I promise." Caleb's never meant words more.

Cora offers him a slight smile before leaving with Mason to head to the vampire council. Caleb and Galina don't have to wait long for Nim to return. The librarian must have noticed Cora and Mason leaving because she doesn't comment on their sudden absence. She gently sets a stack of papers, brown and thin with age, on the table before her.

After carefully leafing through the papers, she finds what they need. She makes a small noise of surprise. "It seems the secret entrance to Purgatory actually lies in a very familiar place."

Caleb and Galina cast a questioning glance between them. "What do you mean?" Caleb asks. "Where is it?"

"The entrance lies in a small temple that was built to worship the Goddess Athena," Nim says. "At least, according to Afonso's notes. I can't be certain if he was there himself, or if this is someone else's retelling he has written down, but I know of the place. Supposedly, this temple also contains the entrance to Atlantis. It says here there is a network of tunnels, once used by the Grail Keepers and dark monsters alike."

Caleb leans forward, but can't make out the writing on the paper. "What sort of dark monsters?" If they're going to this temple, he needs to know what they're up against.

"It doesn't say," Nim replies. "They may not even dwell there anymore, if they were eradicated by the Grail Keepers. You won't be exploring those tunnels, anyway. This note says that to open the portal to Purgatory, the seeker will need to find an object to open the portal."

Deflating, Caleb sets back against his chair. "Where is the object?"

"Again, this doesn't say. The best you can hope for is that it's still somewhere in the temple." Nim sets the paper down. "I'm sorry, but that's all of the information I have available. As far as I know, this is the only way, aside from the Grave, that a person can physically enter Purgatory. Orion is ancient and he may know of this back door, so be prepared to find your way barred once again. For the future of this world, I hope it's not."

Caleb stands. "Thank you for your help, Nim. Your knowledge is invaluable."

A slight blush kisses her cheeks. "It is my duty to serve all who enter Veritas." She bows her head slightly. "I wish you the best of luck."

Once outside, Galina frowns. "It will take us at least a day to get a flight anywhere close to where we need to go, not to mention finding a boat."

Caleb shakes his head. "We don't have the time for all of that. We need to be there today."

"Just how do you propose we do that?" The witch crosses her arms. "Even if we had the money to get such transportation catered to us, it will still take time."

A grin spreads across Caleb's face. "You do know I can run fast, right? *Really* fast." He gathers her in his arms, ignoring her protests, and takes off in a blur of motion.

Galina knows about the speed of vampires, but Caleb's amused at her surprise when they reach the coast and he runs right across the water, kicking up droplets in his wake. Salty wind hits his face and whips Galina's hair back. Her grumbles settle into a deep scowl, but she hunkers down in his arms, conceding this will certainly get them there fast.

They don't know the exact location of the island, but Galina' able to pinpoint it as they draw closer, commenting that she senses the magic. Finally, Caleb slows as they reach a rocky shore. Although they just covered thousands of miles, he's barely out of breath. This is the power vampires hold. Power that could be used for good.

Athena's temple is little more than slabs of rock with an

opening just large enough for a person to pass through. Slowly, they approach the temple. Caleb cocks his head.

"I don't hear anything inside," he says. "Think it's safe to go in?"

Galina leans forward, eyeing the dark entrance. "There's only one way to find out, I suppose." She raises her hand and a sphere of magic appears above her palm to light their way.

Caleb steps inside first, Galina close behind him. The light from her sphere washes across the walls of a roughly circular room. As Nim had said, there are openings leading off to different tunnels. There are also shelves carved into the stone walls with various objects sitting on them.

Galina makes her way around, perusing the shelves as if she's in a shoe store. But each object she eyes is quickly discounted. Caleb isn't sure how she can tell whether it's what they're looking for or not, but he doesn't question her. She hasn't led them astray yet. Plus, what choice does he have? This is his only chance to find Maddy.

Galina steps over to one of the objects—what appears to be a small stone bowl. Her eyes narrow on a series of runes carved along the stone. "This is the one to open Purgatory," she says.

"You're sure?" Caleb steps closer, but he can't decipher the strange markings.

The witch clicks her tongue. "Of course, I'm sure." She glances at him as she picks up the bowl. "I'm going to try and activate it. Are you ready?"

Nerves and eager energy flutter through Caleb's stomach. He rolls his shoulders. "Ready to enter Purgatory? Sure, why not."

Galina closes her eyes, muttering quietly, and then the bowl in her hands begins to glow. Cool air kisses the back of Caleb's neck and in the next instant, a shimmering doorway appears a few feet away.

"Go," Galina says, keeping her eyes closed. "Hurry. I don't know how long I can keep the portal open."

Caleb sets his jaw, then dashes into the portal, hoping to hell he's about to end up in Purgatory.

Alive.

CHAPTER 7

MADELEINE

"Please, you can't do this. Please."

Maddy's teeth grind together as she pulls a whining Quinn along a sidewalk in the empty gray of Mercy City. The soul's constant string of complaints are grating on her last nerve. She tries not to groan at the distance she still needs to travel, or the hours, days, even, that it will take to get to her destination. Purgatory is wearing on her. The starkness, the deafening silence, and the way time seems skewed is messing with her mind, giving her a sense of hopelessness that she will never get out of this place.

"You can't take me to him." Quinn plants her feet, staring with wide, pleading eyes at Maddy. "Please, you don't know what Orion will do to me."

Maddy hisses. "Be quiet, Quinn. You brought this on yourself. So zip it and hurry up." She reaches out and tugs on the spirit again.

Quinn shakes her hands off but with the bracelets around her wrist, there's no use resisting. Tears sting at her eyes and her nostrils flare. "I hate you," she says. "I hate you for doing this to me."

"I haven't done anything to you." Maddy continues down the sidewalk, squinting between the rise of buildings in the business district. She turns, taking a side road that will lead them around the Merrick Group building. "You were the one who decided to take a darker path. What did you think would happen?"

Both women quietly seethe for several more minutes, or perhaps it's a few hours. It's difficult for Maddy to tell.

Quinn stops again as they near the edge of the city. "I'm not taking another step. He'll destroy me. I won't let you deliver me to Orion like some cow to slaughter."

Maddy grabs Quinn's shoulders and spins her around to face her. "Do you honestly think I would hand over the obsidian to anybody, let alone Orion?"

After a beat of silence, Quinn asks, "What do you mean? Isn't that where we're going?"

"Orion may have attempted to sweet-talk me and dangle the promise of a normal life in front of my face, but I'm not stupid or gullible. I want a normal life with Caleb, and someday I'll get it. Right now, I need to get the obsidian out of Purgatory. It's too dangerous. I'm not taking you to Orion, I'm taking you to the Grave and back to the world of the living."

Maddy starts off again and this time Quinn follows her without complaint. Perhaps the promise of not being taken to Orion has her a little less resistant.

"Once we go through the Grave, then what?" Quinn eyes Maddy, suspicion sparking in her gaze.

Pausing, Maddy looks around a corner. There are still no spirits in sight. While she hasn't seen a great deal of the souls dwelling in Purgatory, she hasn't seen any since she captured Quinn. It's strange, as if something has scared them away into hiding. Alert, Maddy quickly and quietly hurries on her way.

"I'll have someone siphon off the obsidian from you and

put it into something more permanent," Maddy says. She ignores the hushed sound of protest from Quinn, the only evidence that the obsidian doesn't want to be drawn from her. Quinn hasn't had another bout of obsidian-influenced ranting since Maddy placed the bracelets on her, but there's no doubt in her mind the evil darkness in Quinn is simply biding its time. "Once the obsidian is removed from you and put somewhere more stable, you will help us recover the Chalice and we will use it to control Orion just as the necromancer had planned."

Quinn shakes her head. "You cannot accomplish such things without the obsidian. Don't you know what sort of power you would hold if you were to use it?"

Maddy grimaces. Perhaps the obsidian isn't waiting in the shadows of Quinn's mind, after all. It seems it's beginning to give up on Quinn and is turning its attention to tempting Maddy. "The obsidian is going somewhere safe," she says emphatically. "Never to be used by anyone ever again. It's too vile and dangerous for this world. Once the obsidian is taken care of you, Quinn, will return to Purgatory. You are a spirit and this is where you belong. Then, we will bury Ileana's body the way she was meant to be from the start."

"No." Quinn's hands fly to her chest and she backs away from Maddy. "You can't make me come back here. You can't. He'll be waiting for me. No matter what you do, Orion will find a way to torture me." Her face pales with sheer panic and her eyes flick around, as if saying his name will draw him to her.

Maddy almost feels sorry for Quinn. The spirit has done so much damage and caused so much strife between everyone, but there is no denying the fear in her gaze is genuine. Maddy offers her a slight smile. "If you help us, Quinn, I promise you we will figure out a way to break the control he holds on you and the other spirits in Purgatory. We can destroy Orion, but we'll need your help. We'll need you to side with us, Quinn, wholly and without any treachery on your part."

The spirit sucks her bottom lip in, working it between her teeth for a moment, then gives a shaky nod. "Okay. I'll let you take the obsidian and then I promise, I'll help you in any way I can."

"Good," Maddy says.

She isn't certain if she believes Quinn—only time will tell if the spirit spoke the truth. The pair continue to travel what feels like miles and days. Maddy's stomach growls ferociously from hunger and her muscles have long since turned watery with exertion. Finally, her eyes spot a familiar cemetery.

She smiles and her heartbeats quicken. "We're almost there." She's so close to getting back to a world with noise and color. She's so close to seeing Caleb again, and knowing he and her friends are safe. Grabbing Quinn's sleeve, Maddy tugs her along as she quickens her pace. "Hurry."

They reach the cemetery and Maddy moves swiftly around the aged headstones, aiming toward the spot near the center where the Grave sits.

"There it is," Maddy says. The mirror image of the Grave in the living world yawns before her, the hole emanating a sort of buzzing energy, as if life from the other world is leaking through. She tightens her grip on Quinn. "Ready?"

Quinn mumbles something that must be a disgruntled agreement. Relief and anticipation flutter through Maddy. She can't wait to be rid of this place.

Just as Maddy's about to leap into the Grave, a flash of light erupts and strikes the ground before her. She and Quinn stumble backward. Maddy blinks several times, attempting to sweep away the effects of the bright light.

"How utterly predictable."

Maddy and Quinn spin toward the voice, and the spirit

makes a noise in her throat like a frightened animal. Orion steps out from behind an above ground tomb, a smile stretching across his face. This time, though, he's dressed in black robes covered in intricate dark blue armor. His black hair reaches far beyond his shoulders, while his piercing blue eyes hold nothing but malice.

Maddy glances toward the Grave and curses. There is some sort of shimmering barrier around it now. She steps in front of Quinn.

"I thought you'd be waiting by the Merrick Group building," Maddy says. It was a gamble. Orion never said he would wait for her there but that was where she'd left him. Apparently, she was very wrong in her assumption.

Orion strides closer to them, his long sleeves flowing, and chuckles softly. "As I said, you are predictable. I saw your life, remember? I know how stubborn you are. You want a life with Caleb, yes, but I knew you wouldn't take the bait. I knew you would bring Quinn here to solve the problem yourself. I've always been good at knowing what people will do."

Maddy scoffs. "What do you want, a reward or something?"

The smile fades from Orion's face. "Yes, Madeleine, I suppose I do. I'll take her." He points to Quinn. "Neither Quinn nor the obsidian will be passing through the Grave again. I will not allow either to escape."

There's no warning as Orion leaps forward, arms outstretched to grab Quinn and the dark power hiding within her. Maddy gasps, reaching back and taking Quinn's arm. She flings the spirit out of the way. Quinn hits the ground and Orion collides with Maddy instead. The pair hit the barrier around the Grave. Cold, biting energy flows across Maddy's back and she traps a scream behind her clenched teeth. She shoves her body forward, pushing Orion away from her. The entity snaps his attention back to Quinn. She's pushing herself up from the ground.

Orion lunges for her, his eyes dark with greed.

"No!" Maddy throws herself toward him and wraps her arms around his waist, groaning as she tries to tug him backwards.

"Get off of me." He whirls, throwing a blast of power into her.

Maddy flies backward and hits the ground hard. Her teeth clamp down on the impact and she bites the edge of her tongue. Warm blood pools in her mouth. Ears ringing, she gets back on her feet and spits. Orion's attention is back on Quinn as he advances toward her. Maddy can't let him get a hold of the obsidian, not when she's so close to bringing it back to her world.

"Quinn, run!" Maddy yells. Thankfully, Quinn actually listens to her for once and bolts to the left.

Orion laughs, his eyes tracking her like a cat watching a mouse try to flee. Maddy hurries to Quinn, grabs the spirit, and once again pushes her behind her back.

"Very admirable," Orion says. "But useless. This is my dominion." He holds his hands outward. "And you will not win here."

Desperation burns through Maddy, and the sensation grows hotter. Her eyebrows pinch together and her pulse races. Something is wrong. The heat is unbearable. What is happening? A deep-rooted instinct unfurls within her. She thrusts a hand forward and then stumbles backward in shock as something bright and burning erupts before her. Wreathed in flames of red and gold, a dragon born of magic and fire rises between Maddy and Orion. The fierce being burns so brightly, it casts away the shadows of Purgatory, illuminating the entire place like a massive beacon of light. The dragon's eyes sparkle like rubies as it dives toward Orion.

The entity is momentarily thrown off by the power which has burst from Maddy. He dodges the dragon, but barely. Maddy draws on more of her magic and the dragon reacts, flames growing hotter and body moving more swiftly. Orion recovers from his shock quickly and begins to fight back. The entity's own fire essence circles around him, then strikes at the dragon like a snake of dancing flames.

Back and forth, Maddy's and Orion's fire battle each other. Heat presses around them, drawing beads of sweat across her forehead. Her muscles shake and the coppery taste of blood coats her tongue from the cut. Maddy's power begins to wane and she realizes she drew too much too quickly. With a final thrust of her arm, trying to urge the dragon forward, it disintegrates.

Her chest heaves and her knees shake. The absence of the fire and light makes Purgatory feel colder and darker than ever. She stares at the empty space between her and Orion.

"I hope you have a better plan than that," Quinn mutters.

Maddy isn't even certain how she conjured such a thing in the first place, or what she can possibly do now. She reaches toward Quinn's hand, ready to tug the spirit and run. How far will they be able to go, though, when Orion's reach extends over all of Purgatory?

Orion advances toward them. Triumph drips from his lips as they curve in a slow, confident grin. He has them trapped and he knows it. Maddy frantically tries to think of something, anything, she can do to stop him. Quinn's fingers tighten in Maddy's hand and she can feel the terror in the grip.

Just as Orion is closing in, hands wrap around his neck from behind.

His eyes widen a fraction just before his head jerks to the side with a terrible snap.

Orion's limp body drops to the ground and Maddy comes face-to-face with a certain vampire king who looks very, *very* pissed.

CHAPTER 8

CALEB

Anger and relief crash together and threaten to wreck Caleb where he stands as his gaze locks with Maddy. Her lips are parted and her eyes are wide with shock as she stares back at him. Behind her, Quinn's gaze darts to him, then to Orion's body.

"Caleb?" Maddy's voice is hushed, as if she can't quite believe he's standing right there in front of her.

He takes two long strides and grabs her shoulders. "What the hell is wrong with you?"

"What?" Maddy blinks, then seems to really register the expression on his face. She reaches up, grabbing his arms. "What's the matter?"

"What's the matter?" Caleb bares his teeth, but Maddy doesn't flinch away when the monster inside him peeks through. "Maddy, you could have been killed. You could have been trapped in Purgatory, forever. Why would you just jump through the Grave like that?"

She jabs a thumb back toward Quinn. "To catch her, which I managed to do, by the way." She props her hands on her hips. "You know, I thought after not seeing me for days and days that maybe—" Her words are cut off as Caleb wraps his arms around her, pinning her to his chest in a tight hug.

"God, Maddy, you had me scared to death. I didn't know what was happening to you. I didn't know if you were lost or hurting." He takes a few deep breaths, inhaling her scent and trying to detect any injuries or fear. He doesn't smell anything other than relief and a bit of awe. He eases her back and tilts his head. "Did you say days?"

"Yeah." Maddy looks around Purgatory, frowning at the monotone landscape. "I was walking forever and while I knew it must just be this place, I'm convinced I've been here for days. At least, it's felt like days."

Caleb lifts a hand and runs the back of his knuckles down Maddy's jawline. "It hasn't been days in the living world. Hours, at the most." Her skin heats beneath his touch. "Are you sure you're okay? Did anything hurt you?"

"I'm fine." Maddy looks down at Orion and swallows. "Is he...dead?"

He knows what she means. Orion's body here in Purgatory may have been broken, but does one ever truly die in such a place? "I honestly don't know for certain." He takes a step away and toes Orion's body. The man's eyes remain dull and lacking any spark of life. "I want you to go back through the Grave to the mortal world and take Quinn with you."

Quinn takes a few steps away from Maddy. "I'm not your prisoner. You can't tell me what to do."

"Is that so?" Maddy crosses her arms and turns toward her. "Those bracelets on your hand say differently. You're coming back with me." She steps closer to Quinn, but the spirit again sidesteps.

"You're going to take the obsidian from me," she says, the words almost a whine. "What if it kills me in the process?"

Maddy's eyes roll. "You're already dead, remember?" She tries to grab Quinn but the spirit keeps her distance.

Impatient to get out of the strange world of Purgatory, Caleb flashes forward and takes Quinn's arm. "We don't have time for this. I need to take care of Orion before he miraculously comes back to life. I have a feeling you wouldn't want to be lingering here, Quinn, if that happens."

She opens her mouth, then snaps it shut. Her retort dies in her mouth, and she decides to glower between Maddy and Caleb instead.

"How did you even get here?" Maddy asks, taking Quinn's hand when he draws the spirit to her. "I thought vampires couldn't go through the Grave?"

"Through a portal, though I'm not at liberty to say where and how in the present company." Caleb smiles when Quinn bristles. "You better get going. I'll take care of Orion and I'll meet you at the Grave on the other side. Please wait for me there, Maddy. I don't want to have to go chasing after you again." He chuckles at the annoyance that coats her scent.

She tugs a reluctant Quinn over to the Grave, then looks back at him. "Are you sure you're going to be okay?"

"I'll be fine," Caleb says. "I'll be close behind you." A look passes over Maddy's face, a sort of yearning that's smoldering behind her gaze. "We'll be together again soon."

She nods. "Come on, Quinn." Without another word, Maddy jumps into the Grave with her and disappears.

Caleb releases a breath, his cheeks puffing out. He recognized Maddy's parting expression and his chest tightens at the thought. She missed him, a concept that feels both strange and freeing. He was frantic to be reunited and it had only been hours for him. Maddy was in Purgatory for what had felt like days on her part. He can't even imagine what she must be feeling. It makes him even more eager to get out of this place and return to her side once again.

He turns his attention to Orion's body. He doesn't know much about the man other than he was a powerful being who nearly destroyed the world. Caleb wishes he had Gabby or Galina to speak with in regard to what to do with Orion's body. Leaving him out in the open feels too dangerous, as if some spirit may come along and prod him awake. Even the reapers may find Orion's body and bring him back to a semblance of life right here in this cemetery.

Pursing his lips, Caleb peers around. There aren't many options available to him. He certainly can't bring the body back with him. That would be more dangerous than leaving Orion here. He supposes he could tear him apart and scatter the broken pieces throughout Purgatory, but that seems unnecessarily messy. Caleb studies the cemetery, an idea finally materializing. He'll bury Orion—this is a graveyard after all.

He makes quick work of digging with his hands, his strong fingers pulling up dirt easily. Within minutes, another large hole several feet deep has been created in the cemetery.

Caleb steps back, surveying his handiworks when a chill has settles on his skin. He glances over his shoulder to find a wandering spirit pause and stare at him. He holds his breath, but the spirit seems to snap out of its daze and continue on its way. But it's a reminder for Caleb. As a vampire, he isn't supposed to be in this place. If he doesn't hurry, Purgatory will learn of his presence and then who knows what will happen to him. He grabs a hold of Orion, the man's head lolling at an unnatural angle, and pulls him over to the freshly dug grave. Then, he rolls the body into the hole and works quickly to cover him up, grateful for vampire speed.

Caleb stands and wipes his dirty palms on the front of his

jeans. Satisfied he's done the best he can, he whirls around and runs. He reaches the portal then rushes through.

Galina jumps when he suddenly emerges back in the temple, nearly dropping the object from her hands. "You made it," she says. She puts the stone bowl back on its shelf. "What happened?"

"I'll tell you on the way back." Caleb steps over to the witch and gathers her in his arms, the need to be back with Maddy overwhelming. "We have no time to waste. We're going back to the Grave."

As the pair run across the ocean in a blur, Caleb recounts what happened in Purgatory. "So, I sent Maddy back with Quinn, then I buried Orion's body right there in the cemetery. I wasn't certain what else I could have done with him."

Galina's arms are tight around Caleb's neck as she glances at the spray of water kicked up by the vampire's feet. "You did the right thing," she says. "There are spells that could have been performed to ensure that Orion stays buried, even in the after-life, but he should be down there a good long while, if not for all of eternity."

Caleb nods, glad to hear that. At least that's one enemy they don't have to deal with.

The journey across the ocean and back to the Grave takes nearly an hour. His heart is racing as he slows down at the familiar sight of the cemetery. He quickly scans the area and lets out a relieved breath when he spots Maddy standing with a sulking Quinn.

"It's about time," Quinn says. "It's getting cold out here and I'm hungry."

Caleb doesn't bother to tell the spirit he had to travel from a secluded island in the ocean. His focus is entirely on Maddy. She notices his stare and he's certain he hears her heartbeats quicken.

"Galina, would you mind taking Quinn off Maddy's hands for a minute?" he asks, not breaking eye contact with Maddy.

The witch walks over and grabs Quinn's hand, then tugs her away. He ignores Galina's muttering about young people and their hormones. She weaves between the aged headstones and stops with Quinn several yards away. Caleb and Maddy may as well be alone, the way she stares at him as if he's the only person in existence.

"Caleb." Maddy's voice trembles and she says his name with such heartbreaking relief, that he crosses over to her.

He pulls her into his arms again. He can feel her heart beating against his chest. Her scent washes over him and he breathes deeper, drawing in every emotion whirling through her.

"I was afraid I was never going to see you again," she says. Shame flickers through her scent. "I didn't want to give up. I knew I had to get Quinn out of Purgatory, but everything was taking so long. I started to fear I'd never get out, and never find you."

"Good thing I found you, then." Caleb's hand curves around the back of Maddy's neck. His fingers play with her hair as he looks down at her, a smile on her face. "Let's not do that again, okay?"

Maddy huffs a quiet laugh. "Do what again, go into Purgatory or be apart?"

"Both." Caleb shakes his head. "God, Maddy, I hadn't realized..." His voice drifts into silence, because how can he possibly put words to what he's feeling?

"Realized what?" Maddy tugs on his shirt, drawing his attention.

He grabs her hand, holding it to his chest as he bares his soul to her. "I hadn't realized just how much you mean to me, and how much it would hurt to be away from you until I saw you jump into the Grave." His other hand continues to hold the back of her neck and his thumb drifts up her skin, then pauses on her quickening pulse. "I never want to be apart from you again."

Maddy's lips quirk in a smile. "I think I can live with that." Her fingers curl in his shirt and then she's drawing him closer, rising up on her toes.

A low growl rumbles up Caleb's throat as his mouth claims Maddy's. Heat rises between them, catching their souls on fire as they deepen the kiss. He revels in her taste and the warm touch of their lips moving together. Their kiss deepens, their hands climb up to clutch each other.

And just like that, Caleb is ruined. There is nothing left of his life but Maddy. He wants to fight with her and live for her. Everything they do, everything they'll face, he knows they must do it together. They've both been fighting against this while yearning for it. They've tried to run from it, while simultaneously opening their arms to the sparks between them.

Now, they've caught fire and there will be no going back.

Maddy is the first to pull back. She rests her forehead on Caleb's chest, her breaths quivering. "Never again," she says. "I don't want to be apart anymore. I don't want to be alone. I don't want to fight against *us*." She tilts her head back, peering up at him with wide, hopeful eyes.

"This is our life," Caleb says. "And we're going to continue it together. No more holding back. No more fighting or doubt. I care for you, Maddy, and I want you to be with me."

Her eyes blink rapidly and she leans her head against him again. He rubs her back and laughs softly.

"Are you crying?" he says.

"No." Maddy scoffs, but doesn't speak again for a moment. Finally, she takes a step back and rubs her nose. "I'm just glad to be out of Purgatory."

Caleb smirks but doesn't say anything about the tear he's certain he notices slide down her face. He shoves his hands in his pockets. "You know, we should really try going out on a normal date sometime."

Maddy laughs as the pair of them start toward Galina and Quinn. "That does sound very nice."

Before Caleb can promise that they'll get through this and find a sense of normalcy again, she halts. He glances down at her, nostrils flaring as he draws in her scent. Alarm permeates her. He follows her gaze to Galina and finds a strange, black smoke billowing behind her. Before he can call out a warning, the dark smoke surges forward and swallows the witch and Quinn.

"Galina!" Maddy rushes toward them.

Caleb races past her but the smoke is gone by the time he reaches it. Galina is lying on the ground, her eyes shut, but her chest rising and falling steadily. She's unconscious rather than dead.

Maddy slows to a stop, then turns in a circle. "She's gone," she says. "Quinn is gone."

"Look." Caleb points to the ground where Quinn had been.

There, burned into the dirt where the spirit had been standing, is an infinity symbol.

CHAPTER 9

MADELEINE

Maddy crouches and studies the looping infinity symbol. It looks like a figure eight but narrower, more refined, somehow. Tentatively, she reaches down to touch it. She hisses and jerks her hand back.

"Is it hot?" Caleb asks, standing close behind her.

"No." Maddy shakes her head. "It's freezing." She straightens to her feet. "What was that...that thing?" There were no words to describe the strange smoke that billowed up in the cemetery. It wasn't just plumes of darkness. There had been something sentient about the smoke, as if it were a living creature and not merely vapors.

Caleb tilts his head, eyeing the symbol left on the ground. "I'm not sure what it was, but it can't be good."

A low moan rumbles from Galina and her eyelids flutter open. Maddy crosses over to her and kneels down at the witch's side. "Galina?" She lays a hand on Galina's shoulder. "Are you okay?"

Maddy helps Galina into a sitting position and the witch rubs at her temples. "I feel like I've been hit by a truck."

"You were attacked with some sort of smoke," Maddy says. "And whatever it was, it took Quinn and left that." She points at the symbol.

The witch narrows her eyes, spotting the infinity symbol. She climbs to her feet and walks over to get a closer look. "I've seen this symbol before," Galina says. Her face is grim, lips pressed together as she stares at the mark left on the ground.

"What is it?" Caleb asks.

"I'm not certain what it means or why it was left here, but this symbol kept popping up when the world was close to an extinction-level event a few months ago." Galina sighs. "I think we need to visit Veritas again. Perhaps Nim knows what this means."

Maddy peers around the cemetery one more time, but there is absolutely no sign of Quinn. "All right," she says on a sigh. "Let's go pester Nim again." She blinks when Caleb grabs her hand, then smiles. His touch is warm, comforting.

And he doesn't let go until they reach the steps of Veritas.

It's so strange to Maddy that not long ago Caleb had infuriated her, made her feel betrayed and unwanted, and now, he's someone who she can't see living without. Maybe that's why he got to her so much in the first place. Because she was so drawn to this strong, determined vampire. She blinks, realizing the one holding the door open to the massive, ancient library holds her heart and soul. Caleb's mouth quirks into a grin, no doubt catching her scent as she passes by him.

Several minutes pass as the three of them search the library for Nim. There are a few other patrons scattered throughout the lines and line of bookshelves. None of them spare them a glance, too focused on whatever it is they're researching. They finally find Nim on the third floor, a stack of books on her lap as she wheels along a bookshelf.

"I had a feeling I'd be seeing you again, though I didn't

think it would be so soon." She turns her wheelchair to angle toward them. "I'm glad to see you've returned safely from Purgatory, Maddy. Were you unable to find Quinn?"

"I found her," Maddy says. "Then promptly lost her outside of the Grave, thanks to some weird smoke thing." Nim lifts an eyebrow, but Maddy doesn't elaborate just yet. "Have you ever seen or heard of this symbol?" She draws it in the air with her finger.

Nim nods as her brow sinks down. "Why do you ask?"

Caleb leans against one of the tall bookcases. "Because it was left etched onto the ground where Quinn was taken. It was cold to the touch, if that makes any difference."

"Cultus Infinitialis," a voice says from behind.

Maddy looks over to find a pair of women approaching them. One is older with blonde hair and blue eyes. There is no supernatural aura around her so she assumes the woman is human. The other is wearing a bright green dress with vibrant hair to match. She smiles broadly at Maddy.

"Hello," the green-haired one says. "My name is Blaise and this is Sierra." The woman gives Galina a friendly, familiar nod. There is something about Blaise and as Maddy looks between her and Galina, she realizes Blaise is also a witch.

"Hi," Maddy says. She tilts her head. "What was that you said?"

Sierra is the one who answers. There is no smile on her face. "Cultus Infinitialis. That symbol is part of a cult that once belonged to an organization named The Tenth Legion. It would seem it's a part of the new mystery organization that is beginning to make waves in the supernatural world." She leans against the railing overlooking the main floor and brushes a tendril of hair from her face. "As if we don't have enough to worry about. You say you've seen this symbol. What happened?"

Maddy glances at Caleb and Galina before answering. These people are strangers, and she isn't certain how much they should know. Caleb gives her a small nod so she recounts the journey into Purgatory and what happened afterwards.

"The black smoke monster, if that's what it truly was, came out of nowhere," Maddy says. "It was quick. The thing knocked Galina out and took Quinn in a matter of seconds. Even Caleb wasn't able to get to it in time. Then, it left behind the infinity symbol." She turns to Nim. "Have you heard of anything like this monster?"

Nim hums. "Perhaps, but I want to find a reference to be certain. I'll check the books."

Craning her neck, Maddy looks up at the endless shelves of books. "That could take days."

"Then, perhaps it will be best if we split up." Nim smiles, then wheels off with Blaise. Galina and Sierra move toward another section, leaving Maddy and Caleb to search together.

As the pair move among the shelves, their footsteps almost silent as they sink in the plush carpet, Maddy finds herself glancing at Caleb. His eyes are on the books, but she's certain he's homed in on every step she takes and every beat of her heart. The aisle they walk down is narrow. Her shoulder nearly brushes his and, unable to help herself, she reaches down and brushes her fingers over his hand.

Caleb stops, first looking down at the fingers Maddy twines with his, then lifting his gaze to her face. Something burns there in his eyes, a need she knows is reflecting in her own stare. She draws in a shaky breath, surprised at just how much she's feeling. It's as if the words they spoke in the cemetery had opened the floodgates and every emotion she's held for Caleb is now pouring out. Drowning in the need to touch and taste him, she hooks a hand behind his head and draws his face down to hers. Their lips meet and the warmth burning between them is stoked into a fiery passion.

Uncaring if anyone happens to walk by and see them, Maddy presses her body closer to Caleb. She aches to feel every hard muscle, to breathe in his scent, and taste him more deeply. Her pulse quickens when his tongue flicks against her lips and she parts her mouth. A moan rumbles up her throat and he becomes unleashed at the sound. He whirls her around and her back hits the shelves. A volume tumbles to the floor but neither of them stop.

Caleb breaks the kiss and for a second, their eyes meet. When he finds no hesitation in Maddy's gaze, he trails a line of kisses from beneath her ear and down her jawline. Her knees nearly give out when his warm mouth presses against the side of her neck, sucking and kissing her. He grabs one of her legs and lifts it up toward his hip. She tangles her fingers in his hair, butterflies erupting in her stomach. He lets out a growl of plea-sure, skimming his nose along her throat, breathing in her scent.

"God, Caleb." Maddy's voice shakes. She wants more of him, so much that she can barely stand it.

A throat clears and the two look over to find Galina passing by with a disapproving stare. Slowly, Caleb sets Maddy back on the floor. There's a challenge in his gaze, as if daring the witch to utter a single word of reprimand.

"I thought you'd like to know, Nim found what she was searching for." Without another word, the witch turns and walks away.

Maddy presses a hand to her chest, her heart racing beneath her palm. What's gotten into her? She and Caleb were alone for mere minutes and she lost herself in a make-out session. Granted, she doesn't regret it, but they have to get their head back in the game before they completely lose their senses.

Caleb lets out a long sigh. "Come on." He grabs her hand, the subtle squeeze he gives her fingers the only reassurance he offers that someday, they'll be able to be together the way they want.

They follow Galina through rows of shelves and then find Nim seated at a small table, a large, age-worn tome open before her. Sierra and Blaise peer down at the yellowed pages. Maddy takes a look and finds a rough drawing of a monster made of smoke.

"When you spoke of the monster who took Quinn, I thought this may be it and I was correct," Nim says. "It is called a cherufe. The cherufe are creatures often associated with volcanoes and magma. They are hard to find, harder to catch, and nearly impossible to control." She tilts her head back, peering at Blaise. "It wouldn't have left the symbol unless it was ordered to do so. I wonder what the cult is up to with such a monster? Cherufe are not ones to blindly give their loyalty away."

"Especially since we thought this cult had been destroyed," Sierra mutters.

Maddy stares at the drawing of the cherufe. "Apparently, the cult has returned. If they have creatures such as this in their thrall, then we are in deeper trouble than we thought."

"Quinn must be found," Nim says. "She has the obsidian within her. We dodged a bullet by getting her out of Purgatory before Orion could get his hands on her, but it's only a matter of time before someone else tries to use her and the power she holds."

"Or before she tries to use it herself." Maddy recalls the way Quinn had been speaking about the obsidian while in Purgatory. The dark influence was already beginning to stain her thoughts.

Galina pulls Blaise aside. "We can do a locator spell. If we do it together, it will be stronger."

Blaise nods and the two join hands. Maddy watches with interest. Sometimes Galina uses powders, stones, and other objects with her spells, but perhaps if there's another witch, they somehow manage to feed off each other's magic. Light swirls softly between their hands as their eyes close. Galina mutters the words for the spell under her breath. The library's silence stretches between the group as they wait, tense, for Quinn's location.

Suddenly, the witch's hands unclasp and Galina shakes her head. "A block was thrown up by a strange power before I could completely lock in her location. I'm certain it was the power of the dreamcatcher that provided the block."

"Damn it," Maddy growls. "What are we supposed to do now? The cherufe could have taken Quinn anywhere."

Galina shakes her head. "No, not anywhere. I saw flashes of a familiar place, however. I believe Quinn may be somewhere in the Merrick Group building."

Before Maddy can mention that everything keeps circling back to the Merrick Group of Industries, Caleb's pocket starts buzzing. He pulls out his phone and answers, walking a few feet away. A muscle ticks along his jaw as he speaks quietly. She tries not to watch or listen, but she can't help but be curious. After a couple of minutes, he ends the call and stuffs his phone back into his pocket.

He gives Maddy an apologetic smile as he walks back to her. "I'm sorry, but I need to leave and meet with the council."

"Should I come with you?" she asks. Caleb is the vampire king, and she knows he has responsibilities with his kind, but if they're going to be together, she wants him to know she supports every facet of his life.

He shakes his head. "No, it's just some vampire business. I'll deal with it and come right back." His cheek lifts in a smile. "Be careful and try not to do anything impulsive like jumping into Purgatory."

Maddy rolls her eyes, but a smile touches her lips. "I promise not to get too crazy if you promise to hurry."

After a quick peck on the lips, Caleb flashes down the stairs and out of Veritas before Maddy can tell him to stay safe, too.

CHAPTER 10

CALEB

The council is still in the same place as the previous time Caleb visited them. He approaches the nondescript building and when he sees a familiar figure leaning against the brick wall, his eyebrows rise.

"Mason?" he pauses beside his best friend, then glances around. "Where's Cora?"

Mason shoves away from the wall. "I sent her off with some of the other vampires to learn some fighting techniques. I figured she could use it."

Caleb nods. He should have thought of it himself. "We'll need to make sure she's told that Maddy is okay."

"You found her, then?" Mason pushes the door open and steps inside.

"Yes." Caleb's tone is sharp, thinking about the fact he'd lost Quinn directly after leaving Purgatory. Mason, sensing the irritation in his friend, doesn't pry for more details.

Elias, the vampire who works closely with the council, steps out of a room ahead at Caleb's approach. "There you are," he says. "The council is growing impatient."

"I came here as quickly as I could manage." Caleb tilts his chin up, his voice hardening. It's a reminder to Elias just who he is speaking to. Caleb may be younger than him, and new to ruling, but they chose him to be their king and he will demand respect when it's due. "Shall we?" He stalks past Elias into the room where the council waits.

The members of the council look up in unison when Caleb enters the room with Mason and Elias.

"Ah, there you are." The man who speaks doesn't glower with impatience or smile in greeting. His face is impassive, as is the rest of the council. They've had years of practice in schooling any emotion from their features, a technique Caleb isn't certain he ever wants to accomplish. Though he's a vampire, losing all sense of emotion takes him much too far from the humanity he wishes to cling to as long as he can. Without it, he's nothing but a monster.

He greets them and takes a seat at the table. It's round, putting them all on level ground. "My apologies for the delay. I've had several matters that needed my attention."

"Tell us about your progress with the mystery organization," a woman says. Her hair is short, almost boyish, but her eyes tell her age and wisdom. "Have you found out who they are and where they hide?"

Though much of it could be unrelated to the organization, Caleb recounts the events since he last spoke with the council, including his trip into Purgatory and the fact Quinn was taken by a cherufe. When he finishes, he looks to Mason. His friend stands nearby and nods.

"It's true," Mason says. "I was there for much of it, though as you know I wasn't in the cemetery when Caleb returned from Purgatory."

One of the council members folds his long, thin fingers and stares at Caleb. "And what are your plans now?"

"Finding Quinn is a priority. She cannot be allowed to run around with the obsidian," Caleb says. "We think she may have been taken to the Merrick Group of Industries."

Elias steps up to the table. "And what of this Orion fellow? I think we need to focus on preparing for his arrival into the mortal world. We cannot afford to be caught off guard if he does, indeed, manage to escape Purgatory."

"He's right," the short-haired woman says. "Orion is a powerful entity. He would not be so easily killed, as you claimed." She turns her bright blue eyes to Caleb. "Do you believe, beyond a shadow of a doubt, that Orion was ended?"

Caleb pauses. "No, I cannot make that promise." As much as he hates to admit it, he can't be certain Orion was truly killed when he snapped his neck. If he is as powerful as Gabby said, Orion would likely return at some point. The only satisfaction Caleb has about the matter is that Orion will need to dig up through six feet of dirt in Purgatory. "Make preparations for a possible attack from Orion if you feel the need to do so, but I am going to focus on retrieving Quinn from the organization's clutches. It will be catastrophic if the obsidian remains with her. It is only a matter of time before they extract it from her or use her to do their will. Maddy and I—"

Elias's humorless laugh cuts through Caleb's words. "You and Maddy." His face is cold as he stares at Caleb. "In my opinion, you are much too preoccupied with that warlock girl to take the needs of your own vampires seriously. Whose idea was it to follow Quinn in the first place? It seems to me you will do anything the girl wants. Tell us, Caleb, what exactly are you receiving in return for the loyalty you seem so willing to give a hunter of our kind?"

Images of himself and Maddy rise in Caleb's thoughts. He reigns in his emotions before the others in the room can scent it. Judging by the curl of Elias's lips, he knows exactly what Caleb had been thinking about.

Elias turns his attention to the council members. "Caleb has informed us that Orion says that the cure for vampirism developed by the Merrick Group is actually designed to kill us. It's their way of 'curing' us, I suppose. We need to find a way to come up with a solution for this problem before it gets out of hand. If the cure gets out, many vampires will unwittingly end their lives before we have the chance to spread the word of this false advertising."

One of the council members, a man who looks old even for a vampire, with graying hair and ancient eyes, peers at Caleb. "This is another problem which cannot be ignored. Perhaps, if this Quinn girl is in the Merrick Group building, you can find a way to destroy the cure while also seeking out Quinn and the obsidian."

Caleb knows seeking out the cure is important, but he also feels it's a distraction from the more important task of finding the obsidian. Before he can say as much, Elias speaks.

"I can send a group of vampires to assist our king on this mission," he says.

The council members lean closer to each other, murmuring for a few seconds before straightening. "While we need every able-bodied vampire preparing for Orion's possible arrival, we are willing to grant your request, Elias. It wouldn't do for our king to end up in a situation at the Merrick Group that he's unable to get out of."

Caleb grinds his teeth. He should have known this would happen. He can already feel the council beginning to slip a leash around his neck.

Elias glances at Caleb, a hint of satisfaction on his face. "And, of course, it will also be a way for us to ensure Caleb stays on task."

Caleb bristles and turns a cold gaze to the smug vampire. "Are you suggesting, Elias, that I am incapable of accomplishing what needs to be done, or that I need a pack of babysitters on my heels?"

"Of course not, my king. I am merely suggesting that, given the company you have decided to keep, you may find some... distractions. All men, no matter how high they rank, often need the council of close friends to keep their minds on their goals."

A symbol. That's what the council is trying to do with Caleb. They wanted a king they could show to their kind as a leader who will bring them to victory, all while they secretly tie strings to him and play him like a puppet. He wants to lash out at all of them at the thought.

"I do not need Elias's men to accompany me to the Merrick Group." Caleb works to keep his voice calm, though he's certain a storm rages in his eyes. "I am more than capable of doing what must be done and you know it, or else you wouldn't have chosen me to be the vampire king."

The woman with the short hair, the only female on the council, stares at Caleb with the first flicker of emotion he's seen from any of them, and it certainly isn't pleasant. Irritation twitches at her thin eyebrows and a slight frown weighs on her lips. "No one here doubts your abilities, Caleb, but Elias's suggestion will stand."

Anger breaks through Caleb's restraint. "Am I not the king?" he says. "Am I not allowed to make my own decisions?"

"You are the king, but you are not a dictator. This council will not allow any more unilateral decisions. We have all of vampire-kind to consider, and not merely the whims and wishes of our king." The woman lifts her chin, steel coating her voice. "You may be the one leading us, Caleb, but all decisions you make must be consulted first with the council. If you cannot agree to this, we will need to speak in length."

In other words, if Caleb doesn't agree to the council's terms, they will simply find a king who is more malleable. There would be no guarantee the new king would allow Caleb anywhere near Maddy, either. He'd have no choice but to do as he was told, so for the time being, he'll go along with the council's wishes.

"Very well," Caleb says tightly. "I'm grateful to have your guidance and will accept Elias's help."

"Find this cure quickly," one of the council members says. "And bring an end to this organization. Keep us informed of your movements and do not stray from the task at hand."

Caleb nods and, clearly being dismissed, leaves the room. Before he has a chance to make it outside of the building, Mason pulls him aside.

"I need you to be careful." His voice is so low Caleb can barely hear him. "There are some who are against you being appointed as our leader."

Caleb scoffs. "Because of Maddy?"

"Maybe in part, but most of the grumblings I managed to catch are because of your relation to Kenna DeVoe. The things she has done to vampire-kind are not easily forgotten." Mason squeezes Caleb's shoulder. "Watch your back with these vampires Elias is sending with you." He drops his hand and takes a step back as others file into the room.

One in the forefront approaches Caleb. The man has dark hair and dark eyes, but an easy smile touches his face.

"My king," he says. "My name is Raul. Elias said you may be in need of our assistance."

Caleb gives Mason a farewell nod, then turns. "That remains to be seen, but I would be glad for your company." He despises the fake niceties but he can't afford to set the council against him.

Raul and his vampires follow Caleb outside and don't speak

as the group heads to Veritas. Caleb pauses on the stone steps and turns to the vampires at his back.

"Wait out here for me," he says.

Raul walks up a step. "We are supposed to accompany you."

"To the Merrick Group, yes, but there is no need for you to shadow my every step. Wait here." Caleb's voice is heavy with authority and he's glad to see Raul give a reluctant nod.

He finds Maddy seated in an armchair in the corner of the library on the third floor. There are no signs of the others, but the papers Nim had found on the cherufe are spread on a table in front of her. A smile lights her face when she spots him.

"That was fast," she says. Then, her smile falters. "What's the matter?"

Caleb plops into a chair beside her with a sigh, then proceeds to tell her about the meeting with the council.

"Damn." Maddy's mouth twists to the side and she's silent for a moment. "But we may need help when we storm the Merrick Group. We won't be able to get in and out as easily as we did the last time. It's irritating that Elias sent men to watch you, but if it helps us get the cure..." Maddy trails off and shrugs.

Caleb leans over, grabs her wrist, and pulls her to him. His mouth is on hers before she can utter a protest. The kiss is short, but no less intense with heat. Maddy seems a bit breathless when she eases back.

"What was that for?" she asks, her cheeks flushed.

Caleb gives her a crooked smile. "Because I felt like it," he says. "And because I like knowing that even when things aren't going our way, you're still at my side. I have a feeling I'm going to need you watching my back before this is all over."

Maddy smiles at him and a fierce glint flares in her gaze. "No one will dare touch you with me around, Caleb."

He knows she speaks the truth, but as they stand, he can't help the uneasiness sliding up his spine.

He just hopes she'll never have the need to follow through with her promise.

CHAPTER 11

MADELEINE

Maddy begins to lean closer to Caleb, wanting to feel his lips on hers again, but she catches the quiet sound of steps approaching and straightens. Galina rounds the corner and her gaze lands on Maddy with a flash of irritation.

"There you are," she says. "I've been scouring nearly the whole library for you." Her accusatory glare takes in Caleb, as well, as if her being unable to find Maddy is somehow his fault.

"Sorry." Maddy gestures toward the stack of papers. "I just wanted to find a quiet corner to do some research. Did you need me for something?"

The witch settles down on the couch in the quiet corner of the library. "I just wanted to let you know when it comes time to storm the Merrick Group, I can find where we'll need to go."

Maddy raises an eyebrow. "Really? I thought you were having trouble using a locator spell because everything keeps getting blocked?"

"That is still true," Galina says. "But Blaise has retrieved an ancient spell and we'll be able to use it once the time is right."

Caleb straightens and his eyes narrow slightly as he

watches Galina work on re-braiding her hair. "That seems fairly convenient. Where did this spell come from?"

Galina doesn't stop braiding as she lifts her eyes to Caleb's. There is a no-nonsense frown on her face. "It's witch business, Caleb, and I'm not at liberty to tell the vampire king every movement we make."

The witch had been with them for so long, Maddy forgot that Galina has her own people and her own alliances. She doesn't have to work with them, but she's chosen to. She reminds herself to make it a point to thank Galina more often. Without her, they likely wouldn't be breathing any longer.

"Thank you, Galina," Maddy says. "And thank Blaise, too, wherever she is. I'm sure the spell will come in handy." She peers down at the papers in front of her and frowns.

Caleb drags his suspicious stare from the witch and locks his gaze on Maddy. "What's the matter?"

Maddy shrugs a shoulder. "I just think we might need to take care of the cherufe. It swooped in out of nowhere and helped to take Quinn. That thing could show up again, anywhere, at any moment."

"Yeah." Caleb picks up a few of the papers, scanning the ancient texts. "I read a little bit about them from Kenna when she was teaching me about monsters of legend. They are supposed to be incredibly dangerous creatures. I didn't even know they existed any longer. No one has seen a cherufe in centuries. People figured they'd died out."

"The dangerous, evil things of this world do tend to return when they are most unwanted." Galina tosses her finished braid over her shoulder. "What we think we're putting down for good today will only rise up to resurface after it has been forgotten. It has been this way since the beginning of everything."

Maddy leans back and rubs at her temples. The witch's

words certainly don't make her feel any better. When was the last time she's eaten anything, or gone to sleep? Determined to ignore the headache forming, she turns her attention to Caleb. "When was the last time a cherufe was seen?"

He tilts his head, lips twisting to the side as he thinks. "I believe Kenna had said the last time it was seen was when it devoured the city of Pompeii."

Maddy's eyebrows lift. "Pompeii was destroyed by a cherufe?" Most people have heard of the destruction of the ancient Roman city, but she had no idea a supernatural creature had been involved.

"Yes," Caleb says. "Of course, it looked like a natural disaster after Pompeii was destroyed, but for those who know of their existence, there is no doubt it was a cherufe."

"I think the bigger concern isn't how it was used in ancient times, but what sort of havoc it will wreak in this day and age," Galina says. "Imagine something like that loose in Mercy City, or anywhere in modern civilization. The cherufe will kill thousands, possibly millions."

Maddy takes one of the papers from Caleb. "It says here that the cherufe has to be summoned. The cult is clearly involved with this monstrosity but why would they summon it? Surely, it wasn't just to kidnap Quinn. That could have been done with or without some sort of smoke-and-fire monster."

"It's hard to say." The witch stands. "But we need to find a way to banish the cherufe, or even kill it."

"I've been looking," Maddy says. "These papers are the only thing so far that Nim has been able to find on the cherufe." She looks at Caleb. "It's probably the same source of information Kenna used to teach you about them. Nim has looked, but she can't find anything in any books, much less information on how such a creature can be dealt with."

Galina peers out toward the rows and rows of bookcases.

"Well, there has to be information out there somewhere. Until we know what we're up against, I think the best thing to do is play it safe for now and hold off on going after Quinn. We cannot even be certain she and the Merrick Group are in their building. It would be reckless of them to hide her there knowing we can get in. I'll be sure to keep Blaise close in case we need to use that spell, but until then, we should focus our attention on the cherufe."

"Good idea," Maddy says, but frowns down at the papers she's already read through. "Where are you going?"

The witch glances over her shoulder as she walks away. "To ask some questions." Without another word, Galina leaves Maddy and Caleb alone.

Maddy groans and settles back in her chair, glaring at the papers. Her stomach growls.

"When's the last time you ate anything?" Caleb asks. Maddy shrugs and he gets to his feet. "Stay here. I'll bring back some books and snacks."

Before she can speak, he flashes away in a blur. Minutes later, he returns with books beneath one arm and a paper sack and drink in the other. "Here. Chinese. Hope that's okay?"

"It's perfect." Maddy's mouth is watering as she opens the sack and pulls out a carton of fried rice. There are egg rolls, orange chicken, and dumplings inside, too. She ignores the chopsticks and picks up the plastic fork, then digs into the fried rice. "This is amazing. Thank you."

Caleb smiles and drops the books on the table. "These are books on monsters, legends, and other creatures that Nim hasn't had the chance to look through yet. I figured we could tag team this research session."

Maddy smiles around her forkful of rice. The situation gives her a sense of dejavu. She and Cora had many late-night study sessions together. Caleb opens a book, the spine groaning as he lays it flat on the table, flicking carefully through the tome's thin, yellowed paper. Maddy grabs one of the other books, the green cover so faded she can barely make out the title, *Creatures of Myth*.

She eats as she reads through the pages. Time slips by and the library grows darker. She's barely aware that soft lights fill the space, chasing the shadows to the corners of the nook she and Caleb are researching in. The words begin to blur in front of her face. She shakes her head, fighting against the weariness.

"Hey."

Maddy jumps as a hand lands on her shoulder. Caleb is peering down at her, his eyebrows drawn together. "Huh?" She tries to remember if he'd spoken.

"You look like you're about to fall asleep. Why don't you stretch out on the couch?" He jerks his head to the faded, floral couch Galina had sat in earlier.

"I can't." Maddy's jaw pops as she yawns, then taps the book in front of her. "This is too important."

Caleb stares at her for a moment, then grabs her hand and tugs her to her feet. "All right, then at least come and sit with me so I'm not trying to read your book upside down." He settles on the couch, pulling her down with him.

Maddy can sense the trap Caleb thinks he's slyly laying out for her, but she settles next to him, anyway. The empty take-out containers litter the table and she scoots the empty rice carton out of the way so she can prop up her feet. She pulls the book into her lap and continues to read. She can sense Caleb reading, as well. After a few minutes he lays his arm behind her on the back of the couch. Unable to help herself, she leans a bit into his side. She reads through several more pages depicting monsters of various islands when Caleb's fingertips start to trace soft patterns on her shoulder.

A small smile quirks at her lips at the tingling sensation his touch leaves on her skin. "If you keep doing that, I'm not going to be able to concentrate on reading."

"Let's face it, Maddy," he says. "You haven't been able to concentrate on reading for the past thirty minutes."

She can't argue with him there. She's so tired it was a wonder she hasn't slumped over from exhaustion already. Caleb's arm suddenly snakes around her waist and then he's hauling her down onto the couch cushions.

"What are you doing?" she hisses.

Caleb shifts so he's lying on his side, his back pressed against the back of the couch. "Just making you more comfortable, that's all." He pulls Maddy up against him, then takes the book from her hands and holds it for her. "See?"

Maddy's lips twitch in amusement. "Uh huh." She doesn't quite trust herself to say anything else, not with the way her body is pressed up against Caleb's and her heart starts to race. She's mortified to think he can likely feel the rapid beats drumming through her, but moving is the last thing she wants to do. In a matter of minutes, she's resting her head on Caleb's arm, reading the book he holds in front of them. Long into the night, they read. The library is so quiet, she can hear someone cough on the other side of the building.

The lights dim further and Maddy closes her eyes, telling herself she just needs a few seconds of rest. Caleb's warm breath brushes the side of her neck and tickles at her ear. She lets the soft sensation carry her farther into darkness.

She can't help it. It feels too good.

MADDY GROANS, her consciousness dragging up from the depths of a deep sleep. Then, she cracks an eyelid when something nudges her foot. She blinks away the blurriness of sleep to find

Sierra and Blaise smiling down at her. Behind them, she notices pale morning sunlight sweeping across the floor from the window just around the corner. The memory of last night rushes back to her and she's suddenly very aware of Caleb pressed against her. She doesn't need to turn and look to know he still sleeps. His breathing is steady as his chest rises and falls against her back.

Slowly, Maddy sits up, her cheeks warming as she swings her feet to the floor. She clears her throat, then glances up at Sierra and Blaise. "Sorry, I was just..." She casts around for an excuse as to why she'd been passed out on the couch with the vampire king. Her eyes land on the book they'd been reading late into the night. It had dropped to the floor beside the couch. She bends over and scoops it from the floor. "We were just reading."

Sierra waves her hand. "There is nothing to be embarrassed about. When I was researching reapers with Ryder, we spent many nights like this, cuddled on the couch until we were too exhausted to read another word. Countless times, Gabby and Colt woke us up on this very same couch."

Maddy can't help but laugh and the sound jolts Caleb from his slumber. He runs a hand down his face and when he shifts into a sitting position, his hair is sticking up on one side. Maddy gives him a crooked grin, then turns to Blaise and Sierra.

"We tried to find out more about the cherufes, but aside from what Nim had already found, there wasn't much to add."

Caleb starts trying to lay his hair down, muttering about irritating mythical monsters. He glances up at Maddy and she swears he catches the sound of her pulse quickening and quickly ducks his head to hide the smirk.

"I'm sure more word will be found soon regarding the cherufe," Sierra says.

Maddy starts to clean up her mess from dinner the night

before. "I wonder if we even have time to be looking into the cherufe. I know it's dangerous to be letting such a creature remain at large, but we could be taking the time to retrieve the obsidian."

"Yeah, unless the cherufe has been set to keep an eye on Ileana," Caleb says. "In which case, we would need to know how to take it out in order to get to her."

"I have some insight in that regard." Galina shows back up, obviously not having the opportunity to rest as Maddy and Caleb had done. Tendrils of hair have worked free from her braid and bags hang under her eyes. "I made contact with a sorcerer in Thessalonikki, a town in Greece. I've known him for quite some time and I figured he may know what we're up against. He told me of an ancient myth about one of the demigods, a child of Athena, who possessed a weapon that could kill a cherufe. This is the same demigod who killed the cherufe who destroyed Pompeii."

Caleb lets out a low whistle of appreciation.

"Did this sorcerer tell you where we can find this weapon, or if it even still exists?" Maddy asks.

"I believe I may be able to help out in that regard."

Maddy turns toward the voice of the newcomer. A woman joins them, her blonde hair a straight sheet flowing down her back and blue eyes warm. Maddy blinks at the sight of her knee-high converse boots covered in writing. She smiles.

"I'm Arielle, by the way."

Maddy shakes her hand, recognizing the name. "You know something about the weapon?"

"Well, I know someone who may have access to the weapon," Arielle says. "Back when I was fighting the Sins, I made a demigod friend named Alexandra. I think it's time I give her a call." She looks at Galina. "I appreciate you calling me in to help."

"We need all the help we can get," the witch says.

"Thank you, Arielle," Maddy says.

The young woman nods. "I'll get a hold of Alexandra and get back here as quickly as possible. Don't worry, Maddy. We've got this."

Maddy watches Arielle leave just as quickly as she'd arrived. Despite everything they're facing, she can't help but feel a small bubble of hope that things may work out for them, after all.

Just like it has with her and Caleb.

CHAPTER 12

CALEB

The little corner where Caleb and Maddy had tucked themselves into for long hours of research is finally kissed by the late morning sun. A few hours have passed since Arielle left to try and get a hold of her demigod friend. The scent of coffee and paper is strong in the air. From where he leans against a bookshelf, Caleb watches Maddy close her eyes and take a long sip of her French vanilla he'd bought from a café down the street.

He knows Maddy had gotten a few hours of sleep, at least. He'd managed even less. Sleep had been hard to win when he'd been holding her in his arms. Never before had a woman fit so perfectly in them. He could spend hours simply holding her, feeling her breathe against him, and listening to each sweet sound of her beating heart.

As if sensing his gaze, Maddy's eyes open and lock on him as she rests the takeaway cup on her lap. Her thoughts, too, seem to drift to last night. He can hear her pulse quicken from across the room. He pushes from the bookshelf, intent on going over to see just how fast he can make her heartbeat, when the sound of footsteps reach him.

Maddy sets her coffee on the table and gets to her feet as Galina walks in, followed by Arielle and a newcomer. Hairs prickle at the back of Caleb's neck as he eyes the brown-haired warrior woman standing beside Arielle. Something in his nature is guarded against the woman who can be none other than the demigod. He steps over to Maddy, who seems to be more enthralled by the woman's beauty than the sense of someone strong and lethal emanating from her.

"I'd like to introduce you to Alexandra, one of Athena's brave children," Arielle says. "When I told her about the situation, she was more than happy to come and assist."

Maddy introduces herself and Caleb. He's polite, but remains guarded against the woman who has the blood of a goddess in her veins.

"You know how to kill a cherufe?" Caleb asks. There is no point in bothering with all of the pleasantries when there is an ancient monster loose, especially one that could very well level a city if it chooses.

Alexandra nods, her hair swaying at her shoulders in a high ponytail. "Yes, of course. One must use this." She reaches into her jacket and pulls out a sheath. Caleb can see it holds an ancient weapon, seeing as the sheath itself is unadorned in any way. There are no decorative touches, but instead the sheath seems to be little more than aged, tough leather. Alexandra draws out the knife, the weapon as plain and unassuming as the sheath that holds it. Light glints off the straight blade as the demigod tilts the weapon back and forth.

"That's effective in killing a cherufe?" Maddy eyes the blade with obvious uncertainty.

"Don't let its simple appearance fool you," Alexandra says. "It will sink right to a cherufe's heart." She smiles, a sort of delight in her gaze. The woman puts the blade back in the sheath and it disappears inside her jacket once again.

"Although, the major downfall with this weapon is that only a child of Athena may use it, so I will need to accompany you when you confront the cherufe."

Caleb doesn't like the idea of this woman being with them, though he knows it's merely his vampire instincts that desire to shy away from the powerful woman. He shrugs. "We'll be grateful for every bit of help we can get." He turns to Arielle. "Are you going to be joining us?"

Arielle tilts her head back and laughs. "Oh, I don't think so. This is as far as my helping hand is going to extend." She gestures to Alexandra. "This isn't my fight. I've played my part and now I'm finally getting to reap the rewards of the life I fought and almost died for. I'm quite happy and content with my college life. I moved into the Mercy Academy dorms just a few months ago, in fact. I'm actually in the same room number as Gabby stayed in during her stint at the Academy. Small world, huh?"

Caleb glances at Maddy, something in the moment drawing his gaze to her. For a split second, he can see the mixture of envy and longing pass over her face. She wants what Arielle has, a normal college life with nothing to worry about other than having assignments in on time and passing exams. He'll do anything to get her back to the normal life she yearns for. She was dragged into this world of good and evil and Caleb's partly to blame. Sure, she would have found out she was a hunter eventually, but he's the reason she's stayed in the fight.

No matter what, he vows to make things right for her, somehow.

First, however, they had to take care of the cherufe and get the obsidian from Quinn. Then, maybe, they'll be able to start down the road of a normal life together.

"Are you sure we can't persuade you to join us?" Caleb says. "We could use an experienced fighter like yourself."

"That's a hard pass from me. My fiancé would have a heart attack if I said yes." Arielle gives him a small smile. "But I won't leave you all hanging, don't worry. I'm going to send someone to help who may be more interested in taking down this cult." She pulls her phone out of her pocket to check the time. "I need to be heading back soon. Where did you get that?" She points at the cup of coffee sitting on the table.

Maddy picks it up. "Caleb grabbed it from the café across the street. It's pretty good."

"Think I'll grab one before I head back, then." Arielle gives them all a goodbye wave, then makes her way down the long stretch between bookcases that leads to the stairs.

Caleb looks between Galina and Alexandra. "I wonder who she's going to send?" he asks.

Before either can answer, Maddy grabs his arm and gives him a little tug. "Can I talk to you for a minute?"

Caleb follows Maddy several rows of bookcases down. They pause and he angles his head, studying her. "Is something wrong?"

She peers up at him. "Are you ready for this? I have a feeling we'll be leaving soon."

"Of course, I'm ready," Caleb says. He gives her a grin. "What, are you saying you doubt my abilities to kick some ass?"

She doesn't smile, however. She glances over her shoulder, as if expecting someone to be standing there, listening. "You'll have to take them with us, you know, the other vampires. The council set their terms and you said you can't disobey them. I don't like it."

"I don't like it, either, but I can handle them."

"Caleb." Maddy steps closer to him and grabs his hand, giving his fingers a squeeze. "You told me about the warning Mason gave you. Please, don't make light of this situation.

Honestly, I don't really understand why the council feels the need to have those vampires watching you, anyway."

For a long moment, Caleb hesitates. He knows part of the reason is because they don't want him making rash decisions as king that would affect them all. In part because he has feelings for Maddy. But they also want the obsidian, and they want him to destroy the cure.

"They likely want to make sure I destroy the cure," Caleb says. "It's the council's wishes that I get rid of it and after learning the truth of what it truly is, I'm inclined to agree."

Maddy's eyes widen slightly and her pulse ticks faster where Caleb's fingers brush her wrist. "You can't do that, Caleb. You can't destroy the cure."

"It kills vampires," he says. Why wouldn't Maddy want it destroyed? She's a hunter, yes, but he knows she has more respect for vampire life than Felix and his ilk possessed. "I have to destroy it."

An irritated huff hisses through Maddy's teeth. "I'm aware it destroys vampires, but I need to have the cure."

Caleb is quiet for a beat. "Why?"

"Well, I kind of have this idea of modifying it so it really does cure vampires of their vampirism. Any vampire who takes it will have the chance to become human again."

"How?" Caleb frowns, unwilling to even put faith in such a wondrous idea. How many times had he had the brief thought of what it would be like to shed his vampire self?

Maddy bites her lip. "I'm not really sure yet, but I want to give it a try." She runs her hand up his arm. "Do you think you could try to get me the cure? If there's a way to help those who don't want to be vampires, then I want to find it."

Caleb isn't certain if Maddy really wants the cure for others, or if she is secretly hoping he'll decide to take it himself. He also knows what she's asking him is to directly disobey the council.

Less than a day has passed since he met with them, and he's already having to choose.

It seems the council were right to be worried, though. There's no hesitation as he nods.

"If I can get it for you, I will." He lifts his hands and frames her face. "But I want you to promise me something, Maddy." She nods in his hands. "Promise me you won't have the Order cure vampires without their consent. Many of us haven't chosen this life, but we've accepted it. Changing back to human isn't necessarily something most will choose. Some will, for sure, but don't leave any of them without a choice in the matter."

This is the only guarantee he has that this decision isn't the wrong one.

Maddy smiles and hooks her hands behind his neck. "I promise, Caleb."

She draws him down to her and seals the promise with a passionate kiss. He allows himself to get lost in the sultry passion that's always existed between them. In the sense of right that he never wants to lose.

How could this decision be wrong?

S tanding beside the railing on the third floor of the library, Maddy contemplates the cure as Caleb and the others make preparations for the raid on the Merrick Group. She isn't certain if he'd be willing to cure himself of vampirism if she were able to change the treacherous cure into something that would actually make them human again. A part of her wants to see him human, if only so their lives would be easier, but then again, Caleb is the vampire king. He has responsibilities to his kind. She can't think of anyone else who could show vampires they can live alongside humans. And besides, being a vampire is a part of Caleb. She could never fault him for wanting to keep his supernatural self.

It still seems odd to her that Orion was the first one to suggest she find a way to change the cure. Her thoughts turn over and over in her mind, trying to see Orion's reasoning for giving her such a valuable idea. No matter which way she looks at it, she can't see any sort of lie or trap in his suggestion, even though he doesn't seem like the sort of person who would give out information for free.

Maddy sighs and steps away from the rail. Perhaps Orion

had thought he was teasing her with something that he believed impossible. He certainly wouldn't have thought she'd make it out of Purgatory, so dangling a happy future in front of her with the promise of her being able to get her hands on a real cure doesn't seem too far-fetched. Orion likely wouldn't have thought she would actually go through with it, anyway.

"There you are."

Maddy turns to find Cora jogging toward her. "What happened to you?" She studies her friend, whose hair looks windblown and has smudges of dirt on her clothes.

Cora slows to a stop beside her and blows a loose tendril of red hair away from her face. She rolls her eyes. "Mason thought it would be a good idea to have a bunch of the younger vampires take part in some training. It was brutal. No gym class growing up could ever compare."

A chuckle bubbles up Maddy's throat. "Not even Mr. Bell's class?" she says. They had weight-lifting in his gym class junior year of high school. The man also made them run a mile at the start of each class.

"Ugh. Yes. Worse than that."

"Well, I don't envy you," Maddy says. She crosses her arms, then studies Cora. "Do you like it? Being a vampire, I mean."

Cora shrugs a slim shoulder. "It's actually pretty great. I like the speed, and the strength." She gives Maddy a grim smile. "The next person who tries to kidnap me won't have such an easy go of it."

Maddy tries not to remember the horror of discovering her best friend had been kidnapped by the ruthless former Master's vampires. "And if you had a chance to be human again?"

"That's impossible." Cora's eyebrows pinch together. "The cure is supposed to kill us, remember? It's just a trick to eradicate vampires."

Hesitating, Maddy purses her lips. She doesn't want to give

Cora false hope, but... "What if I found a way to change the cure so that it can actually turn you human again? Would you do it?"

Cora opens her mouth, then pauses. Her eyes drop to the floor. "I don't know." She runs the toe of her shoe in a circle on the floor. "I know I'm supposed to want to be human again. I want to be able to go back to my family." She lifts her gaze to Maddy. "But so much has happened. My mom won't forget what she saw, even if I walked back into that house as a human. Besides, after gaining these powers...I just don't know."

Maddy smiles and leans over to hug her friend. "It's okay, Cora. The decision isn't something you have to make right now." She frowns. "Or possibly ever, if I can't figure out how to change the cure."

"I'm sure you'll figure it out." Cora glances toward the second floor and spots Galina, who gives her a little wave. "I'm going to see what Galina is up to. Want to come?"

"No, I think I'm going to go outside and get some fresh air." Maddy feels as if she's seen nothing but bookshelves for days. "I'll meet you outside. I think we'll be heading out soon."

Cora nods and heads in the opposite direction while Maddy makes her way down the stairs. She spots Caleb speaking with Alexandra. He gives Maddy a smile before returning to his conversation with the demigod. Morning air greets Maddy as she steps outside of the large front doors of the Veritas library. The day is already shaping up to be pleasant, if a bit cool. She zips up her jacket and spots Arielle crossing the street, a to-go cup in her hand. The woman takes a careful sip as she approaches Maddy.

"Mmm. You were right," Arielle says. "This coffee is divine." She pauses, eyeing Maddy, and tilts her head. "Something bothering you? If you're worried about the raid, I think you'll have plenty of muscle there to back you up if things get crazy."

Maddy shakes her head. "No, it's not that. It's..." She hesitates. Would Arielle have any insight on the matter, or would she caution Maddy against getting involved in vampire business? Deciding to throw caution to the wind, Maddy speaks. "I may be able to get my hands on the cure. If I can, I'm hoping there is some way to change the makeup of it so it will be able to turn vampires human again." She lets out a hollow laugh. "I really should have paid more attention in chemistry. I have no idea how to do something like that."

Arielle sets her cup down on the hood of a shiny car that looks like it hasn't been on the road more than a few months. The tires didn't even look that dirty. "You know, I may know of someone who can help."

"You seem to know a lot of people," Maddy says, smiling. First, Arielle had brought Alexandra to help. Then, she claims she'll send someone along to give them a hand in the raid. Now, she says she knows someone who can help Maddy with a cure. "Who is he?"

"She," Arielle clarifies. "I don't know her personally, but I've heard of this girl, Abigail, who is extremely talented in biotech and biochem. It would be worth giving her a call, though she may not be able to help. I'll dig around and get her contact info for you."

Relief fills Maddy's chest. "I really appreciate it, Arielle." She gives her the number of her cell. "Thank you so much."

"No problem." Arielle grabs her cup of coffee, pulls keys out of her pocket, and unlocks the door of the car. "I better get going. I've got a class at eleven. It was nice to meet you, Maddy. I'm sure we'll see each other again."

Maddy waves as Arielle pulls away from the curb, beeping the horn a couple of times as she leaves.

"It's a shame she's too busy with school to help out." Caleb comes down the sprawling stairs in front of Veritas to join Maddy.

Maddy watches Arielle's car turn and disappear around a corner. "She's been more than helpful," she says. "She brought Alexandra here, a literal demigod. And she's sending someone else here to help, too." She looks up at Caleb and smiles. "I told her about my intentions with the cure. She says she may be able to get a hold of someone who is educated in that sort of field to help us."

As if on cue, Maddy's phone vibrates in her pocket. She pulls it out to see a message from an unknown number. She swipes her thumb across the screen. The message is from Arielle, with a phone number and email attached under the name Abigail.

"That was fast." Caleb leans over, unashamedly reading the text Maddy received.

Maddy adds Arielle to her contacts, then returns her phone to her back pocket. "This is excellent," she says. "This means we're one step closer to the cure, the real cure."

"Yeah, but first we have to find the other cure before it is too late." Caleb stuffs his hands in his pockets. "Maddy, look, I don't want you to be disappointed, but if we can't find it, or if this Abigail person isn't able to help..."

Concern and doubt dull the light in Caleb's eyes and it made Maddy's heart clench. She steps closer to him and wraps her arms around him. "If we can't figure out how to fix the cure, then we'll just destroy it. It doesn't matter to me if you can't become a human again." She leans back and peers up at him. "Caleb, it doesn't matter to me even if we can fix the cure and you decide not to take it. I just want you to be happy, you know?"

His lips curve into a smile and he pinches Maddy's chin. "I wasn't expecting to hear that."

"What were you expecting that I would take the cure and shove it down your throat?" she teases. She reaches up and grabs Caleb's wrist, even as he slides his hand to rest on her jaw.

"Honestly? I wasn't sure why you wanted the cure so badly, but I thought maybe it had something to do with me."

Maddy shakes her head and Caleb drops his hand. "I just want vampires to have the opportunity to change back to human if they want to, including you, but if you want to remain a vampire, then that's fine with me."

Caleb grabs Maddy's hips, giving them the slightest squeeze. "You know, I'm fairly certain I don't deserve you." He gives her a crooked grin and his eyes drop to her lips. Slowly, he starts to lean down and then the doors to Veritas open. He straightens.

Letting out an irritated huff, Maddy turns to see Blaise, Alexandra, Cora, and Galina making their way down the steps. They gather with Maddy and Caleb.

"I've decided to go with you on this adventure," Blaise says.

Maddy glances toward the doors, but sees no one else.

"Oh, Sierra won't be joining us," Blaise says. "Her and Ryder are getting ready to leave for Hawaii for their second honeymoon. They tried to come but we wouldn't hear of it. Those two have earned their time together."

Maddy isn't quite certain who Ryder is, but assumes he's Sierra's husband. "That sounds great."

Blaise sighs wistfully. "Doesn't it? I'd much rather be laying out on the sand, sipping pina coladas and watching the waves than going after supernatural villains."

"It's not too late to stuff yourself in one of Sierra's suitcases," Galina says.

Caleb snorts a laugh, then looks over his shoulder. As if coalescing from the shadows, Raul and his vampires make their way toward the group. Maddy hides a scowl. She'd forgotten they'd be coming with them. Even though she'd been the one to soothe Caleb's hesitancy in bringing them, she still isn't super fond of the idea. Raul, especially, looks like the kind of man who would stab you in the back while pretending to help you up.

"Easy," Caleb mutters. He gives Maddy a look that clearly states she's emanating something negative in her scent.

Maddy clears her throat and flashes Raul a smile. "Hi," she says. The vampire does little more than to give her a curt nod. Cora, to her credit, flat out glares at the man. If Raul notices, he ignores it.

"Quite the gathering you've amassed, Caleb." Raul's sharp eyes take in the group. He doesn't seem pleased by any of them, especially the witches.

Caleb lifts his chin. "Yes, well, I think we can use all the help we can get."

"Fine," Raul says. "Are we leaving, then? The council will be growing impatient."

Maddy scowls, then glances at Caleb. Does he really think it's okay to let someone speak to their king in such a way?

"We were just about to leave." Caleb's words are clipped and cold, his tone carrying a clear warning to Raul that he needs to be careful with his own words. "We were merely waiting on—"

Maddy gasps as something falls from the sky and lands nearby. The ground shakes and a crack runs up the sidewalk and stops right in front of her feet. Her hand flies out to grab Caleb's arm, steadying herself. Then, her eyes widen as a man straightens before them, tucking in a pair of dark red wings.

The man speaks, his gaze sweeping over all of them. "I believe I received an SOS asking for help with some damned cult."

CHAPTER 14
CALEB

The winged man sweeps a sharp gaze over the group standing outside of Veritas. His stare finally lands on Caleb, then flicks to Maddy at his side. There's no denying the protective way he has angled his body so he's partly in front of her, ready to attack should the need arise. Maddy doesn't seem afraid of the demon as he strolls closer, merely curious. Caleb notices the way her eyes linger on the man's red-feathered wings, then recalls Maddy had produced unusual wings of her own.

"Hello," the man says. He's the dark, handsome type women usually fawn over. He seems a bit stoic, but a certain glint in the man's eyes tells Caleb the guy might have a subtle bit of humor. "My name's Reign. I'm Arielle's fiancée."

Caleb blinks. He certainly hadn't been expecting Arielle to send her own fiancée to help. "Congratulations," he mutters.

Reign dips his chin. "Thank you." Then, he smiles and reaches a hand out to Maddy. "And you are?"

"Maddy," she says, shaking it. "I like your wings."

The demon smiles, then leans forward and mutters in her ear. "Thank you. I like yours, as well."

A blush creeps over Maddy's face. Somehow, the man knows of Maddy's abilities. Caleb's lips press into a hard line and the man moves over to greet Blaise and Alexandra.

"You like his wings, huh?" Caleb says, staring down at Maddy.

Maddy's eyes widen innocently. "What? They're neat." After a beat, a knowing smile spreads across her face. "Are you jealous? Do I need to tell you how handsome you are, and that I like your fangs?"

Chuckling, Caleb nudges her with a shoulder.

Reign is still greeting the others. Raul and the vampires seem like they couldn't care less about the newcomer. Caleb clears his throat.

"We can finish this on the way." Impatience sharpens his tongue. "We need to be going." Beside him, Maddy nods. "Galina, have you and Blaise pinpointed the location?"

Galina steps forward. "We have. It isn't in the Merrick building as we first thought, but rather somewhere on the edge of the city. We will know a more precise location as we draw closer."

"Good. Let's go."

There are several cars parked around the corner of the Veritas building. Caleb, Maddy, and Cora climb into his car. The witches, Alexandra, and Reign get into Blaise's car, and Raul and his vampires tail them from behind on foot. They go several blocks, passing through the business district and then through the main shopping hub. Finally, Blaise's car slows and pulls over to the side of the street at the edge of the city. In the distance, a plain, rectangular building stands out among a few older warehouses.

Caleb, Maddy, and Cora climb out of the car and join the others. Galina is staring at the building. "Quinn is in there."

Raul and his vampires join them. The vampire narrows his eyes toward the building. "It looks like the entire building is surrounded by guards. There aren't many windows, either."

"I think we need to get a closer look," Caleb says. "Then, we'll come up with a plan. Let's go this way and come at them from the side." He jerks his head toward a trash-littered alley.

The group follows Caleb quietly, though Maddy and the witches steps scuff slightly. As long as the building isn't being guarded by vampires, he thinks they'll still be able to get close enough to see just what they're up against. They make their way through the alley and around the back of a warehouse before finally coming up near the side of the square building.

Beside Caleb, Maddy gasps softly. "I know them," she whispers. Several men and women stand guard along the gray face of the building. "They belong to the members of the Order that have sworn themselves to Felix." She eyes Caleb. "The cure has to be in there. Why else would Felix's men be protecting something that could take out the vampires?"

Caleb subtly wraps a cautioning hand around Maddy's wrist. He doesn't want Raul to know her intentions with the cure, especially since the council ordered him to destroy it altogether.

Cora clicks her tongue. "Well, how are we supposed to get through them? I'm assuming, if they're members of the rogue Order, then they will have stakes on them. That means they're a danger to over half of our group."

The witches begin to whisper together for a moment, then Blaise straightens. "I've got a spell that should do the trick. It won't last for long, though, so everyone will need to be quick."

Behind them, Reign's wings rustle with impatience. "It's been a while since I've had some fun. Let's get on with it."

Galina and Blaise clasp hands, close their eyes, and begin to mutter. Caleb waits with bated breath for an explosion or something, but nothing happens. Then, a door opens just as the guards outside slump to the ground, one by one.

"Hurry," Galina hisses.

Caleb grabs Maddy's hand. She starts to protest, but he swings her into his arms. They take off toward the building. Alexandra runs beside them, surprisingly fast for a supernatural who isn't a vampire. Reign flies above, his wings barely more than a hush in the air, and Cora, Raul, and the other vampires keep right on their heels. As they approach the building, Caleb finds the guards have been put to sleep.

"Quick, before they wake up."

He leads the way into the building, then comes up short. The witches' spell must not have reached for enough inside because at the end of a long stretch of hallway, a group of people rush toward them. Judging by their sure steps and plethora of weapons, these are no mere guards, but trained mercenaries. The others gather inside. Reign steps up beside Caleb's shoulder.

"Dammit," the demon growls, eyeing the incoming fighters.

Caleb doesn't look away from the charging men and his eyebrows pinch together in confusion when he starts to hear animalistic snarling among their ranks.

"These are no mere soldiers," Reign says. "I've heard of supernaturals such as these. They're shifters experimented on by the organization."

A chill scatters up Caleb's spine when a shifter changes into a hulking bear and Maddy draws out a dagger. Soon, lions, wolves, and other carnivores are running full speed at them. Caleb grabs Maddy's arm.

"You can't fight those shifters with a blade," he says. "Not in these close quarters."

Maddy's heartbeats pick up tempo. "Well, we have to do something."

The shifters are drawing closer, their claws scratching and scraping along the shiny floor. Jaws snap open and closed, eager to taste blood. Caleb's never seen shifters so large or so quick, no doubt due to some sort of genetic alteration on the organization's part. The vampires he has with him, plus Maddy, the witches, Alexandra, and Reign may be able to handle the onslaught coming at them, but certainly not without losing one or two in their number.

"I'll head them off," Reign says. His wings flare out, ready to propel him down the hallway to meet the frenzy of shifters. "You go and do whatever the hell it is you need to do in this place."

Alexandra steps forward. "I'll help you. These beasts will not be able to withstand the wrath of Athena's kin."

"I'll help, too." Cora joins Alexandra at her side and smiles back at Maddy. "I've got this. You go find Quinn and the cure."

Caleb is silent for a moment, then nods, his face hardening with determination. He looks around and points. "There. Let's try that way."

Caleb, Maddy, and the other vampires head through the door. They're met with a stairwell leading up. Maddy's footsteps echo on the metal stairs as they ascend to the next floor. Caleb shoves through the door at the top before she can manage. Her irritation prickles on his tongue but he doesn't care. There's no telling who may be waiting around every corner.

A new scent is all the warning Caleb has before a large man pummels into him. Maddy shrieks, stumbling to the side as he crashes into her. One of the vampires manages to set her upright before he dashes at a guard racing toward them. Caleb shoves the man who attacked him hard enough that the guard's body crunches against the opposite wall. He falls in a heap and then Caleb grabs Maddy's sleeve, tugging her down the hall.

No sooner have they gone another dozen steps when several more guards dash at them. Maddy brandishes her weapons as the guards storm closer. Caleb tries to keep an eye on her but the fighting pulls his attention to the task at hand. One guard down, then two. He catches a hiss from Maddy, but in the next instant, a guard falls dead at her feet. Raul and the others quickly dispatch the rest. Caleb catches Maddy's eye and she gives him a slight nod. She's okay.

"The cure has to be down here somewhere," she says, a bit breathless. "Why else would it be so heavily guarded? I have a feeling if we find the cure, we'll also find Quinn."

Caleb leads the group down the hallway. A few times they're forced to fight off a guard. Finally, they turn a corner and find a row of heavily armed guards standing in front of a glass-faced room. Behind it, sitting in a case, is a large vial.

"The cure," Maddy whispers.

Caleb glances at Raul, knowing the vampire will take every opportunity to try and destroy the cure so he gets the credit, and the favor, of the council.

"Take out the guards," Caleb orders. "I'll go for the cure."

Raul's eyes flash and his upper lip twitches in a suppressed snarl, but he nods. They leap toward the guards and whoever stationed them there obviously knew what they were doing. The men they face are stronger and faster than the others they'd left dead in the hallway at their backs. Caleb grits his teeth as his fist slams into one man's face. In his peripheral, Maddy's blade slashes, the metal glinting in the light as she strikes. A sense of admiration ripples through him at the sight of her, fierce and unfaltering. Raul and his group of vampires are just as lethal, taking out the guards, blood spraying in their wake. It seems as if only seconds pass before disconcerting stillness fills the hallway.

"Cora," Maddy breathes.

Her best friend joins them. "Reign and Alexandra have it handled. It sounded like you may have needed help up here but I guess not." Her eyes sweep over to the glass wall. "Is that the cure?"

Caleb walks over to the door and finds it locked. Taking a few steps back, he flashes forward and slams his shoulder into the thick glass. The hinges snap and the door falls to the floor, smashing into sparkling shards. Maddy, Cora, and the vampires follow him into the room, glass crunching underfoot.

Slowly, Caleb picks up the vial. The colorless liquid inside looks so innocuous. And yet, they just killed to get to it. And they would've died if they failed.

"Smash it," Raul says. "Hurry, before we lose our chance."

Caleb's gaze flicks to Maddy and she peers at him with wide eyes. He shakes his head. "We don't even know for certain if this is the cure they created to destroy us, or if they have it hidden away somewhere else. This could be a decoy for all we know."

"How are we supposed to know?" one of Raul's vampires asks.

"Caleb..." Maddy's voice trails off with uncertainty.

"We need to test it," he says, ignoring how tight his chest feels. "Just to make sure we aren't being tricked."

Raul scoffs. "If you think me and any of my men are going to be your guinea pigs, you can forget it. Just destroy it. If it's a fake and the real cure shows up, well, then we'll deal with it then. If this is the real cure, then our work here is done."

Caleb peers at the vial of clear liquid. "No, we can't risk that." He gives Maddy a grim smile. "We have to know." He lifts the vial to his lips.

Maddy moves to stop him. "No! You could die!"

Before Maddy can reach the vial, there's a blur of movement.

Cora plucks it from Caleb's hand, pops off the cap, and takes a sip.

CHAPTER 15

MADELEINE

Maddy's heart feels as if it drops straight to the pit of her stomach. Cora licks a drop of the cure from her lips, staring at the vial. The seconds seem to crawl by and then she lifts her gaze. Maddy tries to form the words to ask her if she's okay, but she can't bring her voice to work through the shock.

Finally, Cora shrugs. "I don't feel any different," she says.

Raul steps closer to her, head canting to the side. "She's still a vampire." He looks to Caleb. "Perhaps it takes a while to kill us?"

Oh, God. The horror of such a thought sends ice prickling through Maddy's veins.

Caleb sniffs at Cora. "I don't think so. They'd want vampires who take the cure to die quickly and efficiently. A slow death would mean more of a chance for word to get out that the cure is little more than poison."

"Cora?" Maddy's voice finally squeezes up her throat. She takes her friend by the shoulder and studies her for any negative signs. "Are you sure you're okay?"

Giving her a smile, Cora gently brushes off Maddy's touch.

After releasing a slow breath of relief, Maddy peers at the cure. "This has to be a fake, then." Her gaze snaps up to her best friend and she glowers. "You could have died, Cora. Why would you do something like that?" The shock ebbs, leaving a burning sensation in her throat. She swallows it and focuses on her anger.

"I couldn't let Caleb take it," Cora said. "You would be devastated."

Maddy's nostrils flare. "And how do you think I'd feel if I lost you? You're my best friend. You're one of the best parts of my life. I can't lose you."

"Well, you didn't." Cora gives her a gentle smile. "So stop freaking out, okay?"

"You can't do that kind of crap." Maddy's fingers curl in, her nails biting her palms. "Just because you're a vampire doesn't make you untouchable."

Raul crosses his arms. "It nearly does," he says.

Maddy rounds on him. "Don't even get me started on you, you bastard."

He puts a hand to his chest and widens his eyes in a show of innocence. "Me? What did I do? I didn't force it down her throat." He meets Maddy's scowl. "I didn't do anything, so keep your insults behind your teeth."

"Exactly, you didn't do anything," Maddy snaps. She flings an arm out toward Caleb. "He's your king. He's the one who will lead and protect your kind, and yet you were just going to stand silently by while he risked his life. Didn't the council send you along with Caleb to protect him? Why didn't you step up?" She sweeps her glare over the other vampires gathered behind Raul. "Why didn't any of you step up?"

Raul takes a short step toward Maddy and Caleb tenses beside her. "Perhaps none of us are willing to risk our lives for this man." A sneer contorts his face. "Caleb is no king of mine."

Maddy bristles but before she can speak, Caleb's voice growls through the room.

"You will watch your tone and words with me, Raul. You may not like me, but I am your leader and you need to deal with it, or leave." His gaze slices to the other vampires. "That goes for every vampire."

Raul's sneer widens into a grin. "Are you threatening your subjects, *King Caleb*?" He shakes his head. "You're a relative of Kenna DeVoe, a woman who made it her mission in life to eradicate our kind. Do you honestly think anyone related to that sort of monster can ever truly be king of the vampires? Don't you realize what sort of message that conveys?"

Tension continues to build in the room, making Maddy's fingers twitch toward the stake she keeps on her. Her eyes flick between Caleb and Raul, the two strong vampires facing off. She looks to Cora, and her friend's eyes are locked on Raul, as if ready to tackle him if need be.

"My relations do not matter," Caleb snaps. "Kenna is dead and I am now a vampire."

A short, humorless laugh bursts from Raul. "Yes, you are now a vampire. How many know that your turning was a punishment? You were a hunter, raised and trained by one of our greatest enemies. Do you really think you can be rewarded with such treachery by being given the title of king? You may have killed the master and the former kings may be dead, but your appointment into this position will not stand. There are many who disagree with the council's choice."

Caleb's chin lifts, and though Raul is slightly taller than him, he still manages to look as if he's staring down his nose at the other vampire. "I really don't give a shit what some vampires may think of me or if they disagree with the decision to name me king. The council chose me. Those under my rule will either need to deal with it, or I will deal with them."

The threat hangs between the two men. Raul is quiet for a beat and Maddy hopes Caleb's sharp words are the end of the argument, but then amusement quirks at the opposing vampire's lips. "You must be more insane than I thought if you think you were selected to be king because the council deemed you to be the right one for such an honor. The only reason you were selected is because the council thought you would be easy to control. They need a leader they can tie strings to and tug in any direction they want."

"That's not true," Caleb says.

Maddy flicks a quick glance at him. Caleb told her about the meeting with the council and knew there's likely quite a bit of truth to Raul's scathing words. He may have been given a higher-ranking position under the master's rule and had led groups of vampires, but to have been given the title of king, especially to a vampire so young and new, had been a shock to him. Yet not a flicker of emotion passes over Caleb's face.

"Not true?" Raul clicks his tongue. "Come now, Caleb. Did you really want me and my men here, or were you ordered to do it by the council?" A knowing smile lifts his cheeks at Caleb's silence. "That's what I thought. Elias had hinted at as much when he told me I was to accompany you on this mission. What sort of king would allow the council to send him a flock of babysitters to follow him around?"

Caleb bristles. "If I didn't want you here, you wouldn't be. I am grateful for the assistance in finding the cure, and I told Elias and the council as much."

"Yes," Raul says. "But you and I both know it was merely to keep them from crawling even farther onto your back." His lips peel back, revealing his fangs. "I'm only here because I was ordered by Elias but I refuse to bow down to some ragtag puppet of a king."

Behind Raul, a few of the vampires nod. Maddy narrows her

stare at them, wishing she could take her stake and threaten them to within an inch of their lives.

Raul lifts his hand, studying his fingernails as if checking for dirt. "I have a bone to pick with the council, anyway."

"First, you want to deny Caleb and now you want to take on the council?" Cora barks a laugh. "Yeah, good luck with that."

"Nobody asked your opinion, youngling." Raul cuts a glare at Cora. "Especially a female who was changed by this fake king."

Caleb's nostrils flare. "You really cannot think you can fight the council."

"The council is old-fashioned and short-sighted," Raul says. "They want to keep things as they have always been, with vampires scraping by in the dark, hiding from hunters and others who only wish to see us eradicated." He nods at the vial still in Maddy's hand. "I will find the real cure, and then find someone who can alter it not to cure vampirism, but to enhance it."

The hairs on Maddy's neck prickle at Raul's words. "You want to make vampires...stronger?" She loves Caleb and Cora. She doesn't believe any vampire should have an automatic guilty sentence simply for their nature, but if Raul's plans unfold, they would be unstoppable.

"Once a hunter, always a hunter." Raul's eyes take in both Maddy and Caleb. "You see? The girl you care so much for doesn't even want to make you invincible."

"No one should be invincible, Raul," Caleb says. His foot slides forward and he angles himself slightly. Somewhere in the floor below, the sounds of fighting continue.

Raul seems to notice, as well. "The shifters have evolved, being turned into excellent fighters. If they can be better, then so can we. Our kind deserves this gift, and the retribution we've been owed after all these years." He stares at Caleb, a gleam of triumph in his eyes. "And you do not have the power to stop me. In fact, please try. I dare you."

Maddy can't stand the drivel pouring out of Raul's mouth any longer. Caleb is the king of the vampires, and even if the council had appointed him thinking they could use him, he still deserves the respect such a position demands.

She steps closer to Raul. "You had better be careful not to cross the line, Raul," she growls.

Raul chuckles. "Oh? You mean, like this?" In a burst of speed only vampires are capable of achieving, Raul uncoils and rushes toward Maddy. She manages to take a half-step back before Caleb's arm wraps around her middle and whips her out of the way. Maddy stumbles with the quick movement and her shoulder slams into the wall before she's able to catch her balance.

A ferocious snarl rips up Caleb's throat. He doesn't speak, but the dark and terrifying fury in his eyes tells everyone there that Raul did, indeed, cross a line. There will be no forgiving such a transgression. Caleb unleashes on Raul. The two clash in a blur, arms swinging and fangs flashing under the fluorescent lights above.

Barely more than a few seconds have passed and the other vampires follow Raul's lead. They charge straight toward Maddy, somehow knowing if they get their hands on her, Caleb will do whatever they want in order to save her. Maddy stuffs the fake cure into her pocket to dispose of later and braces for the attack.

Cora suddenly dashes in front of her. "Bring it on, boys." A smile plays at her lips.

The other vampires are happy to oblige Cora's command. She dashes forward, meeting them several steps before they can get to Maddy. Her eyes round as she watches her friend. She knew Cora had been training, but she had no idea she was such an adept fighter. She dodges, ducks, and strikes with such accuracy and swiftness, it's as if Cora were destined to be a vampire.

Numbers are not on their side, however, no matter how skilled Cora is in her new supernatural body. One of the men manages to get through Cora's defenses and sends a fist into her gut. She doubles over and stumbles backwards. The sight of her friend's crumpled face makes something snap inside of Maddy. She taps into her power and unleashes fury on the vampires.

Startled yells erupt through the hallway as her magic flows from her palms to wrap around the traitors. Suddenly, their fighting turns into fleeing, but they don't stand a chance. In a matter of seconds, Maddy manages to decimate them, leaving nothing more than a coat of ash on the linoleum floor.

Maddy hears a pained grunt and her stomach lurches. She twists in time to see Caleb yank a wooden stake out of Raul's chest. A final flicker of hatred passes over the vampire's face and then he disintegrates to dust the floor along with the remains of his followers.

Cora recovers and scowls down at the ashes like she wants to spit on them. The sounds of fighting continue below.

"We need to find Quinn and the real cure," Maddy says. "Before it's too late."

Caleb nods. "Let's go." Together, the three of them venture farther into the building.

CHAPTER 16
CALEB

After searching the entire second floor, Caleb, Maddy, and Cora find nothing. They discover a flight of stairs and head up to the third floor, leaving the echo of the fight below. Caleb's hearing is sharp, straining for any scuff of a boot or quiet hiss of breath as they travel down another long stretch of hallway. Each of them check doors as they pass. If one is locked, Caleb or Cora force it open, trying to make as little noise as possible.

"Maybe the real cure and Quinn aren't even here anymore," Cora says. She opens a door only to find nothing more than a cleaning closet. She rubs her nose at the sharp scent of bleach and cleaner as she walks away.

Caleb peers into another room, quickly dismissing the messy office. "Galina and Blaise said Quinn was here. As far as I know, they're still stationed outside. If they'd seen someone escaping with the girl, they would have captured her." He pauses, head tilting to the side. He swears he heard something. His gaze snaps to Maddy just as she's rounding the corner to the next hallway.

A shifter bursts around the corner. Maddy lets out a shriek

of surprise as the man's clothes shred mid-leap and he shifts into a tiger. If Caleb wasn't so worried for her life, he might have laughed when Maddy tries to hit the beast with a right hook. Cora dashes across the floor and slams into the shifter.

"You can't punch a tiger," Caleb chides as he runs to Maddy's side.

"It was the first thing I thought of." She stares as Cora and the tiger fight. The tiger's sharp claws scrape across the floor and his thick tail whips around, keeping him on balance. Cora just manages to avoid his teeth.

Caleb is just about to leap in to help when a tingling on the back of his neck tells him someone is coming. He looks over his shoulder to find a pack of wolves racing toward them. He grabs Maddy's shoulder and whips her around.

"Get ready," he says.

Together, Maddy and Caleb take on the five wolves. She draws out the long daggers she favors. Caleb notes her grim determination never falters even as she nearly gets bitten. He switches his focus to a large black wolf, presumably the alpha of the small pack. Snarls and feral growls echo through the hallway amid the flashes of fur and glinting steel.

Caleb and Maddy fight together, moving around each other in a lethal dance as they protect the other from the onslaught of the wolves. He's never fought with someone where he felt so certain that they had his back. It brings him no small sense of pride to realize that he and Maddy complement each so perfectly in battle. He can only imagine the kind of wonderful life he will have with her when all of this mess is said and done.

Behind him, the tiger's growls turn into strangling hisses. Cora's arms are wrapped around the shifter's neck as his claws scratch at the floor. Finally, his body goes limp and she drops him. Caleb swings an arm, sending the black wolf crashing into the nearby wall with a crack of bones. Maddy yanks one of her daggers from the neck of a wolf who tries to scramble away, then collapses, bleeding out. Caleb sends a bone-crushing kick into the ribs of the final wolf. Its yelps make him want to cringe and he swiftly ends the shifter's life.

Maddy grimaces at the bits of hair sticking to the bloody smears on her hand. "Yuck." She wipes her hand on her pants.

"You know," Caleb says. "If you'd used your magic, you wouldn't have to deal with the mess."

"Yeah, but I don't know what we may face ahead. I want to be sure I have enough energy to face what comes."

Caleb nods. Maddy is an adept fighter, not only because she's strong, but because she also knows when to check her impulses and think logically.

They move on again, not wanting to linger in case the wolves or tiger weren't alone on this floor. The silence presses in on Caleb, tricking him into being certain he hears things. They sweep the third floor, then make their way to the fourth. After barely being there for more than five minutes, he holds up a hand. He listens for a moment, then puts a finger to his lips, and points down the hall. Maddy and Cora nod, creeping along the wall with him. Halfway down the hall they find a room with light creeping out from under the door.

Slowly, hardly daring to even breathe, they close the distance. Caleb catches a beeping sound inside, and then he hears the racing beats of a frantic heart.

"Please, don't."

Caleb exchanges a glance with Maddy. It was Quinn's voice.

Inch by inch, Caleb carefully leans over to peer through the window in the door. Maddy crouches, then makes her way to the other side to look, as well. Her breath catches at what they both see inside of the room.

Quinn is on an inclined bed similar to one found in hospitals. Thick straps band her body. Her right arm is tied to an armrest and the lead of an I.V. is taped to the crook of her elbow. The woman's head thrashes back and forth, and a tear rolls down her cheek as her wide eyes settle on the other two people in the room.

One is a woman and it takes Caleb a moment to realize she's Caroline Merrick, the sister of Ileana, whose body she has strapped down. He hasn't seen or heard any word of her since his brief encounter with her at the Merrick Group building when he was first searching for the cure. She's inserting some sort of cloudy liquid into the I.V., a smile on her face that holds no love for the shell of her sister. The other in the room puts a scowl on Caleb's face.

Malcolm.

The man had nearly taken out Caleb, Maddy, and their friends in the cemetery thanks to his alliance with some sorcerers who raised an army of the dead to fight. Caleb knows he's after the obsidian, so it's no surprise to see him. Malcolm stands with his hands behind his back, watching as that cloudy liquid flows down the hollow tube toward Quinn's arm.

A terrible, shrieking scream rips through her as she jerks against her bonds.

"Release the obsidian, Quinn, and this will all be over."

"Caleb..." Maddy's strained voice reaches his ears.

The rage and anguish rolling through Maddy is enough to have Caleb bolting to his feet and crashing through the door.

Caroline and Malcolm wheel around as Caleb bursts into the room, Maddy on his heels. Cora dashes around Caroline and yanks the plug to the machine out of the wall.

"Well, this is a surprise," Malcolm says. He grins. "I wasn't expecting us to see each other again so soon."

Any further formalities fall away as Malcolm leaps forward.

Caleb strikes out but the strange magic Malcolm possesses is powerful. The man sends forward a burst of energy that punches Caleb in the gut. He crashes against the wall, sending cracks through the paint and plaster. Maddy races toward Caroline but Malcolm pivots. Too late, Maddy sees Malcom's magic ripple outward. The blast knocks her off her feet and she hits the ground, teeth clamping on a scream as pain shatters up her elbow from the landing.

A growl ripples through Caleb as he shoves off the wall and bolts toward Malcolm. He's a mere foot away when the man strikes. Caleb ducks under the attack but Malcolm's powers seem to have the vampire king in their sights. He's hit from behind and sprawls across the floor. Maddy yells his name and then her steps are eating the distance between her and Malcolm.

Malcolm lets out a delighted, manic sort of laugh as he rains his powers down on Quinn's rescuers. No matter how hard Caleb, Maddy, and Cora try, they can't get near him. Caleb can hear Maddy grinding her teeth and he senses a shift in the atmosphere. She throws her arms forward and her own magic flows. Malcolm barely blinks as his hand slashes through the air, cutting through her magic with barely any effort.

Cora is focusing her energies on trying to get between Caroline and Quinn. The sadistic heiress to the Merrick fortune grins widely at the young vampire. The sight of Caroline gives Caleb an idea. Maddy sends another wave of magic toward Malcolm and while he's distracted, Caleb flashes across the room and grabs Caroline. She lets out a startled shriek, drawing Malcolm's attention. He isn't fast enough to stop Caleb from rushing to the window on the other side of the room and tossing Caroline right through the glass. Malcolm lets out an enraged scream and leaps after her, magic swirling around him.

Maddy jogs across the room to peer out of the window while Caleb crosses to free Quinn from the machine. He undoes the straps around her arms and legs, then works on the ones constricting her middle. A quick glance at her face shows tear tracks staining her cheeks.

"Are you okay?" he asks, listening to her heartbeats drumming in her chest.

Quinn doesn't answer. Cora steps up beside her and pulls up the medical tape holding the I.V. port in the crook of Quinn's arm. She carefully draws out the needle and Quinn whimpers.

"I don't see them," Maddy says. She jerks her head toward the window as she joins the others. "Malcolm must have got them both out of here. If we're lucky, maybe some of the others will spot them and stop them from escaping." Her words are laced with doubt and Caleb can't blame her. He continues to underestimate Malcolm and his powers.

Cora helps Quinn sit up, then steps to the side so Caleb can move closer to the woman. "Did they take the obsidian from you?" He notices Maddy's pulse quicken, waiting for Quinn's answer.

After a moment of silence, Quinn shakes her head. When she speaks, her voice is tight and hoarse from screaming. "No, they didn't. I'm neither alive nor dead, remember? I'm a spirit in this body. My spirit is what consumed the obsidian, not Ileana's body." She peers down at her elbow and touches the bruises forming there from the I.V. "They thought they could torture me so I'd give up the obsidian. They assumed they could draw it out of me, but it's not so simple. That's where Malcolm and his scientist minions have failed."

Caleb releases a breath of relief. Quinn still holds the obsidian. He turns to Maddy and Cora. "I want you to get Quinn out of here. If she still holds the obsidian, then we cannot let others get their hands on her."

"What are you going to do?" Maddy asks. She's bending her arm, seemingly testing her elbow.

Caleb wants to ask what's wrong with her arm but something tells him they need to hurry. "I'm going to continue to hunt for the cure. I'll meet you outside as soon as I get my hands on it." He eyes Quinn who doesn't seem like she'll put up much of a fight. "Take care of her and don't let her get away." He ignores Quinn's glare.

Maddy and Cora help Quinn off the bed and hurry toward the door. "Be careful," Maddy says, then leaves.

Caleb dashes into the hall, urgency breathing down his neck. Time is ticking away and he has a feeling if they don't find the cure today, they'll lose it forever. He checks room after room. A lion races toward him, a shifter left on this floor. Caleb strikes hard and without mercy, then leaves the lion to bleed out behind him. The hair suddenly raises over the back of his neck as he nears the final room in the hallway. He catches a scent similar to sulfur and smoke.

He slows his steps, heart racing, then peers into the room. He stops in his tracks and a thrill of fear flickers through him.

The cure is inside the room in a glass vial and standing before it is a massive creature of smoke and bubbling magma.

The cherufe.

CHAPTER 17

MADELEINE

"Cora, go on ahead and make sure it's clear outside," Maddy says. She has Quinn's arm looped over her shoulder and is half-hauling the weakened woman down the last flight of stairs. "I don't want to get her out there only to lose her in the chaos of battle."

"On it." Cora races down the remaining stairs and disappears.

Maddy can sense Quinn's stare on her. "Don't even try to escape, Quinn."

"I wasn't." The young woman's legs seem like they're going to give out any second. For each several stairs they descend, she leans heavier upon Maddy. "I didn't escape at the cemetery, you know. I was taken by...something." A shudder ripples through her.

Sympathy flashes through Maddy. She can't imagine being taken by some sort of creature like that. "It's called a cherufe," she says.

"I don't care what it's called." Quinn lets out a slow breath as they reach the bottom of the stairs. "I never want to see it again."

Maddy shoves the door open with her shoulder and steps out into the hallway leading to the front door. The floor is littered with blood and fallen shifters. It's a gruesome sight, with fur mixed with smears of crimson on the linoleum and cream-colored walls. Maddy can't help but feel some pity. Had these shifters volunteered for this, or had they been somehow forced to work for Malcolm and his twisted cronies? Quinn makes a small, frightened noise in her throat. After listening for any lurking shifters, Maddy helps her outside. The spirit's eyes squint in the sudden light.

More bodies are on the ground, all shifters. It seems Reign and Alexandra have been very effective while Maddy was upstairs with Caleb and the others. A growl reaches her and she turns to find Cora has joined Blaise and Galina where they are taking out the final few shifters. Their demise doesn't take long.

Maddy tightens her hold on Quinn. The spirit's body is shaking, though from exhaustion, fear, or because she's getting ready to bolt, Maddy doesn't know. She hauls Quinn over to the others.

"Cora?"

Maddy's best friend hurries to her side and helps support Quinn. Cora doesn't seem as sympathetic toward the spirit and glares at the young woman.

"Quinn, you could help out a bit more, you know," Cora mumbles.

Maddy shifts out from underneath Quinn's arm. "Can you take her back to Veritas and have her bound?"

"What?" Quinn squeaks in protest. "Why? I didn't do anything."

"You still have the obsidian and from the way you were talking when we were in Purgatory, you have no intention of giving it up. Worse, you want to use it for your own means. You may be weakened at the moment—if it isn't merely an act—and I'm not going to risk you getting away again."

Cora nods. "I'll get her to Veritas but if she does hold the obsidian, how long will she be able to simply be tied up?"

Maddy gnaws on her bottom lip for a moment. "Ask Nim. I'm sure she'll be more than willing to help. The rest of us will be there as soon as we can."

Ignoring Quinn's whining protests, Cora takes her away. The others join Maddy. Both Reign and Alexandra have flecks of blood staining their clothes. Both witches seem unruffled but the paler complexion of their faces suggests they had to use a great deal of magic.

"Where's Caleb?" Galina asks.

"Still inside," Maddy says. "He's looking for the cure. Did you happen to see Malcolm anywhere?"

The witch shakes her head. "We didn't encounter anyone other than the shifters. What about the cherufe?"

Maddy shrugs a shoulder. "No sign of it. Maybe it left when Malcolm fled with Caroline."

The demigod peers over her shoulder toward the building, a frown on her face.

"Is something wrong?" Maddy asks.

Alexandra peers back at her. "I do not think the cherufe would leave so easily. Once they are given a task, they see it through to the end."

The thought makes Maddy's stomach clench. If the cherufe is still in the building, then—

A pained scream breaks through the air from the direction of the building.

Maddy's heart flies to her throat. "Caleb!"

She barely notices that she's running back toward the front door. A pair of arms wrap around her waist and she gasps when she's suddenly being hauled into the air. The upward velocity steals her breath for a moment and she casts a frantic look over her shoulder to see that Reign has her as they fly up the side of the building.

"Where was he going?" the demon asks.

Maddy swallows, finding her voice. "I'm not exactly sure. He was going to finish searching the third floor."

Reign flaps his great red wings and they approach the building. "Hold your feet up." He tightens his grip on her and pauses in front of a window, then leans back. His legs kick out and his heavy boots hit the window. The glass cracks. After a second hit, it breaks. Reign kicks out the shards clinging to the edges, then helps Maddy into the window.

Maddy hears another scream and she runs in the direction of the sound. Reign hollers at her to wait. She glances back, finding the demon struggling to get through the window with his wings. She hesitates only a few seconds, then dashes down the hall, leaving a swearing Reign behind.

Every instinct screams at Maddy to hurry. Her throat is tight and her muscles burn. In that moment, she wishes she had the speed of a vampire. Fear forms like frost along her veins. What if she's too late? What if the cherufe has already killed Caleb? She wants to kick herself for leaving him in the building to search for the cure alone.

Maddy's feet slip on the floor as she turns a corner and then her breath hitches. The cherufe bursts out of a room and carries Caleb to the floor. Its head almost touches the ceiling, its body is rock and lava. Magma roils under the monster's smoky frame. Even from down the hall, she can catch the scent of the cherufe's sharp, burning scent. Long, wicked claws are poised above Caleb's chest, ready to pierce straight to his heart.

Wrath burns away the fear choking Maddy. Her magic wells within her and she holds up her hand, forming a blazing fireball. She pitches it straight at the cherufe like a baseball player, then starts to run before her magic even has the chance to strike. Behind her, she hears the sound of Reign's heavy boots pounding the floor.

The cherufe backs away with a shriek as the fireball hits it in the shoulder. It turns its head, red eyes searing in a face of black. More footfalls accompany Reign's and in the next moment, Maddy is joined by Alexandra and the demon.

Before she can ask where the others are, Galina and Blaise turn the corner. Together, the five of them face the cherufe. Alexandra brandishes the ancient knife that can be used to take down the wretched beast. Reign and the witches hurry toward Caleb while the cherufe's attention locks on Alexandra and Maddy.

It lets out another shriek, the sound shaking through the air with a ripple of heat. Maddy summons another fireball and glances at Alexandra. The demigod can't attack the cherufe head-on. It will see her coming and she won't have a chance to sink the blade into its heart. Maddy quickly catches the attention of the witches and gives them a meaningful stare, hoping they understand her intent.

The pair nod and together with Maddy start to attack the cherufe.

Sweat rolls down Maddy's temple as the monster wheels toward the magical onslaught. Its claws tear through the air, leaving shimmering heat in its wake.

"Come on, you big ugly beast," Maddy says. She doesn't dare risk a glance toward Caleb to see if he's okay, not with the gaze of the cherufe locking on her, eyes burning like red-hot coals. Out of her peripheral she spots Alexandra creeping closer to the cherufe, her blade clenched in a sure grip. Maddy's heart beats with victory as the demigod's knife cuts through the air toward the monster.

The cherufe pivots at the last moment, a long, smoke-wreathed arm swinging out. It lands a hard blow on Alexandra and the demigod soars across the room. She hits a wall and falls to the ground, unmoving.

Maddy hisses a breath in between her teeth as the cherufe takes a swing at her and the witches. They manage to leap back just in time. She glances over at Alexandra but she hasn't moved. The knife lays beside her. Maddy could get to it but the weapon would be no use in her hands. She isn't a demigod.

"Keep striking at it," Maddy says. She has no idea if the creature can understand speech, but she supposes it doesn't really matter. Taking a risk, she leaves the witches to keep the cherufe distracted while she dashes across the room to Alexandra. Their only hope is the demigod. Spells flash through the room as Maddy reaches her. She crouches down and shakes the woman's shoulder, but Alexandra merely lets out a groan.

The hairs rise on Maddy's arms and she peers over her shoulder to see that Reign has joined the witches. She's never met a demon apart from Colt, but his spells fill the air with a dark sort of aura as he fights beside Galina and Blaise to keep the cherufe distracted long enough for Maddy to wake up the one person who can end this.

"Alexandra," Maddy hisses. She shakes the woman more violently and the demigod's eyes flutter open. "Wake up, we need you." She reaches over and grabs the ordinary seeming knife and presses it into Alexandra's hand.

After several seconds, Alexandra's eyes finally focus on Maddy's face. She sits up, obviously a bit weak, and shakes her head as if clearing her foggy mind.

"Please, you need to hurry." Maddy finally spots Caleb. He's trapped on the other side of the cherufe. He holds a hand to his chest and Maddy wonders if the creature managed to get his claws in the vampire. She tightens her hand on Alexandra's, in turn pressing the knife into the woman's palm. "You need to kill the cherufe before it obliterates us all."

Alexandra's mind finally seems to catch up. She climbs to her feet, holding the weapon, and turns to stare at the cherufe. "I was a fool," she growls.

Maddy's heart sinks, hoping Alexandra isn't getting ready to take off and abandon them. "What do you mean?"

"This is a monster of ancient legend. My ancestor did not kill the cherufe of Pompeii alone. They had help. I thought I could take care of this one on my own, but we need to replicate what was done in Pompeii if we are to end this creature."

"What do you need me to do?" Maddy asks.

Alexandra and Maddy duck as one of the witch's spells reverberates off of Reign and slams into the wall behind them. "Try and find a way to hold the cherufe's arms. You cannot do so physically, it will burn you to the bone. Once you manage to get a hold of him, I'll try and get to his heart."

Maddy eyes the cherufe. The monster seems to be growing more enraged by the minute. Blaise falls and Galina nearly trips over her in her effort to avoid a strike. Reign sees Maddy trying to circle behind the monster. Suddenly, a wall of darkness seems to rise between her and the cherufe. Demon magic. Reign is giving her the chance to get at the cherufe from the back.

The cherufe screeches and the ear-splitting sound makes Maddy wince as she creeps around the side of it through her cover of darkness. Finally, she is at its back. Only a brief moment passes while Maddy contemplates the best way to get a hold of the monster without touching it. She shoots her hands forward and fire magic flies toward the creature. She wraps ropes of flames around the monster's arms and pulls, hoping she's left enough space for Alexandra to get to its heart.

Through the chaos of smoke, fire, and shadows, Maddy catches sight of Alexandra dashing toward the cherufe. The monster thrashes violently in Maddy's magical grip, nearly making her lose her hold. Her teeth clench together and her shoes slide across the floor. Caleb is suddenly there, circling his arms around Maddy and holding her in place.

A horrible sound erupts from the cherufe as heat flares through the room. The smoke churns, as if frantic for escape, and then the vicious creature simply falls into a massive pile of ash on the floor. Alexandra stands over it, panting, knife still in her hand.

Maddy grabs Caleb's wrists and tugs on them. He releases her and she steps through the ash toward the other end of the room. A smile touches her lips as she picks up the vial.

They finally have a hold of the cure.

CHAPTER 18
CALEB

The music on the radio plays softly in the background as Caleb heads toward Mercy City. He and Maddy take the trip back alone since Cora's already at Veritas. Maddy is quiet and he glances at her. She peers out the window, smudges of ash on her jeans and bare arms. Loose tendrils of hair have worked out of her ponytail. Her hands rest in her lap and her fingers are clenched around the cure.

He doesn't comment on the glass vial. He's relieved they managed to get their hands on the cure and he hopes she'll be able to find a way to alter the components. He allows himself the thought of perhaps becoming a human again, but he isn't certain if that's what he really wants. Perhaps, months ago, he would have killed at the chance to have his old life back. Now, however, he has responsibilities. He's the vampire king and even if the council wish to use the title to attempt to pull his strings, he can't simply abandon those who follow him. Not when he can change the way things are.

"Are you okay?" Caleb's voice breaks the silence.

Maddy turns to look at him, raising her eyebrow. "Me?

You're the one who was about to be slaughtered by the cherufe. Maybe I should be asking you."

"I'm fine." Irritation flickers through Caleb, not at Maddy, but at himself. The cherufe had been much stronger than he'd realized and he'd nearly lost his life because of it. When he'd seen the terrible beast, he'd completely forgotten Alexandra possessed the only weapon that could be used to end its life.

"Thank God for that knife, right?" Maddy says. "And for Alexandra. She could have ridden back with us."

Caleb gives Maddy a smile and reaches over to take her hand, resting their interlocked fingers on the console between them. "I don't mind it just being us."

"Me neither." She gives his fingers a squeeze then looks back out the window as they enter Mercy City.

Caleb draws in a breath, tasting something akin to longing in Maddy's scent. His hand tightens on the steering wheel as he turns a corner and onto the street that will take them to Veritas. Someday, he'll make sure her life gets back to normal, and then they can be together. They finally reach Veritas and Caleb parks beside the curb. Maddy hops out and glances back. Reign and the witches are close behind.

Maddy starts up the steps. Caleb locks his car and quickly catches up. The large double doors groan as they enter, the rest of their company close behind. Nim comes around the corner and waves.

"Glad you all seem to be in one piece," she says. "The others are in here." She leads the group to one of the private rooms the expansive library has to offer.

Caleb and Maddy head inside after Nim. Cora is there, along with Quinn. The spirit looks less than thrilled at having been captured yet again. Glowing bands wrap around her middle and wrists, binding her to the chair with some sort of magical ropes.

"I always keep a set of these nearby." Nim pats one of the ropes. "You never know when they can come in handy."

Caleb approaches Quinn. She glares up at him but doesn't struggle against Nim's bonds. "We know you still hold the obsidian, Quinn, but we also need to get a hold of the dream-catcher and the Chalice. Those are two very powerful objects that we cannot allow to be at large. Maddy needs the dream-catcher to help heal Zariah's magic, and we need the Chalice to keep it from controlling those in the supernatural population."

"I don't know why everyone always tries to lay the blame on me," Quinn complains. Her voice takes on a mocking tone. "Give us the Chalice, Quinn. Find the dreamcatcher, Quinn. Enjoy living with the obsidian inside of you, Quinn."

Maddy scoffs and plops down in a chair across from her. "Taking the obsidian was wholly your decision, Quinn. It wasn't mine, or Caleb's, or anyone else's. Now, please tell us what you know about the dreamcatcher and the Chalice, then we can see about letting you out of those ropes."

Quinn flicks a glance between Maddy, Caleb, and the rest of those watching her. Then, her shoulders slump in a heavy sigh. "The necromancer was the one who summoned me. As I've already told you, he ordered me to retrieve the Chalice so he could use it to control Orion and make him let his wife go." She pauses and shifts as best she can in the ropes. "So, I retrieved the Chalice. I didn't want to but I had no choice, you know? Not long after, Orion's minions managed to find me and placed me under their control."

Caleb shares a glance with Maddy. If Quinn was under Orion's control for so long, is she truly free now, or could she secretly be feeding him information? "What did Orion first want with you?"

Quinn's throat bobs as she swallows. She's clearly uncomfortable with the interrogation, but Caleb and his friends can't afford to let any information she may know remain a secret. "Orion commanded me to steal back the obsidian from the vampire master. After that, well, you know what's happened since."

Caleb runs a hand through his hair as he peers over at Maddy. "We have to find the dreamcatcher and the Chalice, somehow." Behind her, Galina nods. She, too, is eager to get Zariah the help she needs. Quinn shifts again and Caleb raises a brow at the uncomfortable glance she gives him. "Do have any insight you'd like to add?"

"I don't know where the Chalice is," Quinn says. "But we can get the dreamcatcher,"

"How?" Galina asks. "Do not lie to us, girl. If you lead us on some wild chase merely so you can buy yourself time..." The witch doesn't finish her threat but Quinn shrinks back from the sharp warning in the witch's stare.

"The dreamcatcher will be at one of Ileana Merrick's safe locations." Quinn tugs against the bonds. "Is this really necessary? I'm not in any state to take off."

Caleb doesn't answer her question. "How do you know the dreamcatcher will be at one of these locations? The real Ileana is dead."

"Yes, but I have her memories, remember? I can tell you, or show you, where the dreamcatcher can be found."

"Right." Caleb crosses his arms, contemplating. He doesn't think Quinn is lying. Her pulse doesn't quicken and he catches no nervousness in her scent. "And what about the Chalice? It's probably our focus. Wouldn't you, or Ileana, know where to find it?"

Quinn shakes her head. "No, I cannot. The Chalice is in the hands of the necromancer. He has cloaked himself using his ancient and powerful magic. Even your witches would have a hard time seeking him out. The only possible way I can find him would be to go through Purgatory." She shudders and closes her eyes. "I really don't want to go there again anytime soon."

Caleb can't blame her, he supposes. He thinks he's killed Orion, but there's no telling if someone as powerful as he will stay dead. The others in the room are quiet, weighing Quinn's words. Galina and Blaise mutter to each other about how they would use the dreamcatcher to help Zariah, and Reign rests against the wall, arms crossed and looking a bit bored now that the action has waned.

"Hang on." Maddy leans forward, catching Quinn's attention. Suspicion laces her tone when she speaks. "Before, in Purgatory, I found you waiting at the ruins where the dreamcatcher was initially found. Why were you there?"

Quinn smiles. "Those ruins lie on a confluence of powerful ley lines."

"Ley lines?"

Blaise speaks up. "Ley lines, in the supernatural world, are lines of energy that flow through the earth. Often, if a witch has to perform a powerful spell they will try to find a place such as the one Quinn speaks of, because it can lend them the energy they may lack to perform the spell."

"Yes," Quinn says. "I was there so I could re-energize myself in order to break through the necromancer's cloaking magic. I may be a spirit, but even we are affected if we lose too much."

"So, you essentially re-charged yourself like a battery?" Caleb asks.

Quinn nods. "Crossing through the Grave weakened me and I was unable to rejuvenate as quickly as I usually can. Something is being done in Purgatory, as if the energy is being slowly drained from everyone. It has to be Orion's doing."

Reign grunts from across the small room. "Most likely."

"Those ruins in Purgatory aren't just a convergence of ley lines, though," Quinn says. "They also hold the entrance to the necromancer's location. It's why I chose that place to gather more energy. I could kill two birds with one stone."

Caleb senses Maddy's stare on him and swings his attention to her. "What are you thinking?"

"I'm thinking that I really don't want to have to return to Purgatory again. You found a back way in so you could meet me there if I go through the Grave, but we aren't certain if Orion is truly dead. He likely won't let anyone moving against him slip through his fingers again." Her mouth twists. "But if we have to go through Purgatory to those ruins to find the necromancer, I suppose it's a risk we just need to take."

"Not necessarily." Nim approaches. She has a steaming teacup in her hand and is stirring it with a spoon. "Purgatory is a mirror of the living world. Everything that exists here also exists there."

Maddy straightens in her chair, her gaze brightening with understanding. "Oh."

Nim smiles and takes a sip of her tea. "You see where I'm going with this. If the ruins in Purgatory hold the necromancer's location, then the ruins in the living world will, as well."

"So, you're saying that all we need to do is go to those ruins and find the necromancer?" Caleb asks.

"Well," Nim says. "It may not be as easy as that, but you could probably find clues to the necromancer's location. Once you find him, then you can retrieve the Chalice before he does something with it that we will be unable to mend."

Maddy lets out a sigh. "I guess we'll be heading back to those ruins, then. At least, Caleb and I will be. Galina, are you coming with us to look for clues?"

The witch shakes her head. "I need to check on Zariah and catch her up on everything. If I'm finished with her soon, I'll come and join you."

Nim sets her cup on the table and jerks her head toward Quinn. "What should I do with her?"

"I called Gabby on the way here," Caleb says. "She and Colt are coming here as quickly as they can. They'll know what to do with the remnant of obsidian inside Quinn."

"Very well."

Caleb gestures for Maddy. "There's no point in wasting time. Are you ready to go hunting for a necromancer?"

Maddy stands and follows Caleb out of the door. "There's never a dull moment with you around, is there?"

The two share a grin as they step through the doors of Veritas.

CHAPTER 19

MADELEINE

Maddy cracks the window as Caleb leaves Mercy City behind. The afternoon breeze is a bit cool, but she loves the scents of late fall. Things have been so busy lately she hasn't really had the chance to take a minute and enjoy something simple. She sweeps tendrils of hair away from her face and frowns at the texture. It's been a few days since she's done more than wash her face in the Veritas library bathroom. Thankfully, she was able to convince Caleb to take her home to Creed for a shower and fresh clothes. She wonders with a bit of embarrassment if she stinks because Caleb agreed easily.

She pulls out her phone and looks up Colt's contact information Caleb had given her. She types out a quick message letting him know she and Caleb would be going after the necromancer to retrieve the Chalice of Solomon.

"Do you think they'll be able to help Quinn?" Maddy asks, resting her phone on her lap.

Caleb turns off the highway, heading toward Creed. "Gabby seems to be pretty confident in her abilities, so I hope so."

Maddy wonders to herself what will happen to Quinn once

the obsidian is drawn from her. Will she leave Ileana's body and return to Purgatory, or will she stay in the dead girl's shell?

Several minutes later, they pull into the driveway of Maddy's house. Her mom's car isn't there, but she already knew she wouldn't be around. Maddy had told her she was on her way but her mom had picked up an extra shift at work. They'd have to catch up on everything later.

Maddy notices one of her mom's pumpkins on the porch is sagging in on itself. After the whole business with the obsidian and everything else was dealt with, she'd have to help her get out some more décor.

"Make yourself at home." She unlocks the front door and holds it open for Caleb as he strolls in. "I won't be too long." She heads up the stairs to her room as Caleb drifts toward the living room.

Maddy stops at her room, rifles through her dresser, and then takes the armload of clothes to the bathroom across the hall. She has intentions of hurrying in the shower but once the hot spray of water rains down on her, she finds herself lingering in the relaxing steam. She lathers up with her favorite shampoo and body wash, then takes the time to shave. Realizing she's taking longer than she told Caleb, she rinses and steps out of the shower.

She frowns at the folded clothes she left by the sink. The jeans, t-shirt, and sweatshirt are practical for this time of year, and for whatever situation they're about to find themselves in with the necromancer, but she really wishes she could wear something cute in front of Caleb. With a sigh, she gets dressed and brushes her hair.

Caleb is watching sports highlights when she heads back downstairs. She's quietly amused, thinking how odd it is that the vampire king is into football, then remembers he's a man just like any other.

"Well, I feel better," Maddy says. The ends of her ponytail still soaks into the back of her shirt but she didn't want to take the time to dry her hair. She heads into the kitchen in search of something to eat. They're out of bread and the only thing in the fridge aside from a collection of condiments, half a jar of pickles, and a nearly empty jug of milk is a questionable salad. It seems she isn't the only one who has been busy if her mom hasn't had the time to go grocery shopping.

"We can stop somewhere and get you a bite to eat if you want." Caleb had followed her and is peering over her shoulder into the fridge.

Maddy nods. "There's this great little deli about five minutes away, if we have the time." She hasn't been into Clark's Deli in a while and the thought of a sub sandwich with all of her favorite meats and cheeses is making her mouth water.

Caleb turns off the T.V., Maddy locks up, and the two head back out.

"There it is." She points to the little deli on the corner with the striped awning and a couple of round tables outside. "I used to go to this place all of the time between classes or on my way home. They have the best BLT's around."

Caleb chuckles as he parks along the curb. "How can a place have a better sandwich with bacon and tomatoes than any other?"

"I don't know, but they do." Maddy climbs out and the two head inside. There is a short line and her stomach begins to growl.

"Maddy, where have you been?"

Maddy turns to find a few of her friends from college sitting in the corner, eating sandwiches. She waves and they walk over so Maddy doesn't have to step out of line.

"Hi, Caleb."

At first, Maddy can't place the young woman who

approaches Caleb along with her group of friends, though she does look familiar. Then, she recognizes her as the young woman Caleb had saved from being bullied on campus when Maddy first met the vampire.

"Hey, Stacy, how are you?" Caleb gives her a familiar, friendly smile.

It turns out Stacy is friends with Maddy's circle of friends, as well. Stacy and Caleb drift a bit away to catch up as Maddy's friends follow alongside her in the line.

"We're organizing a sleepover party for the weekend," her friend Nicole says. "If you're not busy, we'd love for you to come." She flicks a questioning glance to Caleb then back to Maddy, obviously wondering who he is to her.

Maddy's other friend, Braelyn, smiles, practically bouncing where she stands. "Darbie is going to be there so you absolutely have to come. You remember Darbie, don't you? She's coming back to Creed."

"Of course!" Maddy thinks of the girl she'd been friends with when they were young kids. She'd always been a nice girl to everyone and had been one of her and Cora's closest friends. She remembers the little fort they'd made in Cora's back yard and that Darbie always brought cookies from her house that they munched on while talking about how gross boys were. Over the years, she'd lost touch with her, a sad fact of life for many people. She would love to catch up with her again.

Braelyn sweeps a glance to Caleb, too, before giving Maddy a suggestive smile. "If you have plans, we'd totally understand."

Maddy smiles. Some girl time sounds amazing. "I think it's a great idea," she says. "I'll definitely be there."

Nicole, who's always had the tendency to be overly exuberant, squeals and gives Maddy a hug. "Darbie will be so excited to hear you'll be there. Do you think you can talk to Cora?"

Maddy hesitates. Cora is a vampire now, and a young one at

that. Spending the night at a party with her friends may not be safe. "I'll talk to her," Maddy says. She's saved from any explanations as she steps up to the counter. Her friends wait quietly as Maddy orders her sandwich and an iced tea. After a couple of minutes, she gathers her food and they drift back toward the table in the corner. "I haven't spoken to Darbie in years. Where was it she moved, again?"

"Well." Braelyn scoots out her chair and plops down. "After they left Creed, her family moved to a small town named Hereford Hall, somewhere to the east of Tallaganda National Park in Australia."

"That's right." Maddy picks the details from her memory. "God, can you imagine moving to Australia from this place? Talk about culture shock. It would be amazing, though."

Nicole nods, fingers wrapping around her drink. "Her parents inherited an estate over there, remember, and Darbie and her mother would stay there on holidays. Last I heard, they were renting an apartment in Canberra, where her father works. He works in marketing and sales, so he travels to places like Sydney, Perth, Adelaide, and Melbourne. Darbie says he even goes abroad to the Philippines and China. Now, Darbie is coming back to Creed."

"So they're not all moving back?" Maddy asks, her mouth full of a bite of her sandwich. She doesn't sit at the table, knowing she and Caleb can't linger long.

"No," Nicole says. "Just Darbie. She wants to meet up here in Creed for a get together. She got accepted at Mercy City Academy."

Maddy smiles. "That's excellent. What's she going to study?"

"She's aiming for theater and drama," Braelyn answers.

Maddy recalls how outgoing and creative Darbie had been. She was always the star of the school plays and she'd have her little group of friends act out shows in their backyard fort. A theater major sounds perfect for her. "I'm excited to catch up with her. It's been way too long. I had no idea she'd still been living in Australia. I bet she has some amazing stories to tell."

"I'm sure," Nicole says. She nods her head toward an empty chair. "Why don't you sit down?"

"I'd love to stay and chat, but I actually have somewhere to be," Maddy says. "I'll definitely be seeing you this weekend, though. It will be great to have some girl time. Is there anything you need me to bring?"

Braelyn smiles. "Just yourself. I've already been loading us up on snacks and drinks."

"Sounds great!" Maddy waves with her fingers, the sandwich and drink still in her hands. She turns to find Caleb's still speaking with Stacy. Maddy slowly makes her way over, sipping tea through her straw and catching their conversation as she approaches.

"You must go and see my mother," Stacy says. Worry is etched on the young woman's face. "She's still sick, worse, actually. You know how bad off she's been. Mom's been asking for you. It would mean a lot to me and to her if you would stop by and see her. Maybe it would even make her feel a little better." There is doubt in her tone, but she stares at Caleb with a hopeful expression.

Caleb gives Stacy's shoulder a squeeze. "I'll stop by and see your mom as soon as I can. I've just got some matters I need to deal with first."

Stacy's blue eyes look behind Caleb and land on Maddy. She smiles. "Caleb, is this your girlfriend?"

Maddy's heart picks up the pace as she waits for Caleb to say something. For a horrifying second, Maddy thinks maybe he'll deny it, even though she feels certain that their relationship has made it to that point. Then, Caleb nods, though he looks a bit flustered.

Seeing Caleb's internal crisis, Maddy steps up. "Hi, I'm Maddy, Caleb's girlfriend." Behind her, she catches the excited whispering of her friends. She swears she hears one of them refer to Caleb as a great catch.

Stacy grins at Caleb. "Good choice." Then, she smiles back at Maddy. "I hope you keep him on his toes."

Maddy laughs. "Oh, definitely."

"I better get back to my meal," Stacy says. "I see we have the same friends, so I'm sure I'll see you again, Maddy." She waves before joining Nicole and Braelyn at their table.

Maddy and Caleb leave Clark's Deli. She takes another bite of her sandwich, hesitating outside as the door swings shut. She can't stop thinking about Caleb's hesitancy. Slightly irritated, she swallows her bite and turns to him.

"Do you have a problem telling people I'm your girlfriend, or is that not what you want with me? I mean, with all of the kissing and cuddling, I just assumed that's where we were."

Caleb blows out a sigh. "I don't have a problem with it, Maddy. Stacy's question just caught me off guard, that's all."

Maddy stares at him for a moment. She doesn't doubt his feelings for her in the slightest, but knows he isn't the kind of guy to easily admit them. Instead, she has to be the one to make the next big step. Her pulse quickens and her heart races in her chest, but she knows it's the right thing to do.

"I love you, Caleb."

His eyes widen and for a moment, she wonders if she was wrong. Perhaps it was too soon, or maybe he doesn't want to take things any farther with her.

Then, a soft smile touches Caleb's lips. "I love you, too."

Maddy grins wide and wraps her arms around him, nearly

dropping her sandwich. When she eases back, Caleb seems almost apprehensive and a bit shocked.

"Don't worry," Maddy says. She heads to the car. "This is a good thing."

Caleb quietly follows and as he gets in the car and turns the ignition, Maddy tries not to worry about his hesitancy. Was this truly what he wants?

Or is Caleb merely going along with this while he figures things out?

CHAPTER 20

CALEB

Mind reeling, Caleb pulls his car away from the deli. In the rearview mirror, he sees Stacy and her friends step outside. They make their way down the sidewalk, watching with smiles on their faces as he turns the corner.

He can't believe how smoothly Maddy made them an official couple. He does love Maddy, but until Stacy asked if she was his girlfriend, he really hadn't put any thought to a label on their relationship. They'd gone through so much together that being called her boyfriend really doesn't do what they have between them any justice. He thought of the way Maddy had stepped forward, voicing that she was his girlfriend. He should have been the one to proudly claim her and instead, Stacy's question had caught him so off guard that he'd nearly frozen like an idiot. Why had he shied away? What if Maddy thinks he doesn't care for her as much as she does for him?

Pressing his foot harder on the gas pedal, Caleb leaves the outskirts of town and listens to Maddy sip tea through her straw. He pulls in a breath through his nose. Her scent is a tangle of excitement, doubt, and even a bit of dread. His fingers twitch on the steering wheel. He should grab her hand and give her some reassurance after the awkward encounter at Clark's Deli, but instead he allows himself a bit longer to get his thoughts in order.

Maddy said she loved him. His chest swells with her proclamation. He knew she cared for him, but he hadn't realized how deeply her affections ran. Perhaps he shouldn't have encouraged those feelings. God knows being in a relationship with him likely won't do her any good. He's the vampire king now, and she's a hunter. She's also Dracula's heir, however, and he's the nephew of the greatest hunter who ever lived. It's ironic, and a bit poetic, if he thinks about it.

Fate, it seems, has an odd sense of humor.

People won't like it. The vampires will detest his relationship with the young hunter, and Caleb can't see many members of the Order who will approve of Maddy loving the king of the vampires. They'll face strife and prejudices. Is he really willing to put her through that? Caleb glances at Maddy and, sensing his stare, she turns to face him. A wide, bright smile graces her face and all of the doubt seems to melt away within him.

Whatever happens, it will be worth it. *She* is worth it.

Caleb grabs Maddy's hand and brings her fingers to his lips, pressing a kiss to her knuckles. "I promise I won't ever disappoint you, Maddy."

A blush creeps across her face but she chuckles. "I'm sure you will. I'm also certain I'll disappoint you now and then, but look at all we've gone through together. We can handle anything that comes our way."

Caleb believes every word and he finds himself looking forward to this new adventure with this strong, amazing, determined young woman.

After driving for a while, they finally reach the spot where they need to hike into the ruins from the road. They climb out of the car and Caleb locks up. Then, the two begin the trek through the forest. Leaves crunch under Maddy's feet as Caleb keeps his ears open. They may not be the only ones going after the necromancer. After nearly thirty minutes, he and Maddy reach the clearing in the forest that holds the ruins.

Maddy props her hands on her hips, surveying the massive stones jutting out of the earth toward the sky. "Well," she says. "We made it. Now what?"

"Let's take a look around for anything strange." Caleb makes his way into the ruins, Maddy at his side.

The ruins are quiet, strangely so. There are no birds singing in the early evening and even the soft fall breeze has stilled. Caleb pauses and looks down at the ground. The spot where he and the supposed Ileana Merrick had dug up the dreamcatcher is still there, the dirt piled up beside the hole. Maddy steps up to the stone beside it and studies the rough surface. Her fingers trace the pattern of a dreamcatcher etched into the stone.

"I don't think this is the right one," she says. "If the necromancer had known about the dreamcatcher, surely he would have already dug it up seeing as it's a powerful object, wouldn't he?"

Caleb tilts his head. "Maybe. Although only a Merrick descendant could get past the wards protecting it. Plus, if he didn't have a purpose for it, maybe he wouldn't have bothered. I'm not really sure who this necromancer is or what kind of person he is, but he has the Chalice to try to get his wife. He may not be a greedy man."

"Let's examine the other stones, then. There has to be a clue somewhere." Maddy moves to the next stone and Caleb drifts to the one on the right.

All of the stones are covered in runes, the markings faded with time and wind. Some of them can only be discerned by running a hand over the patterns. None of them made any sense to Caleb, the curves and lines as strange to him as a foreign language.

"Maybe we should have dragged Quinn along with us," Caleb says. He squints at a circular rune surrounded by nearly indecipherable squiggles. "She seems to know a great deal about this stuff."

Maddy pokes her head around one of the stones. "I don't think that's a good idea. Quinn probably could have helped but until the obsidian is drawn out of her, she poses too much of a risk. Veritas is the safest place for her." Maddy studies the stone in front of her. "Besides, Malcolm and Caroline are still out and about. I didn't see their bodies after you chucked Caroline out of that window."

Caleb lets out a sigh. Maddy's right, but he wishes there was an easier way to find what they were looking for in this place. They continue to search as evening darkens to night.

Finally, Maddy leans against one of the stones. "I need a break. This is crazy."

Caleb peers around, then finds a flat, grassy spot nearby. It isn't directly on the ruins but close enough they can keep an eye on it should anyone come around, including the necromancer. "Let's take a break over there."

Maddy follows him to the little clearing and sits down. She shifts, then tosses some sticks away before settling her back against the ground. "It's not so bad, actually. You know, this one time I went camping with Cora and we were so excited to leave we completely forgot the tent." She giggles, crossing her arms across her chest. "We spent the whole night in our sleeping bags, laughing and looking up at the night sky. We woke up covered in dew and ants."

"That sounds nice."

Maddy raises an eyebrow.

Caleb lays beside her. "The looking up at the sky part." He turns his head to smile at her. "Not the ants."

"It was nice. This place is pretty cool, too. It's quiet here."

A memory flits back to Caleb of him in a clearing, swinging a dull practice sword with sweat rolling between his shoulder blades, his aunt keeping a keen eye on him.

"When I was a kid, Kenna used to take me to a clearing much like this one. It was surrounded by trees and the space was small, but level and grassy. I spent a lot of time there."

Maddy turns to look at him. "What did you do?"

"Train," Caleb says. "In that clearing, Kenna taught me how to fight, and how to survive. She was relentless, yet fair. She pushed me to not only learn my limits, but to overcome them. God, I would be so pissed at her sometimes. My muscles would be burning and I felt like I could scarcely breathe. I'd end those training sessions feeling like I'd lost a battle every time." A smile touches his lips. "And then she'd always get me something as a treat, like ice cream or a new book I'd been wanting. For every effort, she always gave me a reward."

"Kenna sounds like she was a remarkable woman," Maddy says.

Caleb swallows, staring at the stars in the sky, his gaze tracing the lines of the constellations. "Yes, she was. I miss her very much. She died fighting the Sins."

Maddy rolls toward him, resting her head on her arm. "I'm sorry, Caleb. I can't imagine what it's like to lose someone you love so much."

"I've dealt with it," he says, wondering if that's the truth. "I just wish I'd been able to do something to help."

Silence stretches between them for a moment. Caleb listens to Maddy's beautiful heartbeats, then, before he can change his mind, he wiggles an arm under her and pulls her against him. "Are you cold out here?" The temperature is abnormally fair for the time of year, but maybe it has something to do with the ruins.

"I'm better now." Maddy tilts her head and gives him a small smile. She's wrapped an arm around his chest, holding herself flush against him.

"Then I'll be sure I won't let go." Caleb drifts his knuckles across Maddy's jaw, then leans closer. He presses his mouth against her warm, soft lips and his own heartbeats quicken. Maddy's scent, a combination of her minty shampoo and a growing sense of arousal, fill his mind. The latter nearly has him growling in pleasure. His mind starts to dwell on Maddy's teasing scent, and her lips, and the press of her body against his side. Before he does something he'll regret, he breaks the kiss.

"Something wrong?" Maddy asks. Her voice is breathless. Even in the darkness of the night, Caleb can see the bright excitement in her gaze.

Caleb runs a hand down the back of her head. Moonlight filters through the branches and lights upon her hair like a crown. God, she's so damn beautiful. "I just don't want to hurt—"

Maddy sits up, a scowl chasing away the smile from her face. "Don't," she says. "Don't you dare say you don't want to hurt me or you don't want me to regret anything. I can think for myself and I'm more than capable of making my own decisions. If I didn't want this, trust me, I'd let you know. But I do, Caleb." She lays a hand on his chest, her fingers curling in the front of his shirt. "I want this, and I want you."

"Thank God." Caleb grabs her by the waist and hauls her on top of him.

They're kissing again, any soft tenderness replaced by hungry need as they devour the taste of each other. Caleb moves his mouth to Maddy's neck, kissing and sucking her skin. His lips press against her pulse and he can practically taste her sweet blood just beneath. He isn't tempted to bite her, though. Despite her wishes to not hear him say he doesn't want to hurt her, he truly doesn't. He wants to hear Maddy cry out his name, he wants to hear her moan with pleasure, and gasp against his mouth.

Maddy's blood is the most delectable he's ever tasted, but the sounds she starts to make when he peels her shirt off and runs his hands down her bare ribcage, and the heat of her body pressed against his when they're both exposed, there's nothing more delicious.

Their breaths tangle together with their bodies and when Maddy does scream his name, Caleb knows there is no one on this earth more precious to him and he vows to himself right then and there.

He'll never, ever let her go.

Caleb cracks his eyes open, squinting against the slivers of sunlight slanting down to the forest floor. For a moment, he's jarred, wondering where he is and what he's doing outside. Then, the memories of the previous night flood back like a delightful dream. Maddy stirs in his arms and he smiles. It definitely wasn't a dream. He lays there for a few minutes, reliving their moments together. His heart swells at what they shared. He traces idle circles on her bare back, her skin already pebbled with the chilly morning air.

"Maddy?" he says. "Wake up."

She mumbles incoherently, then curves her body in as a shiver trembles through her.

Caleb frowns. "Maddy, you need to get dressed," he says. "It's too cold for you."

Slowly, she opens her eyes and tilts her head to stare at

him. It seems to take her a moment to catch up and remember what they had done during the night. Then, she gives Caleb a sleepy smile and wiggles closer. "You're warm," she says on a sigh.

He chuckles. "You have an ant in your hair."

Maddy sits up, swiping her fingers through the love-tangled strands. "Ew, I hate ants."

"Here." Caleb reaches over and grabs her clothes. "Get dressed."

After shaking out her clothes and inspecting them for more crawling invaders, Maddy quickly gets dressed while he dons his own clothes. Then, he pulls her against him.

"I don't recall if I said it last night, but I love you."

Maddy's smile lights her face. "I love you, too." She raises up on her toes to kiss him, then stops as she glances over his shoulder. A gasp flutters up her throat. "What is that?"

Caleb whirls to see what Maddy is staring at. There, on the face of one of the stones, is a white star. The two walk closer. "That definitely wasn't there yesterday," he says.

"It looks familiar," Maddy says. "I think it's a rune used in necromancy. I swear I saw something like that when I was filtering through books looking for information on the cherufe."

Caleb leans his face closer to the star-shaped rune drawn on the stone. "What do we do now, though? Who drew it, and when?"

"Maybe it's only visible in the morning," Maddy says. She purses her lips. "I wonder..." She lifts a hand toward the rune, and though his protective instinct wants to stop her, he knows he has to put faith in her, as well.

Magic glows subtly on her palm and she presses her hand against the stone. For a moment, nothing happens and her shoulders begin to sag. Then, the earth seems to groan at their feet. Maddy takes a startled step back as lines shimmer on the face of the stone. A second later, a doorway appears where the star had been.

Hairs raise on the back of Caleb's neck. "I think we found the way to the necromancer." He grabs Maddy's hand. "Are you ready?"

She nods and together they walk inside, and into the dark.

CHAPTER 21

MADELEINE

The shadows grow deeper, stretching overhead like a dark cloak. At first, the morning light from the open doorway in the stone shines at their back but as they go deeper, it begins to fade. The cool air is damp and clings to Maddy like a slick second skin. She shivers, even inside of her jacket. For a moment, she contemplates creating a ball of fire with her magic to keep her warm and help light their way, but something tells her she should hold off with her magic. What if the necromancer senses her coming, or they have a big fight ahead and she needs to save her energy?

A tingle brushes the back of her neck. Both she and Caleb turn in time to see the faint light from the doorway disappear. A soft thud echoes through the walls. Maddy swallows.

"I think we're locked in."

Caleb's fingers tighten around her hand. "Don't worry," he says. "We'll make it back out. If there's a way in, then there's a way out."

Maddy lets go of Caleb's hand so she can cross her arms tight across her chest, doing her best to keep warm in the damp place. "How far down do you think we have to go?"

"I'm not sure, but hopefully not too far."

Sensing Caleb's worried frown on her, she turns to give him a reassuring smile. She can barely see his face in the pitch black. Her toe suddenly hits a stone and she pitches forward. Caleb grabs the back of her jacket before she smacks into the ground.

"Thanks." Maddy's heart hammers at the near miss. Smashing her face into the hard ground is not high on her list. She narrows her eyes, trying to focus her vision. There is nothing but inky blackness. "I can't see a thing in here."

Caleb grabs her arm and wraps it around his waist. "Good thing you're with a vampire then. Hold on tight."

"Can you really see that well in here?" she asks as they continue down the uneven path.

"It isn't perfect, but I can see pretty good." He helps her over a rock jutting up from the earth. "I can't make out things like the porous details of stone or flecks in the dirt like I usually can."

Caleb could usually see details to that extent? She's a bit jealous. "Huh. Well, maybe I should get glasses."

He snorts, the sound seeming to be swallowed by the oppressive shadows.

"Can you tell where we are?" She presses close to him. She's beginning to feel uneasy in the dark, unable to tell what is behind them or what may be waiting ahead.

"Only that we're still in some sort of tunnel," Caleb says. "I can't tell how far it goes, but it looks like it may be turning farther down."

Maddy doesn't like the sound of delving even farther down into the earth. Why couldn't the necromancer have chosen a seaside cottage or mountain villa to hide out in? Why do these people always need to hide in places so...creepy? "This is worse than Purgatory," she says. "At least in there I could see where I was going."

"I can't imagine it will be too far. Even a necromancer wouldn't be able to thrive down here." Caleb pauses as they reach the corner and turn. "Maybe he's closer to the spirits down here."

"Maybe." The air grows colder and more damp. Maddy feels like she's sucking in water with each breath. "I hate this place. I can't wait to find the necromancer and get out of here."

The two fall silent for a while, concentrating on catching any hint of a sound and trying to not make any. It seems to Maddy that they walk for hours and she shudders to think how much earth is between themselves and the surface. She never really thought she'd be afraid of being so deep underground but as the time crawls by, the irrational fear that she'll never see the light of day or feel the fresh air on her face begins to creep in.

Caleb stops, placing a hand on her cheek. "Hey, it's okay," he says. "Your heart sounds like it's about to slam right out of your chest. We'll get out of here, Maddy. I promise."

She lifts her hand, holding Caleb's to her cheek. "I know. It just seems so..." She can't think of the right way to describe the endless, oppressive dark. Maybe if she could actually see, she'd feel a bit better.

"I know," he says. "It's alright. I'm here and we'll be back up to the surface before you know it."

The fear doesn't truly leave Maddy, but she's comforted knowing Caleb's with her. They continue on and soon, she begins to feel something strange.

"Do you feel that?" Maddy asks.

"Yeah." Caleb's voice answers her in the darkness. "It's...strange."

A prickling sensation scatters across her skin. It isn't painful, but it leaves her uncomfortable. "It's some sort of magic," she says.

They turn a corner in the darkness and then smack right

into something solid. Light flares outward, briefly scattering across a barrier. Carefully, she reaches her hand out and taps the invisible wall, eliciting another eddy of light and color. Both she and Caleb examine it, tapping the wall to draw out the light. Their entire way is blocked, from wall to wall, and floor to ceiling.

"Damn it." She kicks the barrier with the toe of her shoe. "How are we going to get past this? We don't have Galina, or Blaise, or even Zariah with us this time."

Caleb raps his knuckles on the wall, the light washing over his face, highlighting his frown and pinched eyebrows. "I have no idea."

Chewing on the inside of her cheek, Maddy studies the barrier, occasionally tapping the invisible wall so she can see. She's been learning much from Galina, and had even learned a little from a warlock in Mercy City, but she feels vastly lacking in the knowledge needed for this sort of thing. Galina had mentioned maybe coming to find them after checking on Zariah, but even if the witch makes it to the runes soon, there's no guarantee she'd be able to find the door. Besides, Maddy and Caleb can't just linger down here and wait for help.

Caleb takes a few steps back, then rams into the barrier. Blinding light flashes and a myriad of color spiderwebs across the wall, but nothing happens.

Maddy clicks her tongue. "You're going to hurt yourself doing that. I don't think this can be taken down physically. It has to be done with magic."

Caleb rolls his shoulder and gestures at her. "Well, you're the one with the warlock gifts."

"No pressure," Maddy mutters. She frowns, studying the wall.

Magic is made up of different elements and light, but it all has rules. The power supernaturals wield is all drawn from the same sort of energy. It was why both she and Caleb sensed the wall before they even set eyes on it. If she can figure out what kind of components were used to make the wall, then she should be able to use the same energy to bring it down.

Maddy pulls in a deep breath and clears her mind before placing her palm flat on the wall. It hums beneath her touch and she can sense the energy buzzing along the flat plane of the barrier. She squeezes her eyes shut, learning every nuance of that thrumming rhythm. Though the air is chilly and damp, a bead of sweat rolls down her temple. She can sense Caleb tense beside her, worrying and waiting.

And as much as she doesn't want to let him down, she can't find what she's supposed to connect to.

Minutes drag by until Maddy's certain they'll have to turn around and try a different method to find the necromancer. Then, her eyes flash open. There. She's found it. She releases her magic into the barrier and a cool, silver light spreads from her palms. The light brightens into flames so hot she has no choice but to let go. The fire spreads along the barrier, the flames eating their way along the invisible surface. Caleb pulls her farther back. The tunnel is illuminated, showing Maddy the craggy walls of stone and bits of dirt and roots hanging from the ceiling. In moments, the barrier falls away and the fire fades.

Caleb lets out a low whistle. "Well done. Galina would certainly be proud."

Maddy beams even as she feels a bit weakened. She peers past the fallen barrier. The fading light is quickly being eaten by the shadows again. "Are those stairs?"

"Yes," he says. He steps past the space where the barrier had stood moments before.

A groan rumbles up her throat. "Why does it have to be stairs?"

Caleb chuckles. "Come here." He scoops Maddy up into his arms and proceeds to make his way up the stairs. He doesn't flash up them in a blur of movement, though he's more than capable of doing so. Instead, he moves at a steady pace, being cautious and not rushing into the unknown. Maddy can't help but enjoy his hold on her and her body against his. It makes her think of last night. She has absolutely no regrets. Being with Caleb had felt more right than she could have possibly imagined. A smile touches her lips in the darkness and she lays her head against Caleb's chest as they make the ascent.

"Why would the necromancer come all the way down there only to go right back up again?" Maddy asks. She isn't certain how far up they've gone, but something tells her they'll be reaching the surface soon.

Caleb adjusts her in his hold. "I'm not certain. He likely didn't expect anyone to get past the barrier. Maybe it is just a way of trying to tire out anyone who tries to follow him."

Maddy wiggles out of his grasp when they finally draw closer to light. Even from several yards away, she can see it's natural light and not something born of magic. Relief floods through her at the thought of being above ground again. Slowly, cautiously, the two go up the final stairs and then step into the late morning light.

They enter a clearing, the space similar to the one they'd slept in the night before. The breeze carries the scent of decaying matter on the forest floor, and a few colorful leaves twist and turn in the air before them. Across the clearing stands a man, his back to them.

Maddy exchanges a glance with Caleb. Is it the necromancer? Quinn hadn't given them a physical description of the man, though in hindsight she wishes they'd asked for one. The man's arms are folded behind his back and his blond hair is neat and short. He wears a suit, but even from a distance Maddy can tell the clothing is older, worn. Perhaps he hasn't bought a new one since his wife's passing. Then, she sees what he is holding and Maddy grabs Caleb's wrist.

The Chalice is clenched in the man's hand.

"Who is this who has come to disturb me?"

The necromancer finally turns and his bright blue eyes are like ice. There is no warmth or light in his gaze, only frigid mistrust.

"I'm Maddy, and this is Caleb. Are you the necromancer?"

The man pauses for a moment, then nods. "I am called Xeros." He glances behind them. "How did you find me?"

Maddy swallows. "Quinn told us to look at the ruins. She gave us the idea."

Xeros grimaces, his handsome features twisting with irritation. "That damn spirit. So, she thinks she can send someone else to do her dirty work for her?"

Maddy doesn't bother to point out that the necromancer had done the exact same thing to Quinn. "Look, I know you have your own needs for the Chalice but we're going to have to take it back now."

"Is that so?" Xeros's gaze lands on Caleb and he sneers. "Vampire." He holds up the silver cup.

Beside Maddy, Caleb gasps. His body goes rigid, back straight. Only his wide gaze darts to Maddy.

"I want you to kill this young woman, vampire," Xeros says. "And then I want you to kill yourself."

Slowly, body twitching as if Caleb were fighting against something, he turns to face Maddy.

CHAPTER 22
CALEB

The Chalice glows subtly in the hands of the necromancer. Caleb's teeth grind together. He can feel the influence of the Chalice sink into his skin, score his muscles, and wrap around his bones. Xeros's command plays over in his mind.

Kill this young woman, vampire.

He wants to shake his head, to yell and rage at the man with a smirk on his face, but instead, Caleb's gaze sweeps over to Maddy. She watches him with wide eyes, slowly shaking her head. He can't do it. He can't kill her. He tries to shove the command from his mind, but with each passing second, the Chalice's influence spreads, clinging to him like sticky spider webs that hold him in their tangled strands.

Complete and utter horror rages inside of Caleb as he takes a staggering step toward Maddy. The necromancer's command makes him feel tight in his own skin, almost to the point of pain. He knows if he obeys, the agony will cease. His fingers open and close into fists, the only outward sign that he's struggling against the Chalice's influence. Even his face holds nothing but cold blankness.

The tread of Caleb's heavy boots scrape through the debris

of fallen leaves and twigs in the clearing. He's trying to stop moving, but his legs seem to carry him forward on their own accord. His eyes drop from Maddy's face to her neck and his throat burns. As if it can read his deepest desires, the commanding influence of the Chalice teases him with an image of his fangs sinking into her delicate skin. He can drink his fill of her delicious blood.

"No." The word drags up Caleb's throat as he takes another step forward. He wants to plead with Maddy to flee but his throat closes up. *I love her*, he tells himself. *I love Maddy. I won't hurt her*. He repeats the thought over and over, as if it will be enough to bury Xeros's sadistic command.

Caleb's stare flicks to the necromancer for a moment. The man's face is subtly lit from the Chalice. Caleb wishes more than anything that he could strangle the man, or rip his head clean from his shoulders. There is no reasoning with the necromancer, even if Caleb could speak.

Xeros's lips press into a thin line. He holds the Chalice aloft. "I command you to kill this girl. Now."

Caleb's chest tightens on the scream he wants to unleash. He turns toward Maddy once again. His thoughts shout at her to run, but it would be no use. She'd never be able to outrun him. He would chase her down like the predator he is and tear into her before she has a chance to go more than several feet.

He twitches, a slice of agony ripping through him like a knife. The necromancer's command is tearing him apart. Lips peeling back, Caleb continues to clench his teeth together, unwilling to unleash his deadliest weapon on the woman he loves. Another flash of pain wracks through him and he draws in a sharp breath. He scents the tang of fear as he watches Maddy. He wants to tell her it will be okay, but his arms start to spread out, his legs bending slightly, preparing to pounce.

"You can fight this, Caleb," she says. "I know you can. You don't want to hurt me and you don't want to hurt yourself."

Caleb tries to shove words past the lump in his throat but the influence of the Chalice forces them back down. Maddy's right. He doesn't want to hurt her. It's killing him just thinking about it. The only solace he has is the fact that if he does take her life, the necromancer's command to then take his own will offer him a way out of a doomed life of loss and guilt.

"You are quite a fighter, I see," Xeros says. "I must say, this is not something I expected. A vampire trying not to slay a human girl? I thought your kind lavished in the thought of such warm, delicious blood on your tongue? Don't you want to taste her, vampire?"

Caleb's eyes clench shut for only a moment before they're forced to snap back open. He's no fool. The necromancer is trying to taunt him into acting on the violent thoughts beginning to crowd his mind. Caleb tries not to look at Maddy, but his gaze is drawn to hers like a magnet. She has so much blood to offer him. When was the last time he drank? Doesn't he deserve something after all he's gone through? If he's going to kill her anyway, shouldn't he be allowed to drink his fill?

A strangled growl crawls up his throat as he tries to dash away the poisonous thoughts.

"I love you, Caleb," Maddy says, her eyes imploring him.

Her words saturate Caleb with a mixture of shame and desperation. What is wrong with him? Why can't he be stronger than the Chalice? Why isn't he strong enough to fight for the woman he loves? Are his feelings for her so weak he cannot overcome Xeros's command? A garbled plea rolls off his tongue as his body begins to lean forward. He can already practically taste Maddy's blood on his tongue, washing away the scents of fear and love emanating from her.

His eyes shutter closed again. He can't live with killing her, and he doesn't want to see the light leave her eyes when he finally commits the violent act. His body trembles as he rallies every last scrap of strength in his possession to fight off the Chalice's influence. He won't be able to hold back for long.

Mind lingering on Maddy, Caleb thinks of all of the times they've spent together. Since the very moment she'd stepped out of the coffee shop and collided into him, he's never had a day where she hasn't lingered in his thoughts. She came into his life and changed it so completely. He never thought he'd find reason to truly live in this world anymore, but Maddy had become the anchor he needed. She'd brought him purpose again. He dwells on the feel of her in his arms and the touch of her lips on his. He thinks about the night they spent together in a clearing much like this, bearing their hearts and souls to each other. God, he wanted those moments with her to last forever. How can it end this way?

His fingernails bite into his palms. The dam of memories and thoughts he'd desperately been trying to build against the Chalice is finally starting to crack. He can't last any longer. His body stops shaking and the last fragment of his true self is washed away, bringing bloodlust flooding into his mind.

A hand presses against Caleb's forehead. The touch startles him, reigning back the necromancer's command ever so slightly. His heart begins to tick faster as he catches Maddy's scent much stronger than it had been a moment before. She's the one pressing her palm to his forehead. What is she thinking? All he has to do is reach out and she'll be dead in a matter of seconds. Caleb's desperate thoughts are snuffed out under the Chalice's influence. He begins to lift his hand to Maddy's throat.

A gasp shudders through him as something begins to beat at the necromancer's hold on him. A strange sort of power tears at the invasive thoughts and rips through the magic of the

Chalice latched on his bones. Xeros's command is torn from his mind and the pain of it nearly sends Caleb to his knees. His legs shake but he doesn't dare open his eyes. If he sees Maddy, the influence of the Chalice will race back ten-fold.

Another wave of the unknown magic courses through Caleb as his hand finds Maddy's throat. Her pulse thrums under his fingers. All he needs to do is squeeze, but he doesn't. The power of the Chalice is weakening. His touch softens on her throat. He doesn't want to kill her.

He isn't going to kill her.

Caleb's heart leaps when the necromancer's command is completely shoved from his mind with another push of magic.

There's silence, and heat. Caleb is almost afraid to open his eyes, still caught in disbelief that, somehow, the influence of the Chalice has been swept away from him. He pulls in a few shuddering breaths, drawing on Maddy's scent. There's something strange about her. Slowly, he opens his eyes.

Caleb drops his hand from her throat and takes a step back with a startled gasp.

Rising up behind Maddy are a set of wings, though these are not the same as the bat-like wings she'd had in the cemetery. These seemed as if they were molded from the fires of Hell itself. Thousands of flames lick along the wings like feathers and heat shimmers in the air around their impressive expanse. They scorch the air with their brilliant orange, red, and gold light. Her wings tuck in tight to her back, drawing Caleb's attention to Maddy's face.

He swallows as she stares back at him with eyes that are no longer her own. Instead of the familiar, comforting brown he's grown to love, they're brimming with fire. The irises have been swallowed by flame to match the wings on her back. His gaze drops to her hands, where claws have grown where her finger-nails once were. Caleb isn't certain what sort of power Maddy has unleashed to become so altered, but he lifts his stare back to hers, awestruck and a little bit intimidated.

Something flickers over Maddy's face, regret, perhaps, or even guilt, and then she turns to face the necromancer.

Xeros stares at her with enormous eyes. His face pales and he staggers backward. The Chalice falls from his hand, rolling in a half-circle on the ground before stopping beside his foot. Slowly, he shakes his head, as if he can't believe what's standing before him. Then, he lifts a finger toward Maddy and his shout echoes around the clearing and into the still air.

"Dracula!"

CHAPTER 23

MADELEINE

The wings on Maddy's back feel strange as she tucks them in. They weigh at her shoulder blades, pulling on her back muscles. The heat of them presses on her neck, but they don't burn her. Instead, the warmth of them is almost a comfort. She stares at Caleb, her eyes picking up details she's never noticed before, like the slight whirl in his pattern of stubble along his jaw and the scar below his left ear, so tiny it's no wonder she's never noticed it before. Then, she notices the flicker of unease on his face.

Guilt swirling in her stomach, Maddy turns her back on him. She glances down at her hands, noting the claws. They seem both alarming, yet natural to her. She wants to grimace but keeps her features neutral as she turns her attention to the necromancer. It's no wonder Caleb seemed a bit afraid of her. She doesn't want him to be. Her new form is jarring, however, and probably terrifying.

Maddy isn't even certain how she managed to grow wings and claws. Something just burst through her when she tried to save Caleb from the influence of the Chalice. She gave in to the sensation and let instinct drive her forward. Now, she's this creature.

Xeros stares at Maddy with wide eyes. He lifts his finger to point at her and she braces herself for an attack. Instead, he shouts out a single word.

"Dracula!"

Maddy blinks, uncertain what he means. Does he know she's the only living heir to the Dracula legacy, or is he mistaking her for the famous vampire himself? She isn't certain, but either way, the necromancer stares at her the same. Cold, seething hate fills the man's gaze. She can practically feel the animosity in the air like the biting static of electricity. It nips and prickles along her skin, making her grind her teeth.

She glares at Xeros. What in the hell has she ever done to him? Neither she nor Caleb attacked the man when they found him, but only stated they wanted the Chalice. Then, he dared to use it to control Caleb into killing her and then himself? The thought makes Maddy's blood boil and the flaming wings at her back burn hotter. She advances forward a step and the remainder of the shock evaporates from the necromancer's face.

Xeros mumbles something too quietly for Maddy to hear. Then, a strange bluish light glows around his fingers. She glances at the swirls and then the man flings his palm forward. Dirt sprays into the air as a blast of magic rushes toward her. She barely has time to flap her wings once before she's struck. She folds and hits the ground. Her teeth click together, narrowly missing her tongue.

"Maddy." Caleb rushes toward her but she shakes her head.

"Stay out of this," she growls. Anger fuels her as she gets back onto her feet. They just wanted to speak to the necromancer and get the Chalice. His attacks are uncalled for, but if he wants a fight, she's all too happy to oblige.

Maddy draws on her own magic, letting the tendrils of

energy coil around her hands. Her nostrils flare as she stalks closer to the necromancer and plants her feet. She narrows her focus on him, drowning out the clearing, the surrounding forest, and even Caleb. All of her focus goes on the man who nearly destroyed everything.

She unleashes, thrusting her fist forward with a yell. Magic swirls through the air. Xeros sends forth his own magic and the two powers collide with a *bang* and flash of light. Maddy squints in the brightness, already rallying another blast of magic. The hair on the back of her neck rises, a sign she's learned means other magic is being drawn. The necromancer's next attack arcs through the air and she strikes the blue magic with a burning streak of fire magic.

Several times, Maddy and the necromancer try to take each other down, but they're at an impasse. Neither one backs down and neither one weakens. Maddy doesn't give an inch of ground. She pushes her magic forward, again and again. A bead of sweat rolls down her spine, tickling her skin. Behind her, she can sense Caleb pacing back and forth. Then, there's a flash of movement. Caleb races for the Chalice, taking the opportunity to retrieve the relic while the necromancer is distracted with Maddy.

Caleb is too quick and Maddy can't yell out a warning in time. Xeros's eyes flick to the Chalice and in the next moment, a streak of his magic spears into Caleb. He's flung several feet away and hits a tree before crumpling to the ground. A groan hums from him and Maddy turns eyes burning with hatred toward the necromancer.

"Don't you dare touch him again." Maddy's voice is steady, and laced with heavy warning.

Xeros sneers at her. "I do not take orders from the likes of you."

Maddy doesn't risk a glance toward Caleb. She hears a twig

snap, however, and figures he must be climbing to his feet. She hopes he'll stay out of the way until the necromancer is defeated. "The likes of me?" She barks a humorless laugh. "Don't like girls with wings, or is it just ones who fight back?" She thinks of Quinn and the control the necromancer had placed over her.

"Your kind should not be allowed to live on this earth," Xeros says. "You are an abomination."

Maddy steps to the side, trying to find a better angle to attack the necromancer than head on. He's too good at defending. She needs to try something different, perhaps trick him, somehow.

The necromancer lashes out again before she can come up with a plan. Her heart lurches as a twisting torrent of magic cuts through the air towards her like a bullet. She flings her arms up, curling her wings inward and wrapping herself in fire. A wince flickers over her face as a flash of pain courses through her. She nearly falls and quickly regains her footing. The wings unfurl from around her and she glares at the necromancer.

Xeros bares his teeth. "Wings. Talons. Warlock magic. Yes, you are an abomination, just as Dracula was himself."

Maddy blinks, uncertain what the necromancer is even referring to. Did he know Dracula held warlock powers, the same magic which has been passed down to Maddy?

The man across from her chuckles. "What's the matter, girl? You don't know your history?"

Girl. Maddy despises the term. She draws on more of her magic, but keeps it just beneath the surface, ready to unleash should the necromancer attack again. Caleb stands near the edge of the clearing, watching the pair of them, waiting for the opportunity to get to the Chalice.

"Why don't you enlighten me, then?" Maddy says. "Since you seem to know so much."

Xeros stares at her for a moment, his palm glowing slightly with his restrained magic. He gives her a tight smile. "Very well. A bit of a respite before I end both you and your lover."

Maddy bristles but holds back from attacking as the necromancer begins to speak.

"There once was a dark faction of the Knights Templar," Xeros says. He lifts an eyebrow. "I'm assuming you know who the Knights Templar were?" His lips twitch at Maddy's obvious irritation before he continues. "This rebel faction managed to sneak vampire blood into a warlock, turning the warlock into a vampire with magical abilities, much like yourself."

"I'm not a vampire," Maddy snaps. She glances at Caleb, hoping he doesn't take her statement the wrong way.

Xeros shakes his head. "Not in the same sense, but you are nonetheless a creature much like Dracula. Powerful. Stubborn. Nearly unstoppable." He tilts his head, studying Maddy with a scrutiny that makes her uncomfortable. "I wonder..."

Magic hums within her, yearning to be set free. She keeps a tight hold on it, not wanting to do something foolish and lose their chance to take the necromancer down. "Wonder what?" she asks.

"Dracula was only killed because Van Helsing got his hands on a special blade," Xeros says. "This blade was made of dark iron. It is the strongest infernal metal in existence and could kill many of the most powerful supernatural creatures in the world. As a result, much of those weapons are now rare and can only be found in faerie dimensions." He falls silent, pursing his lips as he continues staring at her with his scrutinizing gaze.

Maddy flexes her fingers, magic sparking at her clawed fingertips. "Cool story," she says. "But I'm afraid I really don't see the point."

"Don't you?" Xeros glances at Caleb, who watches with a stony stare. "I bet your boyfriend has made the connection.

Many tried to slay Dracula, and through many different means. Only Van Helsing and his blade worked. If dark iron was the only weapon capable of killing Dracula, then what about you?"

Pulse quickening, understanding clicks into place in Maddy's mind. Dracula could only be killed with dark iron. She's the only recipient of the famous vampire's legacy, which means...

"I can only be killed with dark iron?"

Xeros shrugs. "It's merely a theory," he says. "One cannot know for certain. Of course, I'm more than happy to test it."

Nothing but pure malice fuels the necromancer's attack as he sends forth a volley of magic so massive, Maddy has no choice but to hide in a shield of fiery wings and her own power. Her teeth bite down on the cry of pain as Xeros's magic rips at her shield and wings. Maddy can take the pain but when she hears Caleb let out a hiss, she knows the attack from the necromancer has hit him, too. As soon as Xeros's magic stops beating at her defenses, she looks to him from within her cage of fire.

Pure rage pounds through her heart and must be showing on her face, because Xeros begins to look uncertain. He hurt Caleb. The necromancer could have killed the man she loved. A dark and dangerous sort of magic rises up within Maddy, creeping from the shadowy corners she didn't even know were there. In her peripheral, Caleb stills but she doesn't turn toward him. Her eyes, flaming a few seconds ago and now dulled to an inky black, stay locked on the necromancer.

The dark magic seeps to Maddy's fingertips and she holds her hand up. Coal-black swirls rise up from her palm like a snake crafted of shadow and vengeance. She releases the magic. It moves strangely toward the necromancer, twisting and turning, moving unhurriedly, as if the magic itself were seeking out the best place to attack.

The magic strikes, rushing toward Xeros from the side. He

releases his own powers but his magic passes right through the darkness. He lets out a yell as the magic wraps around him, pinning his arms to his sides. His feet shuffle as he struggles to remain standing.

Maddy stalks forward, wings flaring slightly as she glares at the necromancer. He lifts his chin and glares down at her, a spark of challenge in his gaze. *Do it*, his eyes seem to say. *Kill me.* She raises her hand toward Xeros, then curls her fingers into a tight fist. As she does, the dark magic constricts, the shadowy coils tightening around the necromancer's body. He lets out a gasp, mouth opening. Then, his eyes squeeze shut and his face begins to darken. All Maddy can think about as she watches the man struggle is his command to Caleb to kill her, then end his own life. No one deserves life after such treachery.

"Maddy."

She blinks, and looks over to find Caleb picking the Chalice up from the ground. He peers at her, his gaze intense, almost pleading.

"Let him go, Maddy." He walks toward her on slow, easy steps, his arms held out slightly. He's trying not to look threatening.

Caleb's behavior confuses her. She would never harm him. He steps up beside her and touches her arm.

"Let go," Caleb whispers.

Maddy sweeps her gaze from him, down to the Chalice, then over to the necromancer. His face has turned purple and his knees are beginning to sag. What is wrong with her? She isn't a killer. In the heat of battle, yes, but not like this. She reigns in the dark magic and sends it back down into the shadowy recesses of herself.

The moment Xeros is released, he begins to draw on his magic.

Caleb holds up the Chalice, glaring at the necromancer.

"Not so fast," he says. "I order you to stand down. Put your hate aside for a moment."

Xeros stops and his arms drop limply to his sides. He glares, but says nothing.

"I want to know about everything," Caleb says. "Tell us how you came to be here with the Chalice, and your plans."

The necromancer tilts his face toward the ground and sighs. "Very well, but it is quite a story."

CHAPTER 24

CALEB

T he clearing is quiet. In the hush of the night, Caleb can hear Maddy's heartbeats. He glances at her again, wondering if the self that's influenced by Dracula's legacy is going to come back. Her wings are gone, along with the claws. Even her eyes are back to normal. Not that he minds the transformation, of course, but she almost seemed as if she were losing herself to something dark.

"Tell us your story," Maddy says. She stares at Xeros with caution, but Caleb has a strong hold on the man's mind, thanks to the Chalice.

The necromancer lifts his gaze to Maddy, then to Caleb. "If I tell you my story, and let you take the Chalice, will you release me?"

Maddy sniffs but says nothing. Caleb can scent the irritation prickling over her. He can sympathize. Xeros had tried to get them both killed, and yet he wants them to let him go?

"Tell us." Caleb pushes a bit of power through the Chalice, urging the necromancer to begin speaking.

"The world almost came to extinction, you know, thanks to a dark fae sorcerer named Orion." Xeros pauses, noting Caleb's rising eyebrows. "I see you know of whom I speak. Yes, he nearly destroyed everything when he opened the breach that let the Eldritch into the world. Those were dark, treacherous times. The heroes of the day worked hard and trapped the Eldritch darkness into the cage and locked the gates of hell permanently. They also ended up killing Orion, but..." He wavers and a breath shudders through his chest. "I lost my wife to that darkness. I tried using mediums and psychics to communicate with her spirit, but I could never do so."

Maddy crosses her arms, the chilly air getting to her. "Is that why you became a necromancer, to find your wife?"

Xeros's shoulders slump. "Necromancy is a very dark magic and it certainly wasn't something I'd ever considered dabbling in, but...I suppose her loss drove me down a dark path. She had always grounded me. She was a witch, you know, and she was very bright. My wife was my entire world."

The necromancer falls silent for a moment and Caleb watches a tear roll down his cheek. Clearly, the loss of his wife is still an open wound on his heart.

"She was so beautiful," Xeros says. "She had this long, wild hair that was impossible for her to keep neat. She'd throw it in a braid, but by the end of the day she always had leaves or spider-webs clinging to it. My wife was a free spirit and was happiest outside in the garden, barefoot and singing."

Caleb exchanges a glance with Maddy. Pure sympathy shines in her eyes. The necromancer had loved his wife so much he'd been willing to play with dark magic. What would Caleb be willing to do for Maddy? The thought terrifies him a little, because he can imagine doing all sorts of treacherous things to keep her in his life. Love can be such a beautiful, damning thing.

Xeros sniffs, then continues his story. "When the mediums and psychics continued to fail, I had no choice but to take things into my own hands. I began to use the dark arts to communicate with my wife. I found her languishing in Purgatory. The reapers had refused to reap her soul and take her on to heaven." He shakes his head, clearing a lump in his scratchy throat. "She doesn't deserve such a thing. I tried to speak with the reapers and begged them to take her soul to heaven, or even to hell, so she could find some semblance of peace instead of being tortured in endless limbo. The reapers insisted it was not in their hands."

Caleb nods. "Yes, we've heard some disturbing rumors about the reapers."

"I have heard the same," the necromancer says. "I'd heard word that the reapers were commanded to stop ferrying souls to heaven and hell. Such news had confused me. Why would the higher ups refuse to take the souls? Then, through the veil of my dark magic, I saw Orion commanding spirits to do his bidding, including my wife." His hands curl into fists and a muscle ticks along his jaw. "I could not allow such an atrocity to stand. First, Orion unleashed the darkness that took my wife from me in the first place, and now he was torturing her in the afterlife? I couldn't stomach the thought. I knew I had to free her from that vile sorcerer spawn. I returned and delved deeper into dark magic. Learning such things took time, and I worked night and day. I could barely sleep thinking about Orion with his clutches on my wife's soul. Food was little more than ash in my mouth. My whole focus sharpened on freeing my wife."

"Hang on," Maddy says. "Where does Quinn come into this?"

The necromancer fixes Maddy with a flat look. "I was getting to that part. I summoned Quinn's spirit from Purgatory. I put her in the body of Ileana Merrick and asked her to find the Chalice of Solomon, an object I'd read about in my father's books. She worked more efficiently than I could have hoped. Quinn retrieved the Chalice and I used it to control Orion. Then,

Quinn disappeared. I learned she'd gone into Purgatory and when she came back out, she was bearing the obsidian inside of her."

"So, then you found another prize," Caleb says.

Xeros narrows his eyes at Caleb and his body twitches, but he can't move under the Chalice's control. "I'm not the vile monster you are making me out to be. I didn't want the obsidian for selfish means. I was going to use the obsidian to resurrect all of the spirits in Purgatory in order to get them out from under Orion's control. I wanted to free them along with my wife."

"You can't just mess with spirits in Purgatory like that," Maddy says. "They're meant to be in the afterlife. Outside influence should have no sway in that place."

The necromancer turns steely eyes to Maddy. "And yet you went in there yourself. I had control of Orion when he gave you the magical bracelets to put on Quinn. Orion did manage to break my control for a time and he taunted you with the possibility of having a normal life. He told you about the cure, though I cannot see his reasoning for doing so."

Caleb isn't certain, either. Maddy left the cure at Veritas for safe keeping and he wonders if her determination to change it is somehow playing into Orion's hands.

"But you ended up regaining control of Orion?" Maddy asks.

"Yes. Once I had control of him again, I had him ask you to retrieve Quinn. I used his idea of giving you a normal life to try and bait you with the promise that you would have your wishes fulfilled." Irritation flashes over Xeros's face as he peers at Maddy. "Instead of returning Quinn to Orion, and thereby to me, you instead attempted to take Quinn back to the mortal world via the Grave. Then, your vampire showed up and got in my way. He snapped Orion's neck and buried his body."

Caleb scoffs. "How was I supposed to know Orion was being

controlled by a necromancer? He was a threat to Maddy. I wasn't going to allow that to stand."

Xeros bares his teeth at Caleb. "Since your stunt in Purgatory my work has doubled. I had to control spirits to get Orion out of his burial ground you stuffed him into, then work to place control over him again. It took a lot of work and he slipped through my hold several times. Each time I used the Chalice on him, however, it became easier. Eventually, I was able to sever the link between Orion and the spirits, which is how he was able to exert control over them."

Head canting to the side, Caleb asks, "Do you know the purpose behind Orion's control of the spirits? I can't imagine a bunch of dead souls in the afterlife would be of much use to him, especially trapped in Purgatory."

The necromancer's gaze flickers between disgust and sadness. His lips pull down as he shakes his head. "Orion was draining the spirits of their energy. It made them listless, barely more than ghosts without thought or feeling. If he had managed to steal enough of their energy, he would have been able to use it to free himself from Purgatory, then resurrect himself in the living world." Xeros lifts his gaze first to the Chalice, then to Caleb. "And now I no longer have the Chalice, which means Orion is free of my influence. He will once again take control of the spirits and start draining them of every last ounce of their energy."

Caleb looks to Maddy. She meets his gaze but remains silent. Orion is just another problem, albeit a disastrous one, to add to their list.

"Why do you think I tried to be rid of you before you got your hands on the Chalice?" Xeros's nostrils flare and his frame shakes as if the wrath inside of him is working to break free. "You have no idea what you've done. I spent hours, days, *months*, working on this plan. In a day or two, the spell I've been crafting would have been complete."

"What spell?" Maddy asks.

Caleb listens to her quickening pulse and draws in her scent. It's laced with uncertainty and even he begins to wonder if they've made a mistake.

The necromancer lifts his chin. "I found a spell in an ancient text that would have resurrected everyone with the exception of Orion. He would have remained trapped in Purgatory for all eternity and I would have my wife back in my arms." His voice cracks, emotion breaking through his exterior of fury and hate. He peers at Caleb, his eyes a well of loss. "She would have been in her garden again, singing and picking flowers, with spider-webs in her hair and dirt between her toes. Instead, she remains trapped in Purgatory under Orion's fist. You two had to get involved in my life, and now Orion has what he needs. His return to this world will be solely on your shoulders."

The necromancer's words rankle Caleb but he doesn't dwell on Orion's potential escape from Purgatory. Instead, he peers at Xeros with sympathy. "I am sorry about your wife. I cannot imagine the heartache of losing the person I love." He can sense Maddy's gaze on him. God, he'd come so close to losing her thanks to the man before him. "But there are other ways to honor your wife. You are not the only person in the world to have lost a loved one in those dark times."

"I'm aware." Xeros's eyes seem to burn and he tugs against the Chalice's hold. "I vowed to kill the one responsible for her death. Orion brought the darkness into this world, and that darkness swallowed my wife whole. Orion took her from me, and you and your woman took that revenge from my hands."

Maddy takes a step toward the necromancer. "Revenge is not the way to honor your wife, and neither is using the Chalice to control others to do your bidding. You rant about Orion and his control over the souls, yet you did the same with Quinn. Don't you see? You are stooping to the same level as the evil you swore to vanquish. Would your wife really want this for you?"

Rage contorts Xeros's face and his complexion pales in his fury. "Don't you utter a single word about my wife. She would want us to be together, by any means necessary. Yes, I took control of the spirit named Quinn. I would rip her from Purgatory and bind her under my powers over and over again if it means I can get my wife back." His voice is cold and sharp. "This is not going to end here."

Caleb tightens his grip on the Chalice. Something tugs at its power and he realizes Xeros is trying his best to break free. "There are other ways to kill Orion."

The necromancer barks out a humorless laugh. "The heroes tried that with dark iron. While such a weapon has been used many times to take down powerful supernaturals permanently, Orion merely returned to Purgatory to hatch out new plans. I'm not going to allow that to happen."

Caleb hisses in a breath as the necromancer's power suddenly snaps through the Chalice's influence. Xeros takes a step toward him, the necromancer's magic already encircling his hands. Beside Caleb, Maddy's breath catches. There is a blur of movement behind Xeros.

Quinn bursts out of the forest, leaps forward, and drives a long knife into the necromancer's back.

CHAPTER 25

MADELEINE

Shock roots Maddy's feet to the ground. Quinn yanks the knife from the necromancer's back and the man stumbles forward, eyes wide. Then Quinn strikes him again and again. Before she can sink the blade into Xeros's back a fourth time, Caleb flashes to the spirit and yanks the weapon from her hands. She yells and shoves him away as the necromancer falls to the ground.

Maddy finally shakes herself into action and hurries to Xeros. She drops down beside him, blood soaking the back of his shirt. He lets out a final, rattling gasp, and then his body stills.

"He's dead," Maddy murmurs. She peers up at Quinn. "You killed him." A dark thought enters her mind but Caleb speaks, voicing her concern aloud before she has the chance.

"What happened at Veritas?" Caleb snaps. "How did you get out and find us?"

Maddy's pulse quickens and a sick sensation slides into her gut. She eyes the knife Caleb had taken from Quinn, the sleek blade crimson with fresh blood. God, what if Quinn had killed their friends? What about Cora and Galina? Maddy can't think through the horror careening toward her to even recall who else was at Veritas guarding Quinn.

Quinn smiles. "I have the power of the obsidian inside of me. Did you really think you could keep me in that place? It took me a little time, I'll admit, but I managed to free myself of the binds." She tilts her head to the side, her grin widening. "What's the matter, Maddy? You seem worried about something."

Stalking forward, Maddy wants nothing more than to wrap her hands around Quinn's neck and demand answers. Caleb holds an arm out and bars her way. She narrows her eyes at him but he's staring at Quinn with a face of stone.

"What happened to the others?"

Quinn rolls her eyes and waves her hand. "Don't worry. I left everyone in Veritas alive. Snuffing them out would have been all too easy but I had more important things to do. I tracked you down, which wasn't easy. I knew you were going to the ruins but I hadn't expected you to find the necromancer's hidden doorway so easily. You'll have to tell me the story sometime about getting through the tunnel. I managed to arrive just as Xeros was finishing up with his story."

"I didn't hear you out there." Caleb jerks his chin toward the forest.

Maddy wonders if his pride is hurt that he didn't hear Quinn, or if he merely wants to know how she managed to sneak up on them. Maddy couldn't walk through the forest without leaves crunching beneath her shoes.

"The obsidian allows me to do a great many things." Quinn peers down at the necromancer as blood seeps into the ground around him. "And I'm glad I have it inside me. It helped me to take down the man who thought he could control me. What sort of person uses an innocent spirit in his own personal vendetta? Perhaps he spared me from Orion's touch, but Xeros was no better. He used me as if I were nothing more than a means to an end. I heard what he said at the end. He would have used me over and over to get what he wanted. Xeros pretended to care about me and tried using careful, soft words to get me to feel sympathy for him. A part of me wonders if it wasn't the thought of having his wife returned to him that made his drive so hard, or if it was the revenge on Orion he craved for most."

Mulling over Quinn's words, Maddy can't help but wonder the same thing. She recalls Xeros's speech. There was no doubt he loved his wife, heartbreakingly so, but in the end, his focus on revenge had clouded his judgment to the point he'd used an innocent soul to do his bidding. The necromancer's love for his wife had been great, and that deep love had twisted into something dark and deluded.

"What about you, Quinn?" Maddy asks. "I have a feeling there's more to your story than what you're putting out there."

Quinn winks at Maddy. "Women's intuition. We can always tell when something is being held back." She sighs, turning her face skyward. The moon has moved high enough in the sky to send beams of soft light into the clearing. "I've missed the moonlight. It doesn't shine in Purgatory." After another quiet moment, she continues. "When Reign and Arielle closed the breach, they made a mistake. In the chaos, they overlooked a small rip between Purgatory and Earth. Not many spirits knew about the rip, and those who did stayed away out of fear. Who knows what could have come through and snatched them away? I wasn't afraid, however. Instead, I went to the border of the rip and stayed there."

"Why?" Caleb asks. "If the others were so afraid, why would you risk hovering around the rip?"

"Isn't it obvious?" Quinn lifts an eyebrow and crosses her arms. "I was hoping for a time when some necromancer or dark sorcerer would seek entry into Purgatory. I knew it would only be a matter of time before some supernatural being would try it. Once the door to the rip was open, I could take the opportunity to slide through and come back into the world of the living. I'm not certain how long I waited, but eventually, he showed up at the rip." Quinn glances down at the necromancer's body. "He performed a spell to communicate with his wife and I watched the entire exchange between him and the reapers. I saw how distraught he was that the reapers refused to take his wife to a life of eternal peace and rest. I used that broken part of him."

Maddy's forehead wrinkles and she purses her lips. "What do you mean? You used Xeros? I thought it was the other way around."

"Oh, he thought he was using me," Quinn says. "And perhaps he ended up with a bit more of a grip on the reins than I'd intended. You see, I used his despair to convince Xeros that he needed to use necromancy to resurrect his wife. The more dark magic he performed, the more the rip into the living world opened. Eventually, the door between worlds opened wider. I took the chance to come into the mortal world. When I left Purgatory, I found myself near the grave of Ileana Merrick. It was a new grave and the footprints around it were fresh. I could even still smell the lingering scents of perfume from the mourners so I knew she'd been buried that morning. I sank into her body and then after some difficulty, dug myself out of the ground."

Maddy blanches. The entire thing is such an intrusion. Once she's dead, she wants her body to stay that way.

"So, the necromancer didn't put you into Ileana's body against your will?" Caleb says. "Why had he, and you, said as much, then?"

Quinn shrugs. "Because that's what I wanted him to believe. It served my own purpose to be labeled as a helpless victim. You know the rest of the story, of course, with the Chalice and whatnot."

An owl hoots in the distance and Maddy listens to the melancholy sound for a moment. "And what about the obsidian? Had obtaining that always been in your plans? In his story, Xeros seemed surprised that you possessed it."

"Getting the obsidian had never been a part of my plans regarding the necromancer," Quinn says. "I did that on my own." Something changes on her face. She smiles, teeth bright in the darkness of the clearing. Her eyes are sharp and she uncrosses her arms. "Once I had the obsidian, I fell under its influence. It gave me so much power, however, and I loved having such strength. Do you know what it is like to die and hover in Purgatory? The reapers refused to ferry souls to the next life. Lingering in between this world and the next is more of a hell than you can possibly imagine. I never want to be so weak again, and now that I have the obsidian, I will always be able to look after myself."

Maddy grinds her teeth together. Even if Caleb flashed forward to grab Quinn, the spirit could use the obsidian on him. The fight with the necromancer has left Maddy feeling drained of energy so she isn't even certain if her own magic would be of much use at this point. They can't let Quinn get away, but Maddy can't think of a way out of this mess.

"I could kill you." Quinn lifts a hand, studying her fingernails. "It would be easy, especially with the power given to me by the obsidian. But..." She trails off, giving them a smirk. "You did help me find the necromancer and weakened him enough for me to deliver the final blow. He deserves it for trying to use me."

Maddy wants to point out Quinn did the same to him, but provoking the spirit at this moment doesn't seem to be a wise decision.

"I'll spare you as a thank you for your help." Quinn walks towards Maddy and Caleb tenses. The spirit reaches into her pocket and pulls out a glass vial.

Maddy's heart jumps. The cure. "What are you doing with that?" She reaches out and Quinn drops it in her hands.

"You should be more careful where you leave that," Quinn says. "You never know who may come along and steal it. Perhaps I'll come back to you if you manage to get the cure altered. Who knows what kind of potential such a miraculous concoction may possess?"

Caleb openly glares at Quinn as she approaches him. "You know, your girlfriend has her own ideas for the cure, but I've heard rumors about others wanting to make vampires stronger. As the king of the vampires, it is your duty to bring your kind to its fullest potential." She pats his chest. "That's just some friendly advice."

Maddy scowls and Quinn smiles at her.

"It's the truth," Quinn says. She rolls her shoulders back. "Anyway, it's been fun kicking it with you guys but from here on out, we're on opposite sides of this game. Don't cross me again." Without warning, Quinn vanishes into thin air.

"Damn," Caleb growls.

Maddy's cheeks puff out as she sighs and props her hands on her hips. "Well, this went to hell in a handbasket."

Caleb snorts. "People don't say that anymore, do they?" His features soften and he draws Maddy against his chest. "God, Maddy, I thought I was going to kill you."

"Well, you didn't."

"Thanks to your badassery."

Laughing, she eases back from him. "Is that what we're calling my crazy transformation? Badassery?"

Caleb shrugs. "I like it." His phone begins to vibrate in his back pocket and he pulls it out. "Yeah?" He listens for a moment, worry rising into his gaze as he watches Maddy. He nods. "Yes, I'll be there. Thanks for calling, Mason."

"What is it?" Maddy watches him apprehensively as he pockets his cell.

"I've been summoned to the council," he says. "No doubt they want to confront me about the fiasco regarding Raul."

Maddy lifts her chin. "I'm coming with you this time. I was there and I can vouch for you."

"Are you sure you want to step in that viper den?" Caleb asks. "Once they get to know you, you'll have a hard time getting out of their radar."

Maddy smiles, raises on her toes, and presses her lips to his mouth. "I'm the vampire king's girlfriend. It's high time I was on their radar."

CHAPTER 26

CALEB

Caleb's car eases up to the curb outside of the building in which the council is held. Mason had told him they'd moved again, doing their best to stay hidden from the Order. It wasn't merely Felix's rebellious faction they had to worry about, but the actual Order, as well. Although most wouldn't worry about vampires as long as they weren't causing trouble, discovering the whereabouts of the council could be another matter altogether.

"God, I could go for a cheeseburger and fries right about now." Maddy unlatches her seatbelt and frowns as her stomach lets out a gurgle.

"We can grab something after this." Caleb gives her a tight smile. He's uneasy about taking her into the council, a place always reserved for vampire kind only. He shoves his door open and shuts it a bit more sharply than he'd intended. As the vampire king, he's allowed to bring whoever the hell he wants to the council, right?

Maddy watches him from the other side of the car, a knowing expression on her face. "Don't be so worried," she says. "I'm just here in case you need a witness, okay?" She bites her lip as Caleb rounds the car. "If you want our relationship to stay hidden…"

"It's not that." Caleb reaches up and tucks a stray curl of hair behind her ear. "I'm just not certain what we can expect in there. If they find me guilty for something, they can vote to dole out dire consequences. I don't want you getting caught in any crossfire, Maddy."

He hears the soft scuff of footsteps and turns to find Mason approaching. His friend gives him a wave, but his face is pinched with worry. "You better hurry and get in there. They aren't happy." He leans over to look at Maddy, raising his eyebrows. "Uh, is she going to wait out here, or…?"

"She's coming with me." Caleb takes Maddy's hand and gives her fingers a squeeze. "And they can just deal with it."

Mason lets out a low whistle. "Bold," he says. He jerks his head toward a door with peeling green paint. "Good luck. I've been put on guard duty so I'll see you later."

Caleb and Maddy enter the building. There's a lingering smell of dust and mold. She coughs then wrinkles her nose as they walk toward a door on the far end of the wide hall. "The council used to have a permanent residence, but after the fall of the previous king and the masters, they've chosen inconspicuous locations to meet."

"Makes sense," Maddy says. She eyes a cracked bust of some ancient scholar.

Pausing at the door, Caleb peers down at her. "I'm not going to tell you to sit back and be quiet," he says in a hushed voice. "But try not to say anything that will piss them off."

Her lips quirk. "I can't make any promises."

Despite her bravado, he can hear the quickening beats of her heart. He pushes the door open and steps inside, Maddy on his heels.

The council has arranged the furniture like they do in every new place they go. They sit at a wide table with a single chair across from them. Unwilling to take a seat as if he were giving testimony in front of a jury, Caleb walks forward and stands beside the chair. The council note Maddy at his side but they quickly dismiss her. No doubt they think she's his feeder, a vile practice some of the older vampires still cling to. Elias, however, stands beside the wall and he lifts an eyebrow as he studies Maddy.

A vampire seated in the center of the council members clears his throat. "Something worrisome has come to our attention." He folds his hands on the table and spears Caleb with a scrutinizing stare. "There have been accusations of treachery regarding you. We sent a party of vampires with you to the Merrick compound, and it seems there is a rumor that you slaughtered your own men. These accusations cannot be ignored. There are some who are even calling for your head."

Maddy's feet shift beside Caleb and he lightly touches her wrist in warning. "If there are some calling for my execution, I would think you would be questioning them for treason. As for Raul, yes, I did kill him and his men, or most of them. It appears one may have gotten away if you have heard about what happened at the Merrick compound."

"And what, exactly, happened there?" a female vampire on the end asks.

"Things were going according to plan," Caleb says. "We reached the compound and got inside without a problem. Once there, we were attacked by shifters. I headed upstairs with Raul's group to search for the cure. It was there he attacked me, saying I was unfit to be king. His men fought, and died, with him."

The council members mutter, cursing and whispering to each other. Then, the head of the council speaks. "We should have expected resistance when we chose you to be our king, given your history and your ties with the Order. However, you should have also been more judicious about killing Raul. He was a strong vampire, as were his men. We will need all of our strength if war is to come. The better option would have been to simply capture Raul and his men, then let them meet their punishment after questioning."

"They did meet their punishment." Maddy takes a small step forward, drawing the attention of the council. "They committed treason and attacked their king. It doesn't matter how they felt about the leader you chose, those vampires got the justice they deserved."

Annoyance flashes across the council. One of the men waves a hand at her. "Who is this?"

Near the wall, Caleb sees a slow smile creep across Elias's face. Before the vampire has a chance to speak, Caleb touches the small of Maddy's back. "This is Madeleine Grimes," he says.

"Ah," the head of the council says. He watches Maddy with a disapproving stare. "So this is the girl who has decided to tangle herself in vampire business."

Maddy scowls. "Excuse me?"

"She has offered invaluable help to your king." Caleb's words are sharp. "And she deserves your utmost respect. I will not tolerate anything less."

A female vampire with a pinched, shrewd face and jet-black hair leans forward. "My king." Her words sound respectful, but Caleb still catches the undertone of derision. "I feel it is our responsibility to inform you to tread lightly in regard to your... alliances. Already, the leaders in the vampire community are beginning to put forth their names in the running to be the next king. You hold a valuable position, but do not make the mistake of believing you are beyond replacement."

Maddy bristles beside Caleb. "Are you threatening your king?"

The shrewd woman flashes a white smile, light glinting off her slender fangs. "Of course not. I'm merely informing him of the treacherous path he is walking. Consorting with you, a hunter of the Order, is not something Caleb's subjects will take kindly to. You, Madeleine, are not only endangering his position, but also his life."

Elias pushes away from the wall. "She is no mere hunter, though, is she, Caleb?" He stalks toward Maddy on fluid feet. Caleb tenses, ready to rip the man's head off if he so much as makes a wrong move. Elias leans down, drawing in Maddy's scent. Caleb lets out a warning growl and Elias smirks. "Oh, you've been naughty, Caleb, hiding such a person from us."

"What are you talking about?" The elder of the council peers at Maddy. "Who is she?"

Elias folds his hands behind his back and turns to face the council. "Madeleine Grimes is no mere hunter of the Order. She is also the descendant of Count Dracula, and the sole heir of his legacy."

The entire room falls silent. Caleb wants to smash Elias's face into the wooden floor at his feet for revealing such information to the council without his or Maddy's permission. The secret is out, however, and he needs to regain control of the situation before it is too late.

"I thought she would be a valuable ally," Caleb says. "She is loyal, intelligent, and with her abilities passed down from the greatest vampire in our history, she is incredibly powerful."

"There are many in the supernatural world who view her kind as nothing more than abominations," the woman with the pinched face says. "However, I feel much of those prejudices are born of jealousy." Her eyes narrow as she studies Maddy. "Do you possess both vampire and warlock abilities, as Dracula did?"

Maddy nods, but doesn't expand.

Elias looks between the council and Caleb. "This will get out in the open eventually. We need to prepare for the fact that a bounty will likely be put on both of their heads. Many vampires will not want Dracula's heir to live." He turns his attention to Maddy. "No matter your intentions, you will be seen as a threat."

"Dracula's heir is the least of our worries." The head of the council stares at Caleb. "There is another threat we have to worry about. The cure. Did you manage to find it?"

Caleb can hear Maddy's pulse quicken and he hopes none of the others in the room notice. "We did. At first, we found a bottle that contained a false cure. The real one was found being guarded by a cherufe. The creature was killed and I destroyed the cure." Caleb hopes that by peppering his statement with truth, the council will believe his lie. "Now that the threat of the cure is out of the way, I propose we begin working toward strengthening the position of the vampires once again. Our numbers have weakened and if there is indeed a war coming, then we will need a strong point from which to fight."

The council nods, obviously pleased with his intentions. "If you can find a solution for vampire kind, then you have our blessing to proceed in whichever way you see fit."

Telling them the cure had been destroyed had been the right thing to do. The council has a little more trust in Caleb and he knows the leash they'd attempted to loop around his neck wouldn't be strangling him after all.

The council dismiss him and Maddy and they leave the building and climb into the car.

"Why did you do that?" Maddy asks. She doesn't look at Caleb but stares at her hands in her lap.

Caleb starts the car. "Do what?"

"Tell them you're going to work toward strengthening the

vampires," Maddy says. "Don't you think that's at least something that we should have talked about first?"

Caleb lets out a sharp sigh as he pulls away from the curb. "I'm only trying to protect my kind. I know you worry about them, but I'm their king, Maddy. If Orion and his minions manage to get into this world, we're going to need to have the numbers to keep from being wiped out. Not to mention the Merricks are creating those evolved shifters. We need to do something to make sure we can stand against them if the time comes."

Maddy is silent for a moment. When she speaks, determination coats her scent. "Caleb, I know you want to protect your kind. Trust me, I support you. I just want you to understand that I'm still going to have the real cure made. It's not going to be something that will strengthen vampires."

"I'm not against you fixing the cure," Caleb says. "If any vampire wishes to become human again, then that is their decision."

"It's not just that," Maddy says. She clears her throat and glances at Caleb with uncertainty. "I might be Dracula's heir, but I'm also still a member of the Order. There is only so much I can condone. I know there are good vampires like you and Cora and Mason, but there are also men like Raul. We won't have any choice but to force those like him to take the cure."

Caleb's jaw works side to side and his fingers tighten on the steering wheel. "Okay," he says. He knows the logic of Maddy's decision. Balance is needed if their world is to survive. A vampire like Raul becoming king would be devastating.

Yet, as he pulls away, he can't help but feel their paths are beginning to diverge.

CHAPTER 27

MADELEINE

addy's fingers drum on her thigh as Caleb drives her to
a small park in Mercy City. She'd called the woman,
Abigail, and fixed up the meeting. She hopes with Abigail's skill
in biotech she'll be able to alter the cure. There will be no telling
until she speaks with her, however.

Flicking a glance toward Caleb, Maddy chews on the inside
of her cheek. He's been quiet since they left the council. She
doesn't like the tense sensation between them. "Are you okay?"
she asks.

He looks at her. "Of course. Why do you ask?"

Maddy turns to peer out the front windshield as they come
to a stop at a red light. "You just seem like something is bothering you." Her eyes drop to the vial on her lap. "Is it because of
what I want to do with the cure?"

"I just don't want you to be disappointed if it doesn't work,"
Caleb says. He hesitates, hand tightening on the steering wheel
as he stares at a truck idling in front of them. "I know as a
hunter of the Order you want to fix what you see as a problem."

Maddy hasn't really put much thought into Caleb's view of
the situation. She was a part of the Order, yes, but that didn't

necessarily hold the amount of sway on her decision to fix the cure as Caleb seemed to think. She knew how dangerous vampires could be and that a cure that would turn them all human would be appealing to the masses of the supernatural community. Vampires, however, were much like humans in that there were good ones and bad ones. She knows this, and if she's able to fix the cure, she'll make certain those in the Order understand, as well. She just hopes this doesn't cause a rift between her and Caleb.

After a few more minutes, they arrive at the park. He pulls into a vacant parking spot in the shade. "You go and talk with her," he says. "I'll wait here. I have some calls to make myself."

She gives him a tight smile before climbing out of the car. "Be back soon," she says. Butterflies wing in her stomach as she heads toward a gazebo on the left side of the park where Abigail said she would be waiting. Maddy's wanted to alter the cure for so long, but now she begins to wonder if it's the right decision. She shakes her head and tells herself it will be a good thing. No one is going to force the vampires to take it, unless they're criminals like Raul.

As she approaches the gazebo, she spots a young woman sitting inside, bobbing her head to whatever song she's listening to on her phone. "Hey," Maddy says. The woman doesn't hear her so she waves her hand.

Blinking, the honey-haired woman smiles then pulls out her earbuds. "Hey! Sorry about that." She sets her phone down and rises to her feet, holding out her hand. "I'm Abigail, and you must be Maddy."

Maddy returns the smile and shakes her hand. "Nice to meet you." She jerks her head toward the cell phone. "Must have been a good song."

"I do love me some alt rock," Abigail says. "So, you

mentioned on the phone that you had something you wanted me to take a look at?"

"Yeah, I do." Maddy glances around. Caleb still sits in his car a distance away, but she isn't certain there are any others around. If a vampire had been tailing them, they'd be able to hear what they're about to discuss. For all she knows, they may run out and take it from her before she has a chance to hand it over to Abigail.

The young woman leans forward. "Don't worry, the area is secure." She grins. "Trust me."

Maddy nods, then pulls the vial out of her pocket. "This is a substance that was supposed to cure vampires and turn them human again, but we were given false information. This 'cure' will actually kill vampires instantly."

Abigail's eyebrows rise. "May I?" She takes the vial Maddy hands her and holds it up, squinting at it as light filters through the glass and clear liquid. "Where did you get this?"

"It was developed by the Merrick Group."

Abigail lowers the vial. "Shit."

"I take it you've heard of them?" Maddy says. She takes a seat on the bench.

Abigail sits, as well, and sets the vial between them beside her cell phone. Music still plays through the earbuds and she taps the screen a couple of times to turn off the screaming band. "Oh, I'm very aware of the Merrick Group. They're well known in my circles." She lifts her gaze to Maddy. "I'm an evolved werewolf, of a sort. The Merrick Group of Industries has been creating problems in the shifter community by evolving shifters."

Maddy thinks of the shifters they encountered at the Merrick's compound. "Yes, we learned as much." She pauses, eyeing Abigail. The young woman doesn't seem like a werewolf, with her golden blonde-brown hair hanging to her shoulders, slender build, and dark blue eyes. Of course, Maddy hasn't had the chance to meet shifters since being yanked into the supernatural world. "Did the Merrick's evolve you?"

"No," Abigail says on a sigh. "It's actually pretty complicated, but someone I know made himself strong, then scratched me and turned me into a werewolf. Afterwards, we were ostracized from the packs."

"I'm sorry." Maddy isn't certain what else to say. It's clear to her Abigail has feelings for the man who scratched her but something tells her the relationship is complicated. Being ostracized from the pack likely makes it much worse.

Abigail waves a dismissive hand. "It's a long story, too long to discuss now." She picks up the vial with a small smile playing on her lips. "I'd much rather discuss this. I've always been into biotech and biochem. I love the science and complication involved. What do you know about this?"

"Not much, unfortunately," Maddy says. "All we know is the Merrick's developed this cure saying it would cure vampirism, but once ingested the vampire would die instantly. Obviously, we haven't tried it out, but we heard about it from a valuable source."

"Hmm." Abigail purses her lips, studying the liquid. She takes the cap off, holds it under her nose, and sniffs. "It doesn't have an odor, which is strange. I suppose they wouldn't want the vampires to scent anything alarming. I'll need to take the cure back to the lab and run several checks so I can map out the components. What exactly are you wanting me to do with it?"

Maddy glances toward the car again, certain she can sense Caleb's stare on her. "I want to see if it can be altered so that it can actually turn vampires into humans again, should they choose to do so. Imagine all of the vampires who were turned against their will. They'd have a chance to get back to a normal life."

Abigail nods slowly. "Many likely won't choose that path, but the option would be nice." She sticks the vial in her bag. "It won't be easy, but fortunately I have access to magic."

"Oh?" Maddy is certain werewolves are incapable of possessing magic, which leaves limited possibilities. "Do you know a witch?"

"Quite a powerful one," Abigail says. Her smile widens. "She has half the power of the Grail and half the power of the obsidian."

Maddy jumps as a woman steps into the gazebo as if out of thin air. The woman, who Maddy assumes is Abigail's witch friend, has jet black hair and bangs so long they nearly obscure her eyes. Even her clothes are black, giving her major goth vibes.

"Maddy, this is Dinah," Abigail says.

Dinah nods at Maddy. The witch doesn't seem too friendly, but Maddy wonders if she's perhaps just a bit shy. Either way, she has a feeling Dinah isn't someone to cross. Perhaps it's intuition or maybe it's the warlock side of Maddy, but she's certain she can sense the deep and powerful magic hidden inside of the witch. Suspicion wells up in her. Had the witch been coming here to meet with Abigail, too, or had she been sent to watch and listen to the meeting without Maddy's consent? She watches the witch closely as Dinah sits across from them.

"Abigail says you have both the power of the Grail and half the power of the obsidian inside of you?" Maddy asks. If it's true, then the witch is powerful, indeed. She wonders if the Grail nullifies the darkness of the obsidian.

Dina crosses a leg over her knee. "It's true."

"Where are the other halves?"

"Inside Arielle, of course." Dinah glances at Abigail, then back to Maddy. "I'm assuming you know Arielle?"

"We've met," Maddy says. She tries to keep the shock from

her face. She had no idea Arielle held such power within her, as well. Maddy decides she really needs to catch up on the history of the supernatural world.

Dinah points at Maddy. "Gabby told me about you, and your situation. Some spirit has possession of a fragment of the obsidian."

Maddy nods. "Yes, her name is Quinn. She's a slippery sort and keeps disappearing." Her thoughts go to Gabby, then flicker between Dinah and Arielle. Pieces begin to fall into place. "Was Gabby going to take the remnant of the obsidian from Quinn, halve it, then place it inside you and Arielle?"

"Yep," Dinah says. "She's already informed us both of her intentions."

That is some plan. Maddy isn't certain how they can handle having so much power inside of them, but apparently the obsidian is safe within Dinah and Arielle.

Abigail clears her throat and pats her bag. "I'll work on this, Maddy, and try to have the cure ready as quickly as possible. It may take some time, but I'll be sure and give it my utmost attention." She pauses, then glances over her shoulder toward Caleb's car. "Be sure and stay on your toes. I can't imagine Malcolm and Caroline Merrick will be thrilled to learn their creation is at large. They'll want to know where their cure disappeared to and what your plans are. Don't underestimate them."

"We won't," Maddy says.

Abigail scoops up her phone, stuffs it in her pocket, and heads out of the gazebo. Dinah joins her.

"I'll be in touch," Abigail says, waving.

Maddy returns the wave. "Thank you so much!" As Abigail and Dinah head off in the opposite direction, Maddy jogs back to Caleb's car. She slides in and reaches for her seatbelt.

"Well?" Caleb says, starting the car.

"She's very nice," Maddy says. "She's working with a witch named Dinah and they're going to get started on altering the cure."

"That's great." Caleb reaches over and squeezes Maddy's hand, drawing her eyes to his. "Really, Maddy. I think this is a good thing."

Relieved that the possibility of a true cure being developed doesn't seem to be bothering Caleb as much, Maddy smiles. "Everything will turn out okay, you'll see."

"Where to?" Caleb asks as they pull away from the park.

"Back to Veritas, I guess." Maddy leans back, adjusting the seat belt across her shoulder. "I want to check in on everyone, especially after Quinn's stunt."

The return drive to the library is short. It's late afternoon and the building will be closed to the public in less than thirty minutes. Caleb parks his car and then the two head inside. Caleb's jaw pops as he yawns.

"I think I'm going to find a couch upstairs and get some sleep," he says. He eyes Maddy. "Want to join me?"

Maddy's heart flutters at his invitation and she thinks back to their time together in the forest. Nothing sounds better to her in that moment than curling up with him, caged in his arms and their bodies pressed together. Caleb's lips twitch in a knowing smile, catching her scent.

"There you are." Galina approaches them. "I was hoping you were okay. I'm so sorry about Quinn, the trickster."

Caleb pecks Maddy on the cheek, gives her a smile, then flashes upstairs. Maddy supposes there will be plenty of time to be together later. She turns to the witch. "It's not your fault. Where are the others?"

"Nim is around here somewhere. Blaise had to go on some Archivist mission. I'm not sure where Cora has wandered off to," Galina says. She eyes Maddy. "So, tell me all about what happened."

Maddy and Galina head toward one of the private rooms where Maddy tells the story of what happened with the necromancer, Quinn, and the vampire council.

The witch nods slowly, eyebrows pinched together. "This is a concern," Galina says. "There are rifts popping up in the vampire community and those who are willing to do dangerous things to infiltrate the leadership."

Maddy can't help but agree. "The question is, what do we do about it?"

Galina's gaze weighs heavily on her. "It's time we got the Order back together."

CHAPTER 28
CALEB

Darkness seeps around Caleb like shadows reaching out to take hold of him. He peers around, heart racing, uncertain of where he is or what is going on. Then, he squints as a bright light chases away the inky black. Orange and yellow flicker across the walls. He sits up to find Maddy striding toward him, her wings bright and burning at her back, eyes like spheres of fire, and claws clicking at her fingernails.

Hairs raise on the back of his neck and he peers around for the danger that had urged her to transform. He finds nothing but four blank walls.

"Maddy?" Caleb's voice is strange, hollow. Something isn't right, he can feel it.

The woman striding toward him doesn't utter a word. Even her footsteps don't make a sound as she crosses the room toward him.

"Are you okay?" Caleb asks. He's growing more uncertain by the second. He loves Maddy, but the way she's looking at him makes his skin crawl.

She doesn't answer him. She pauses a few feet away, staring down at him with emotionless eyes, as if the fire in them had burned all sense of joy and love from her stare. She leaps and in the next moment, she's sitting on him. Caleb shifts, surprised at Maddy's strength. Then, he stills and wonders if perhaps she has some plans to repeat the time they had together in the forest. Maybe she wants to try things in her other form?

Caleb starts to reach for her face, wanting to draw her down for a kiss, but she grabs his hand. Her fingers squeeze and the bones in his wrist pinch painfully. He jerks against her hold.

"Maddy, what are you doing?"

She doesn't relent and he tries again, confused. Has something happened to her? Has the darkness of Dracula living within her taken hold?

Maddy suddenly jerks her other arm down and lunges her hand into Caleb's chest. He screams, feeling her fingers wrap around his heart. He peers at her, eyes stinging with tears of agony.

"Wh-what…" He can barely get a word out.

Maddy leans down, and her eyes burn hotter. When she speaks, however, her words are coated with ice. "You broke my heart, Caleb. It's only fair that I break yours."

His head thrashes back and forth, but her hand tightens in his chest. A final, throat-shredding scream rips from his lungs as she pulls out his heart.

Bolting up, Caleb sucks in a lungful of air. He sits, gasping, in the dark corner of the library. He's nearly fallen off the couch he'd been sleeping on and he shifts back on to it with shaking arms. His eyes dart around the space and after several more breaths he realizes the whole thing had been a terrible nightmare.

He drops back against the couch, grimacing at the worn cushions. He adjusts, trying to avoid the loose spring poking at his ribs.

"Man," he groans. Closing his eyes, he throws his arm

across his face. The amount of relief coursing through him at the fact the nightmare wasn't real is nearly palpable. Slowly, his racing heart begins to ease. He thinks of Maddy in her other form, and while she's a bit terrifying to behold, he knows she would never hurt him. She certainly isn't the kind of person to rip a man's heart right out of his chest, let alone his.

Caleb lowers his arm and twists on the cushion. It's still dark in his corner, but he can see a blush of light across the rich wooden floors several feet away. He sits up, realizing it isn't the buttery fading light of the afternoon sun, but the bright, crisp light of a waking day. He'd been exhausted, mentally and physically, but he hadn't realized just how much he'd needed the rest. He'd slept through an entire afternoon, evening, and night.

The library is quiet. There are no hushed voices or whispers of turning pages in books. Perhaps the others are still asleep. Caleb climbs to his feet and stretches, arching his back. It's a shame Maddy hadn't joined him during the night. He would have enjoyed waking with her in his arms, especially after the horrid dream he'd been having. Fighting off the dregs of the nightmare, he quietly walks toward the railing that overlooks the main floor.

It is still too early for Veritas to be open to the public. The lamps on the little desks scattered throughout the area are still dark, though in the far corner, Caleb spots a faint glow that tells him someone other than himself is awake in these early hours. He heads toward the stairs, stuffing his hands in his pockets. There is a slight burn in his throat that tells him he'll need blood soon, but he can hold off a while longer yet. Maddy, he knows, will wake up hungry, however.

She'd enjoyed the coffee he'd gotten from the café across the street so he quietly heads out of Veritas.

The morning is still early enough that there isn't much traffic, but the café already has people trudging inside for their caffeine. Caleb follows an elderly man inside, the bell above the door chiming. The line isn't too long, but he'll still need to wait for a few minutes. As he stands in line, drowning out the nearby chatter and breathing in the scent of coffee and cinnamon rolls, his mind drifts to the council meeting.

He doesn't regret taking Maddy, but he knows her presence there certainly didn't do him any favors. The council had warned him others were after his position, but whether they wanted to replace him or not, he isn't certain. Seeming as if he curries favor to the Order thanks to his relationship with Maddy would make him look bad. There isn't anything he can do about that, however. He isn't going to hide her like she's some lover he's ashamed of, because he isn't. He's proud of Maddy and if others can't agree with the two of them being together, that was just too damn bad.

The line moves closer to the counter as Caleb worries over the vampire factions. There's definitely a schism in the vampire community. Many, like him, want to try and dwell peacefully in the world. Then, there are those like the former master, and even Raul, who want to better the vampire kind by any means necessary. Caleb can only imagine the kind of bloodshed there will be if he doesn't get control. As much as he despises the idea, he needs to do something to curry their favor and bring those who oppose him being king to his side.

Caleb needs a way to unite the vampires while also not losing Maddy at the same time. Letting her take the cure to Abigail had been a sign of trust between the both of them. Still, he feels deep in his gut he needs to find a way to make the vampires stronger before war breaks out. But he has no idea how to make his kind stronger. Maybe he should find someone like Abigail to help him work out a solution. After all, if there is a concoction to kill vampires, or even cure them of vampirism, surely something can be made that will make them stronger?

The elderly man in front of Caleb gives the cashier his order and Caleb starts reading the menu, eyeing the specials scrawled on a chalkboard on the counter.

Would Galina help him figure out a way to help his kind? He dismisses the thought as soon as it blooms in his mind. Galina is a witch, and technically witches are not tied down to any certain faction, but he knows she favors the Order. It's why she was so keen to take Maddy under her wing and work with her regarding magic. No, if he's going to strengthen the vampires, he'll have to find a solution himself. He is, after all, their king. The vampires are his responsibility and his alone.

"Good morning!" The young woman behind the counter is clearly trying to be perky, but dark circles hang under her eyes and the scent Caleb breathed in from her was laced with irritation and exhaustion. "What can I get for you?"

Caleb glances at the specials again. "One tall lavender latte, please, and a dozen lemon blueberry muffins." He isn't certain if Nim or any of the others who may be around in Veritas drink coffee, but most people wouldn't say no to a muffin. When the cashier gives him the total, he hands her the cash then steps to the side to wait for his order. A few minutes later, he's heading back across the street, a cup of coffee in one hand and a paper sack laden with muffins in the other.

He jogs up the steps leading to the massive doors and shakes his head as he approaches, still in disbelief that Quinn had managed to escape not only the witches but also get out of Veritas on her own. The place may appear to be a mere library, but he knows it can also act as a fortress if need be.

Caleb thinks of Quinn as he eases open one of the doors. Before she'd managed to slip from their clutches yet again, he remembers the words she whispered so quietly to him, even Maddy hadn't heard them. Quinn had told him the dream-catcher is the solution to his problems. He shuts the door quietly behind him. The dreamcatcher does have restorative properties. Would it be possible to use it to strengthen the vampires? He would have to study the artifact to be certain. Quinn told him that the dreamcatcher was hidden in one of Ileana Merrick's safe locations, but he has no idea where to start looking.

Nim spots him and points to a room to the side, presumably letting him know where to find Maddy. He makes his way over, noting the light creeping under the closed door. He shifts the bag of muffins to his other arm and opens the door. Maddy looks up at him from a chair in the corner. Her face is pale and shadows hang under her eyes. There is a pile of books around her and Caleb notes nearly all of them are on the recent history of the supernatural world.

"Did you get any sleep?" He hands her the latte.

She smiles, wrapping her hands around the cup. "Yeah, here and there. I was doing research." She inhales the steam drifting from the cup. "This smells divine. Thank you."

"Muffins?" Caleb sets the sack on the end table beside her.

"Someone's been busy," Maddy says. She takes a sip of coffee then reaches into the sack and grabs a muffin. "Wow, these are huge." She peels the paper back and takes a bite, making a noise in her throat that sends Caleb's pulse quickening.

"I thought you'd need something to wake you up." He takes a seat in the opposite chair.

She eyes him as she takes another bite of muffin. "So, what've you been up to?"

"Thinking," Caleb says truthfully.

"About?"

Caleb leans forward, propping his elbows on his knees. "I want to find the dreamcatcher. I think there may be a way it can be used to strengthen the vampires."

Maddy swallows her bite and her gaze drops to the floor. Caleb watches her mouth work as she chews on the words she's unwilling to speak. He knows how she feels about making the vampires stronger, but perhaps someday she'll see his side of things. Finally, she lifts her gaze and holds his. After a moment, she nods.

"We do need to find the dreamcatcher. It may be able to restore Zariah to her full powers again. I know Galina has been worried about her." Maddy takes a sip of her coffee, then mutters about how delicious it is.

Caleb smiles softly. Despite their different beliefs and opinions, he's glad they have found a common goal.

Perhaps, despite all of the things trying to work against them, it will be enough to hold them together.

CHAPTER 29

MADELEINE

Maddy lets out a sharp sigh amid the stacks of papers, books, file folders, and empty coffee cups from the café across the street. Caleb has kept her well fueled on caffeine as they delve deeper into their research on the Merrick Group. They've taken over a room on the top floor where they can concentrate in the peace and quiet without the distraction of those visiting Veritas. Nim was kind enough to let them use a room furnished with a pair of sofas, a few chairs, tables, and even a mini fridge in the corner. The fridge hums now and then, but other than that, the room is nice and quiet.

Caleb's sitting beside her on one of the sofas, a laptop in his lap. Maddy's own lap is full of clippings from several articles regarding the Merrick's.

"I don't understand," Maddy says. "The Merrick Group of Industries is such a successful organization. Look." She grabs a paper from a nearby stack. "These are all of the industries the Merrick Group has a foothold in. And check these out." She fans through the articles. "They've contributed to the welfare of humanity on numerous occasions and are known for participating in several worthy causes. Do you think it's all just a cover?"

Caleb leans over, eyeing an article where the Merrick Group had hosted a gala to benefit an organization that helps children with rare diseases. "I don't think it's necessarily a cover, at least in regard to humans. But according to my research, the supernatural histories paint the group as dark and evil. It seems the Merrick Group has even been involved with the Tenth Legion."

Maddy slumps back against the couch. "Well, that's just fantastic. How are we supposed to go up against an industry that looks like saints on one side, and evil beings on the other?" She reaches over and picks at a muffin, now stale from the morning. She nibbles on a pinch of crumbs, then moves the stack of articles and replaces it with a file folder.

Caleb reaches over and squeezes her knee. "Everything will turn out." He pauses, studying her face. "Maybe you need some rest, Maddy. We've been at this for hours."

"We don't have time for rest," she says. "We need to learn about the Merrick's so we can find something on Ileana. Otherwise, finding the dreamcatcher will be nearly impossible." She turns back to the file folder and pulls out several pages to look over. Caleb's hand drifts down her thigh and Maddy turns narrowing eyes to him. "What are you doing?"

Caleb gives her a grin. "Sorry. Am I distracting you?"

He very much is distracting her, but she can't let his obvious flirtations pull her from the task at hand. She understands. They've hardly been able to spend real quality time together since their night in the forest. If they didn't have so much riding on their shoulders she'd toss the papers away, say to hell with it, and pull him down with her on the couch.

Instead, she leans over and gives him a quick kiss. "I love you, Caleb, and we'll have plenty of time to catch up with each other, but we need to focus right now."

Caleb groans and leans away. "I know. It's just, well, you're driving me crazy."

Maddy laughs as she starts to read the pages in her lap. "I'm just sitting here."

"Yeah, sitting there looking all cute with your eyebrows pinched in concentration and smelling like heaven." He starts scrolling through a website. "It's downright rude."

Shaking her head, she scans through the first page, then a second. Then, something catches her eye. "Hey, did you know the Merrick Group used to be headed by someone named Warren Merrick? This paper shows accounts of payouts going to Warren. I thought Malcolm had always been in that role?"

"Hmm." Caleb taps away on the laptop and then turns it so Maddy can see the screen, as well. There's a photo in front of a large house of a man, woman, and three small children. "That's right, it seems. This is a photo of Warren Merrick, his wife, and their three kids right before they did a vast expansion of the company."

Maddy studies the photo. "That's Caroline." She recognizes her, even as a child. "And Ileana. Not sure about the brother."

"Tyler," Caleb says. He does some more clicking and follows a link to another page. Then, he frowns. "Huh. That's strange."

Maddy, forgetting about the boring pages regarding payouts and taxes to the Merrick Group of Industries, scoots closer to Caleb. "What's strange?"

His gaze scans the screen. "It seems at some point, Warren Merrick disappeared. No concrete evidence of foul play was ever found. He left no note or instructions. He simply...vanished. It looks like there are a lot of rumors and hardly any seem plausible. Some seem to think he ran off with a mistress while others think he's still alive, avoiding taxes and prison time for fraud. Most seem to think he died in some accident or something."

"That is pretty odd," Maddy says. "If he died in an accident, wouldn't someone have witnessed it? I mean, unless he was alone at the time. Still, even if he went out boating by himself, or went hiking or something, someone would have known where he was heading. People don't just disappear."

Caleb snorts. "Quinn did."

"Yeah, well, normal people who aren't possessed by a manifestation of evil don't just vanish." Maddy peers at the laptop. "So, how did Malcolm come into the picture?"

He scrolls down the article on a business news page. "According to this, there were a lot of rumors and speculation over who was going to head the company. None of Warren's children were old enough at the time. Then, Malcolm suddenly announced himself as one of the Merrick's, saying he was a brother to Warren but had been estranged due to some former family drama."

Snorting, Maddy searches for her latest cup of coffee. "That's convenient." She takes a sip, grimacing. It's gone cold. Then, she remembers Malcolm's words that day in the cemetery when they fought him and his army of revenants. Malcolm had said he'd been blessed by the archangel Raphael. Could that have something to do with the fact he was able to take over the Merrick Group of Industries, despite being out of the picture and uninvolved for so long?

"We need to find out more about this," Maddy says. "Something isn't right. We need information on the whole family's genealogy. It may give us a clue about what really happened with Ileana."

Caleb passes the laptop to Maddy. "I have an idea. Genealogy information is hard to get a hold of but I think I may have a solution. You keep up the research and I'll be back." He stands and flashes out of sight before she could ask him what he has planned.

Frowning, she turns back to the laptop to try and find out

the Merrick family history on her own. She clicks several links and scrolls through numerous pages but finds nothing on any siblings for Warren. There isn't even any mention of any cousins he was close with, or adopted siblings. Who is Malcolm and is he even a Merrick?

Caleb returns in less than thirty minutes with a fresh coffee in one hand and a large manilla envelope in the other. "I compelled an official to get this information."

Maddy sets the laptop on the coffee table and takes the envelope Caleb holds out to her. She takes out the papers on the Merrick genealogy. After scanning through it, she confirms the lack of information she's found online.

"There is no mention of Malcolm anywhere," she says. "These are completely accurate?"

Caleb nods. "Yes. All genealogy information is precise. Even children born of mistresses and adoptions are listed. If Malcolm isn't mentioned, then he isn't a Merrick in any way."

Pursing her lips, Maddy scans the papers again, just to be sure. "So, Warren vanishes and is presumed dead. Then, his daughter Ileana suddenly falls ill of a mysterious illness and dies. Tyler and Caroline don't suspect foul play at all? They just take Malcolm, a man they didn't even know, at his word?"

Caleb rubs the back of his neck. "I guess if they have the same goals as Malcolm, why would they even bother questioning him?"

"But what about Ileana?" Maddy says. "Do you think she opposed him and he got rid of any resistance?"

Before Caleb can answer, there's a knock on the door. Nim pokes her head in. "Hey, a package was just delivered for you, Maddy."

Maddy glances between Caleb and Nim. Who would even know she was here aside from Cora and her mom? Neither would send her a package, either. They would just text or call if they had something for her. Maddy takes the package from Nim and thanks her. There is nothing on the front aside from Maddy's name so she has no idea where the package came from.

"Hang on." Caleb stands and takes the small box. He lifts it to his nose and sniffs. Then, he shrugs. "I don't smell anything off. It seems safe to open."

God, she hadn't even thought about the fact someone could have sent her something harmful. She's making new enemies at every turn. Maddy opens the box and rifles through foam packing peanuts. Then, she pulls out a journal. Her heart hammers as she opens it and begins to read.

"This is Ileana's journal. Here, you read faster than me." She hands the journal to Caleb.

After a few minutes, Caleb relays what he's read so far. "Ileana knew Malcolm was no relative. It seems I wasn't the only one to get my hands on the genealogy records. She had planned to reveal as much at a board meeting."

Maddy's heart sinks, already knowing where the story was going. "Clearly, she didn't have the chance."

"No, she didn't. Malcolm started using poison on her." His face darkens. "I've heard of the methods Malcolm used. The dark Knights Templar faction used the same poison on Count Vlad who became Dracula. The poison doesn't work instantly, but instead makes the victim more and more sick, making it look like an illness they can't recover from."

"That's horrible," she says.

"Yes." Caleb peers at the open journal in his hands. "As Ileana became sicker, she knew Malcolm was going to kill her. She couldn't turn to Tyler or Caroline since they were already enamored with Malcolm and figured they wouldn't believe her." His head tilts as he flips the page. "It seems only one person did believe her, an imaginary friend."

Maddy raises an eyebrow. "An imaginary friend?" Perhaps Ileana was so sick from the poison, she was seeing things. Or maybe, in her desperation and loneliness, she simply wanted someone to talk to, even if that someone was just in her head.

Caleb falls silent and when he looks at Maddy, his eyes are wide with shock. "You're not going to believe this."

"Oh, great," Maddy says. "What now?"

"That imaginary friend of Ileana's that no one else could see?" Caleb flips the journal around to face Maddy, then taps the page. "Her name was Quinn."

CHAPTER 30

CALEB

Maddy paces on the other side of the coffee table and Caleb's eyes track her as she moves back and forth. Every time she turns and walks a few steps one of the floorboards creaks slightly. He hasn't spoken since he told her that Ileana's imaginary friend was Quinn. Everything is beginning to stitch together but he isn't certain he's ready to learn where this all leads. Had Quinn and Ileana planned for something bigger than what they are seeing, or was their friendship and everything that happened with the obsidian merely a coincidence?

"It's possible that this isn't even the same Quinn," Maddy says. She doesn't sound convincing, even to herself. She finally stops and looks at Caleb. "But I know that probably isn't the case."

Caleb listens to Maddy's heartbeats and studies her pale face. She's gone too long without much rest. The coffees he'd brought her had helped her stay awake while they researched the Merrick's but it's only a matter of time before her body gives out due to exhaustion. He twists on the couch so that his back is against the armrest and holds out a hand.

"Come here for a minute."

Maddy frowns. "Why?"

"Because I want you to," he says. He gives her his most charming smile. "Please?"

Obviously suspicious, she rounds the coffee table and sits on the couch. She lets out a squeal when he wraps an arm around her and pulls her back against his chest so the pair of them are stretched out on the couch. He tightens his hold on her when she wiggles.

"Just lie still for a few minutes, Maddy. You look dead on your feet. We can still talk. I just want you to relax for a bit."

Slowly, her body sags against his and she sighs. "I guess this is pretty nice."

Caleb agrees and his fingers drift a bit along her abdomen where her shirt has ridden up slightly. He doesn't take things any farther, knowing she won't rest at all if he distracts her. Deciding it's best to stay on track, he lifts the journal from the coffee table and continues to read.

"It looks like Ileana and Quinn kept speaking. She wasn't certain who or what Quinn was at first, but then she found out Quinn was a spirit from Purgatory."

Maddy grabs a corner of the journal and tilts it so she can see it better. "It doesn't make any sense, though. How is it possible for a spirit in Purgatory to be seen by Ileana? Do you think Ileana had some sort of supernatural ability? Maybe she was a seer like Nim."

"It's possible, I suppose." Caleb continues to read. "They became close friends while Ileana grew sicker. Quinn had been trying to help her." He turns the page. There was another line stating Ileana had a plan. After fanning through the rest of the journal, he finds it empty. "It ends right before she died," he says, noting the date at the top of the page.

"That's really sad," Maddy says. She takes the journal and flips through it herself. "And a bit frustrating. I know her journals mention several safe places she's hidden things, but I wish she'd been more specific. I guess by the time the dreamcatcher was found, though, Quinn was already in her body. If only we had more information we could pick apart."

Caleb tightens his arm around Maddy's middle, then leans over and grabs the box the journal had arrived in. He digs through the packing peanuts, hoping they'd perhaps missed something. Sure enough, there is another journal at the bottom. The cover on this one is newer, lacking the scuffed edges of Ileana's journal.

"Clearly someone is looking out for us," Caleb says.

Maddy shifts, scooting closer to him and tucking herself under his arm as he opens the journal. "That doesn't look like Ileana's handwriting."

"No, it doesn't."

Before they have a chance to start on the new journal, Maddy's stomach lets out a tremendous growl. Caleb can scent the embarrassment from her as her cheeks flush.

He chuckles. "My god, woman. How much do you eat?" He notes the empty papers where the muffins had been scattered on the tables throughout the room.

"I can't help it. Research and studying makes me hungry." She crosses her arms tight, as if she can smother the gurgling of her complaining stomach.

Caleb starts to ease Maddy off of him. "I'll go and grab you something. What do you feel like eating?"

"No." Maddy wraps a hand around his arm. "I don't want anything right now. I can deal with it in a bit. We need to know what happened with Ileana and Quinn."

Caleb hesitates, then picks up his cell from the table. He sends out a quick text, then pulls Maddy back against him. "Shall we?" he says, cracking open the journal again.

They start to read and it doesn't take long for them to

realize this journal belonged to Quinn. Maddy taps the page. "Look. Quinn says that once in Purgatory, she fused herself with Ileana. She knew that Orion would find a way to come back. And she was right. Orion returned even after Arielle killed him with an iron dagger." She cranes her neck and tilts her head back to peer at Caleb. "Do you think the necromancer was right about me, that I can only be killed with an iron dagger?"

Caleb can't stop the shudder that ripples through him at the thought of Maddy being killed in such a way. He presses a kiss to her forehead while he lifts a hand to cup under her jaw. Her pulse jumps against his fingers. "I'd really rather not find out, if you don't mind."

A smile touches Maddy's lips, and it's so damn warm and full of love that he wants to take her mouth right there in a deep and passionate kiss.

"Would you miss me?" she asks.

"I'd be devastated." Caleb shakes his head. "I really don't want to talk about your death, Maddy."

She turns her attention back to the journal. "Speaking of devastating, let's find out what happened with Quinn."

"It looks like after Orion came back, but Quinn headed toward the Rip before he had a chance to exert control over her," Caleb says. "She's lucky he didn't spot her. Given the amount of power he possesses, he probably has ways of keeping tabs on everyone in Purgatory." He turns a page in the journal, trying not to lose himself in Maddy's intoxicating scent as she lays her head back against his shoulder. "The necromancer came into the picture shortly after she reached the Rip. We know what happened there."

Maddy starts running her fingers up and down Caleb's forearm as he holds the journal in front of them. "Yeah, she ended up taking the obsidian and being totally corrupted by it. I actually feel sorry for her. Was she just trying to get out of

Purgatory to help Ileana? I mean, we don't even know if Ileana was dead at this point, right? Quinn didn't write any dates down in her journal. Can you imagine? Once she was out of Purgatory, that could be when she found out about Ileana. I bet it tore her up, as close as they had become."

"It makes me wonder how much the necromancer knew about Quinn and Ileana. He put Quinn's spirit in the recently deceased heiress. Was it because he knew he would be able to use Quinn if she was in her friend's body, or had Quinn convinced him to put her in Ileana?" Caleb's skin pebbles under Maddy's touch. He shifts slightly and clears his throat. She's driving him crazy with the subtle touches, her scent, and the familiar sound of her heartbeats.

She shrugs. "Who knows? It's too late to ask the necromancer, now, thanks to Quinn. I still don't really understand why she killed him. Whether she asked the necromancer to put her in Ileana's body or he made the decision, either way it helped Quinn. At this point, with Orion running rampant in Purgatory, she's safer in the world of the living and she had the necromancer to thank for that." She pauses, tilting her head back to eye Caleb again. "Am I bothering you, lying like this? If you're getting uncomfortable, I can move."

"You're fine," Caleb says. The last thing he wants in that moment is for Maddy to move away.

She smiles, then presses a kiss to the side of his neck. "Good." She turns back to the journal. "Do you think she really hated the necromancer?"

"I think that she was being influenced by the obsidian." Caleb flips another page. "Yep. See here? She says the obsidian had latched onto her's and Ileana's fused spirits and became too strong to resist. She tried fighting it, at first, but the power and darkness became too tempting. It looks like she killed the necromancer because he'd asked her for the obsidian. Perhaps she didn't want to give it up, or feared he may take it from her."

Caleb's pulse begins to quicken as they scan the journal. The scrawls across the page are erratic, the letters jagged and the pages torn in some places as if Quinn had been pressing too hard with the pen. This page holds information from after the necromancer's death.

"She still has the obsidian inside of her," Caleb says. "She's started to try and fight it again, but she can't let it go. She wants to be free of the obsidian, and yet there are times when she gives herself over to the darkness. That's why she ran away, it seems. There's a part of her that doesn't want to hurt us, even if the larger part of her, the part influenced by the obsidian, just wants to stay out of our grasp." He turns the page.

Scrawled in large, nearly illegible letters are the words, "I hate this inside of me." The heart-shredding emotion left in ink practically bleeds from the page. For a long moment, the both of them fall silent, staring at Quinn's words. They're the last ones in the journal.

Maddy swallows. "God. Poor Quinn," she says.

"Both Quinn and Ileana have been trapped by the obsidian's influence," he muses.

"Yeah, and it doesn't seem like it's going to be getting any better for either of their souls." Maddy takes the journal, closes it, and drops it back into the box. She sits up and twists on the couch to face Caleb. "Do you think we should try and find Quinn? Maybe Galina can try a location spell."

He straightens on the couch and drops his feet to the floor. He stares at his dark boots, noting their scuffed appearance and fraying laces. He'll need to replace them soon.

"I know you're worried about Quinn," he says. "And at some point we'll need to find her so we can have Gabby draw out the obsidian, but I think for now, we still need to go after the dreamcatcher."

Maddy reaches over and takes his hand. "Caleb, I know you want to find a way to strengthen the vampires..." Her words trail off and she bites her lip, hesitating. "Just don't let that cloud your judgment as far as the rest of this mess goes. I'll support you no matter what you choose. I just want us both to do what is right."

For a moment, Caleb thinks. He does want the dream-catcher to see if it can aid the vampires, but Maddy has her own reasons for wanting it, as well. "At this point, I think finding the dreamcatcher is our best alternative. Who knows? Maybe its restorative properties will even work on Quinn."

Maddy stands and picks up Ileana's journal. "Okay, then." She opens it up, scanning the pages for a minute, then taps the paper. "I know where we can start."

CHAPTER 31

MADELEINE

Maddy and Caleb head downstairs just as a pizza delivery guy walks into the library. Caleb walks over, pays him, then sets the box on the front counter. Nim frowns at him from behind her desk.

"There isn't supposed to be food in the main library," she states. Still, she steps over, flips up the lid, and takes a slice.

"I forgot I'd ordered it," Caleb says. He slides the box closer to Maddy. "Take a slice and let's head out."

She does so, taking big bites of the cheesy pizza as they head down the front steps, then climb into Caleb's car. A warm feeling nestles in her chest at how unconsciously he looks after her.

"Where to first?" he asks, pulling away from the curb.

Maddy studies the journal then directs him to the closest location within Mercy City. The two head to a small warehouse. The building is crowded with weeds and the windows are dark and dusty.

"There isn't even a lock." Caleb pushes the door open and bats away a spiderweb. The warehouse is small, hardly more than a storage building. They search through sagging boxes with water stains, crates piled with musty file folders, and a chest that holds nothing but a collection of empty jars.

"Well, this place was a bust," Maddy says. "If Ileana had hidden something here, she must have moved it."

Caleb picks a sticky spider web out of her ponytail. "Yeah, I think we need to move on to the next one. Is it in Mercy City?"

"Yeah, over on the other side by the train station," Maddy says. "Let's go."

They search Ileana's safe house by the train station, then two more scattered throughout the city. None of them hold much beyond half-empty boxes and dust, let alone the dream-catcher. Maddy starts to lose hope. She flips through Ileana's journal again, certain they've missed something. Then, her eyebrows pinch together.

Caleb catches her expression. "What is it?"

Two of the pages in the journal are stuck together. As carefully as she can, Maddy peels them apart. "I think this may be it." She tilts the journal, squinting at the illegible writing. "Ugh, I can't tell what it says."

"Perhaps I can help."

Maddy and Caleb whirl around to find Galina leaning against the doorway of the place they'd just searched.

"I'd really like to know how you're capable of sneaking up on me," Caleb says.

The witch doesn't pay him any mind as she strolls over. "Nim mentioned you two were off to search for the dream-catcher. I'd like to help. We need it to help Zariah, after all. If we do have a war breathing down our necks, we'll need her back to her normal power state."

Maddy holds the journal out to Galina. "We've searched all of the other safe locations mentioned. I think this may be the one where we'll find the dreamcatcher but I can't read her words. The pages were stuck together."

Caleb steps closer as Galina takes the journal and peers over her shoulder. "Do you have some sort of spell to fix it?"

The witch puts her palm over the hasty, messy words and closes her eyes. Her hand glows as she mutters. For a few moments, Maddy fears it may not work. Then, the letters begin to straighten into the elegant penmanship of the rest of the journal.

"That's incredible," Maddy says. "I can read it perfectly now."

Galina hands the journal back to her with a disapproving frown. Then, she glances at Caleb. "I thought I saw someone peeking into your car." The vampire takes off and the witch turns back to Maddy. "You know, you would be able to perform such a spell if you were to fully embrace your warlock powers."

Maddy shifts uncomfortably and looks at the ground. A caterpillar crawls by and she watches the fuzzy bug for a moment before it disappears under a cluster of leaves. "I know. It's just, well, it kind of terrifies me. You didn't see what happened during the duel with the necromancer. It brought out a different side of me. I think even Caleb may fear me when I'm like that. I don't want to hurt anyone."

"My girl, you cannot fear that which is a part of you," Galina says. She gives Maddy a kind, reassuring smile. "The best thing for you to do is embrace your powers, and learn to control them."

Maddy isn't so certain, but perhaps the witch is right. After all, her powers are a part of her now.

Caleb returns, scowling. "I didn't see anyone."

"Hmm. Strange," Galina says lightly. She heads toward the car. "We best be off now that we have the new location.

Caleb glances at Maddy with a question in his eyes but she waves a dismissive hand and mouths "girl talk".

From the back seat, Galina directs them to the nearby town

of Grove Hill. They drive through the quaint streets, then on the other side, they turn down a narrow lane. A small house sits at the end, surrounded on three sides by brown fields. The windows are dark and the place has clearly been unoccupied for some time. Caleb parks the car near the sagging front porch and eyes the house.

"The place looks like it may crumble on our heads any moment," he says. "We'll need to be careful."

The front door is locked but Caleb is able to ram it open. The three head inside. Dust covers the old, worn furniture and the floorboards creak and groan under their every step. Maddy jumps when a rat scurries across the counter in the kitchen to the left.

"Gross." She scans the kitchen for any more vermin.

"Let's split up," Caleb says. "It will make this faster."

Maddy agrees and drifts toward the living room, hoping the rats like to stick to the kitchen area. She listens to Caleb and Galina poke around the rest of the house. Maddy goes over to a bookcase, the shelves laden with books. She starts to pull on them, half-expecting one of them to be a lever that opens up a secret room but nothing extraordinary happens. Leaving the books, she peers under the coffee tables and searches behind the single couch. It's old, the fabric patterned with something that looks like it would have fit well in a grandparent's house. She starts lifting the cushions and traps a scream when a mouse scurries out of a nest of stuffing from the cushion.

Shuddering, Maddy drops the cushion, then pauses. Lifting it again, she notices the end of a feather sticking out. Heart pounding, she picks up the neighboring cushion. A smile spreads across her face. The dreamcatcher sits on the sagging springs of the couch.

"I found it," she calls.

Caleb and Galina join Maddy as she gently lifts the dream-catcher. "Well done, Maddy," Galina says.

Caleb gives her a one-armed hug. "Good job."

"Thanks." Maddy hands the dreamcatcher to Galina, who puts it carefully inside one of her many inside pockets of her clothes. "Let's get back to Veritas and see what we can do with this."

Maddy and the others head outside, then stop dead. They're no longer alone.

Malcolm stands in the driveway, a wicked sort of smirk on his face. Caroline stands behind him and she eyes Caleb with hate. She clearly remembers just who shoved her through that window back at their compound. Arranged to the side of Malcom are men and women, their eyes vacant and expressions somewhat slack.

"Revenants," Galina whispers.

"Shit." Maddy scans the area. At least they aren't in town where innocent people would be hurt.

Malcolm takes a step forward. "I know what you have," he says. He holds out his hand. "Hand it over and I'll let you leave in one piece."

In answer, Maddy draws an incredible amount of her warlock magic to the surface. She feels the weight of the wings as they appear on her back and the claws that grow on her hands ache for the touch of blood. Without a word, she dashes toward the revenants. Magic ripples in the air and she senses Galina's energy as the witch attacks the other side. Caleb, too, begins to tear into the revenants as Malcolm's army rushes forward.

The numbers of revenants are greater than they had been in the cemetery, but Maddy has more power coursing through her veins. She takes them down easily, claws ripping through flesh and magic sizzling to their bones. After another revenant falls at her feet, Maddy sets her sights on Malcolm. She dashes forward but halts when Caroline runs in front of him.

"Get out of the way." Maddy spits the words through clenched teeth. She has to pivot and take down another revenant before he can attack from behind. She wheels back around, but Caroline hasn't moved.

Caroline lifts her chin. "You stay away from him."

Maddy lets out a humorless laugh. "Don't you understand what he's done? He killed your sister."

No shock spreads across Caroline's face, only stark refusal to believe Maddy's claim. "He did nothing of the sort and you clearly don't know what you're talking about. Ileana was sick. She'd been diagnosed with multiple psychotic illnesses, primarily schizophrenia."

"I read what Ileana wrote about him." Maddy jerks her head toward Malcolm. "Even Quinn can back me up." Not that they knew where the spirit has gone, of course.

Caroline scoffs. "Quinn is nothing more than Ileana's imaginary friend, born of her mental problems. This Quinn you've met is Ileana. I thought she was dead, but apparently she faked her own death."

Caleb and Galina continue to fight the revenants around them. Maddy is quiet for a moment, letting her mind wander to the possibility that Caroline could be right? What if Quinn wasn't Quinn at all, but merely Ileana? She shakes her head. It doesn't make sense, not with everything that happened in Purgatory and afterwards.

"You're either lying or delusional," Maddy says.

"I'm not." Caroline's hands curl at her sides. "I only want to take care of my sister. My father captured her, you know? We want to save her from the darkness of the obsidian."

A cold sensation drops into the pit of Maddy's stomach. The Merrick's have Quinn? That would mean they may be able to steal the obsidian. She flicks a glance to Malcolm but the man is preoccupied with the fighting. Caleb is getting closer to him with each revenant that falls.

"Caroline, Malcolm is not who you think he is," Maddy says. If she can get Caroline to believe her, maybe she'll come to their side.

Caroline shakes her head. "He's family." The young woman suddenly dashes forward with a ferocity that surprises Maddy. There is a knife in her hand, the blade dark and sharp.

Maddy leaps out of the way, her wings fanning out to provide balance. Caroline spins on her heel and stares at Maddy with a wrathful glint that says she doesn't want Maddy to leave this place alive. There will be no convincing Caroline Merrick to join their side.

Hand slicing through the air, Maddy's claws narrowly miss Caroline. The Merrick heiress straightens, her bravado from moments earlier beginning to falter on her features as she realizes just what she's up against. Behind Caroline, Caleb finally reaches Malcolm and the two begin to fight. No words are exchanged, but the dark look that passes between them speaks volumes. They both intend on it being a fight to the death.

Maddy swings her gaze back to Caroline just in time to see the blade cutting toward her face. She ducks and fans out a wing. Her teeth bite down on a scream of pain as the blade pierces the webbing. It burns, but in her desperation to get distance back from Maddy, Caroline loses her grip on the blade. The knife flies in the opposite direction as Maddy flaps a wing and turns a searing glare toward Caroline.

The revenants continue to pour in from wherever Malcolm had stationed them. Caleb has gotten to their leader but how long can he last before he's overtaken by Malcolm's army? Galina continues to fight the revenants, but her magic doesn't shoot from her hands as swiftly. The use of her gifts is beginning to take its toll. Suddenly, two figures dash into the fray. Maddy's heart leaps.

Cora and Mason have found them.

Together, the pair of vampires rip into the revenants as they help Galina. Maddy looks to Caroline and the young woman's face pales, realizing that, perhaps, this won't be as easy as she had believed. Maddy starts to advance toward her when a terrible shriek breaks through the air. Caroline turns, eyes already widening.

Malcolm's body is bending backward as if a giant hand was pressing him toward the earth. His legs falter and he hits the ground. Caleb turns to glance at Maddy, clearly shocked and having nothing to do with whatever ails Malcolm.

Everyone stops. The revenants fall where they stand, collapsing to the ground. They no longer move or blink or breathe. Caroline lets out a choked gasp and runs over to where Malcolm is half-sitting on the ground. Her hands grasp his shoulders.

"What is it? What's wrong?" She peers around, eyes wide with fright.

Malcolm can barely speak without screaming. Pain flashes across every inch of his face. "Something is happening...to my source...of power."

Galina hurries to Maddy's side and together they inch closer to Malcolm and Caroline. Maddy leans over to the witch. "Do you know what's happening?"

"We know Malcolm doesn't exactly possess powers himself. He needs to channel them from a different source, such as a sorcerer. Wherever he keeps his source of power must be under attack."

Caroline shakes her head, her flawless hair swaying. "It can't be. There are powerful wards protecting it."

A fierce shudder wracks Malcolm's body and he curls

forward, groaning. "The wards are broken. I could feel someone cutting through them. They're doing something to the source of my power." His eyes clench shut and he screams again. When he speaks again, his voice is hushed and hoarse. "It's that damned angel. She's been after me ever since my tryst with the demon weapons and my alliance with the Grigori."

Maddy blinks and looks to Caleb. He mouths the word, "Gabby."

Once again, Maddy's friend has saved the day.

Cora and Mason join Maddy, Caleb, and Galina. Caroline stares at them, seething, as she cradles Malcolm's head in her lap. He doesn't try to get up, but he reaches into his pocket and presses something into Caroline's hand. Her fingers curl around the object as she stares at them with cold fury.

"This isn't over," Caroline snarls.

In the next instant, they disappear.

Maddy turns to Galina. "Do you still have the dreamcatcher?" The witch nods and Maddy breathes a sigh of relief. She turns to the spot where Caroline and Malcolm were a moment before. "I wonder if she will ever realize that Malcolm is the man who murdered both her father and her sister?"

"I don't know." Caleb crosses his arms, peering around at the fallen revenants. "I kind of wonder if she would even care if she did learn the truth."

The cell phone in Maddy's back pocket rings. She pulls it out and blinks at the name flashing on the screen. "Oh," she says, not quite sure what to do. "I forgot about the sleepover."

CHAPTER 32

MADELEINE

"Are you sure you don't mind?" Maddy slides into the front seat of Caleb's car and settles a bag on her lap. She turns to her house and gives her mom a wave.

"Maddy." Her name rolls off of Caleb's tongue with a chuckle. "You've already asked me a dozen times and again, no, I don't mind in the slightest. You need this. You deserve it." He backs out of her driveway then heads down the street. The occasional streetlight sets the damp road glowing and a brisk wind sends leaves whirling in front of them.

Maddy smiles. She's never been a prideful person but she has to admit to herself, a break is well-deserved. They got the cure and it's being studied in a lab where it will hopefully be molded into something that can help vampires. The dream-catcher is safe in Galina's hands. The witch is already beginning to perform spells to see just how it can be used to restore Zariah to her full power once again. Quinn is still missing, but thanks to Malcolm showing up, they now know she's in his clutches. That's another battle for another day.

"What are you going to do while I'm at Nicole's?"

Caleb turns on his right turn signal and heads down

another street. "I think I'm going to go and visit Stacy's mother. I was always close with their family and she's been in poor health."

"Aw, poor Stacy. I bet she needs this sleepover, too."

They arrive at Nicole's house in a few minutes. The windows glow with light and as they pull into the driveway, Maddy can already hear the blast of music. She unbuckles her seatbelt and Caleb reaches over and grabs her hand.

"I mean it, Maddy," he says. "You really do deserve this. I know it's difficult to put things on the back burner given everything we still need to face, but you need to find balance. Being a hunter or warlock or vampire isn't easy. Trust me, I saw Kenna struggle enough times to be a warrior and yet have a normal life. You need to enjoy the little things like sleepovers and trips to your favorite café with friends. Have fun, okay?"

Maddy smiles and squeezes his fingers. "I will." She leans forward and presses her lips to his.

Caleb cups Maddy's face, his fingers sliding up her jawline then cradling the back of her head as he deepens the kiss. Her pulse quickens and she suddenly wants to have a sleepover with *him*.

A wolf whistle reaches them. Maddy and Caleb break apart to find Nicole sticking her head out of the front door.

"Come on, Maddy," she calls. "Your man will survive without you for a night."

Maddy laughs. "I guess I'd better get going." She gives Caleb a final peck on the lips. "I love you."

"I love you, too." He curls a stray lock behind Maddy's ear. "Go and have fun."

She climbs out of the car, gives him a parting wave, then jogs up Nicole's front steps.

"Ready to get this party started?" Nicole asks, holding the door open for Maddy.

"Hell yes." Maddy grins as she steps inside. The living room is overflowing with pillows, blankets, and snacks.

Nicole drops into an armchair. "My parents are gone for the weekend so we have the house to ourselves."

Maddy spots Stacy in the corner and the young woman gives her a shy smile. Braelyn gives Maddy an enthusiastic wave as she stuffs a handful of popcorn into her mouth. A body suddenly slams into Maddy and she stumbles backward, laughing as she's trapped in a tight hug.

"Darbie!" Maddy hugs her friend back. "Oh my God, it's been ages."

Darbie, who has a wide smile splitting her face, steps back. "I know, right! It's so good to see you."

The two head over to plop down on a couch. "I want to hear all about Australia," Maddy says.

Nicole crosses her legs and leans forward. "I want to hear all about the hottie you were kissing."

Maddy glances at Stacy. Caleb has been her neighbor for years and she isn't certain how Stacy feels about him. What if she has a crush on him and resents Maddy? She finds Stacy smiling, though, and Maddy tells her friends about him. She doesn't mention that he's a vampire or anything about her life as a hunter. Instead, she says they study a lot together and he always gets her favorite coffee.

The girls listen to music and watch movies. Darbie talks about Australia and the boy she had to leave behind so she could go to school.

"Honestly, I think he was more torn up about it than I was," Darbie says. "He wanted to try the whole long-distance thing, but that never really works out."

Braelyn kicks up her feet, setting her fuzzy socks on the coffee table. "Yeah, you're here for a new adventure and that means scoping out what Mercy City has to offer." She winks at her friend. "Maybe you'll be lucky enough to find a catch like Maddy did with Caleb."

Maddy laughs. "I didn't catch him, he caught me, remember?" She'd already told them how they met and the fact she'd barreled right into him as she left the café.

Nicole gets up and heads into the kitchen. "I'm starving," she says. "I'll be right back."

The snacks hadn't lasted long with five teenage girls, who Maddy is certain could pack in more food than any man. Nicole comes back a few minutes later and shakes her head.

"Nothing," she says. "Anyone fancy going out and finding something to eat?"

Maddy gets to her feet. "Sounds good to me. You live a lot closer to restaurants than I do. We can walk."

The girls pull on shoes and jackets. "I saw a Chinese place not far from here on the drive over," Darbie says. "Anyone down for that?"

"I'm not much of a sushi person," Stacy says. "But I think crab Rangoon and dumplings are to die for."

Maddy zips up her jacket. "I think that sounds fantastic." Her chest is nearly swelling with happiness as the group heads outside. Caleb was right. She really needed this. It's amazing to feel normal and to, however briefly, forget about things like rebellious vampires and dark obsidian. She knows that come tomorrow she'll have to dive back into that stark reality. Galina may need her help with the dreamcatcher and Maddy wants to check in with Abigail on the status of the new cure. Tonight, however, she's going to stuff herself with lo mein and eggrolls, laugh until her stomach hurts, and enjoy something as simple as time spent with a few friends.

"Wow, it's getting chilly out," Braelyn says. They jog down the steps and start across the lawn, leaves crunching under their feet.

They reach the edge of the street and bright light flares over them. Maddy turns as a roaring sound fills the air. Just as she looks over her shoulder, a massive ball of fire crashes into the house. The explosion is deafening. The blast knocks her off her feet and she slams into the pavement. Screams fill the air as the house cracks apart. Maddy sits up with a groan, the heat of the burning house reaching her face. Her stomach lurches and her heart pounds in her chest. Frantic, she looks for her friends.

Nicole sits a few feet away, her mouth open and eyes wide in shock. Stacy sits beside her, hands clamped over her mouth.

"Darbie! Are you okay?"

Maddy's head whips toward Braelyn's voice. Darbie is pushing herself up with Braelyn's help.

"I think so," Darbie says. "Ow!" She touches her forehead. Blood smears under her fingertips.

Braelyn inspects it as Maddy gets to her feet. "It doesn't look too bad. Just a nasty scrape."

Maddy staggers toward the house. Where the hell had that fireball come from?

"M-Maddy, what are you doing?" Nicole's voice shakes. She doesn't get up.

The neighbors are rushing out of their houses, many of them already calling for ambulances and police.

Stacy is trying to choke back sobs. "We were just in there. We could have died. What was that?"

Several neighbors surround the girls, asking if anyone was hurt and what had happened. Maddy quickly learns she was the only one who had seen the fireball as it struck the house. Whatever it was, it was clear to her it was no accident. None of the others notice as she drifts toward the house.

The heat is nearly unbearable. Pieces of shattered glass and broken wood litter the front yard. One of the trees near the porch was nearly blown over, the roots on one side ripped from the ground. The alarm in the car in the driveway is blaring, it's staccato alarm shrieking in the chaos. In the distance, she can hear sirens as emergency teams already make their way toward the house.

Maddy looks over to her friends, her heart still in her throat. Stacy was right. They had almost all lost their lives, but why? Who would do this? She isn't certain what she's searching for but a feeling of dread slides into her stomach and leaves a sour taste in her mouth.

It's no secret to her that she's been making enemies. Malcolm and Caroline could have done this. Orion is a definite possibility. It could have even been some of the vampires who were against Caleb being king, or even Felix's rebellious faction of the Order.

Flames heat her face as Maddy approaches the house and then she stops as something catches her eye.

There, etched on the ground and glowing slightly, is the unmistakable loops of the infinity symbol.

CHAPTER 33
CALEB

C aleb rocks slightly on his heels, hands stuffed in his pockets, as he waits on Stacy's mother's front porch. After a couple of minutes, the door opens and a middle-aged woman in maroon scrubs patterned with pawprints answers.

"Yes?" She scans him, eyebrows slightly raised. She obviously hadn't been expecting company.

Caleb hadn't realized that Stacy's mother is in such poor health that she has a nurse visiting to take care of her.

"Hey, I'm Stacy's neighbor." He jerks his head toward the house next door. "I've been a friend of the family for a long time and thought I'd stop in for a visit."

"Are you Caleb?" the nurse, whose name tag says is named Mary, asks.

Caleb nods. "Yes, ma'am."

Mary opens the door wider and steps back so he can walk in. She offers him a friendly smile. "Stacy said you may be stopping by. I'm sure Katherine would enjoy the company. She hasn't been getting many visitors these days."

The house has a sharp lemony scent coupled with bleach that makes Caleb's nose twitch. Mary must also do some cleaning for Stacy's family because the wood floors are gleaming and every surface is sparkling. A reality show plays on the T.V. in the living room, but other than that, the house is eerily quiet.

"She's down the hall in her room," Mary says. "I'm afraid she doesn't really get out much anymore. She's awake, she's just eaten her dinner." She makes her way over to the kitchen table where an array of medications and a weekly pill box sit. The nurse had been in the middle of getting Katherine's medications organized for the coming week. "If you need anything, just holler."

Caleb makes his way down the hall, eyeing the framed photos as he passes. Many of them are of the various stages of Stacy's life, from photos of a chubby-cheeked baby to a more recent photo of Stacy and her mom sitting on the back deck, the summer sun crowning their hair and grins on their faces. He reaches the last door on the hall and knocks softly before easing it open.

"Katherine?" he says as he enters. "It's Caleb."

The woman sitting up in bed is not the one he remembers. Her face is haggard and pale, and her hair is cut short, likely so it is easier to care for. A thick quilt covers her lap.

"Caleb." Katherine's eyes shine as he approaches. "I was wondering if you'd made it out of the dark."

Caleb clears his throat, uncertain of what she's speaking about. Does she know about the obsidian, somehow? "How are you doing?" He eases into a chair beside the bed. "I'm sorry I haven't been around as much as I'd promised. I've had a lot of things come up lately." A pang of guilt hits his chest. Katherine had been Kenna's best friend, and he should have visited more often. He'd had no idea she was deteriorating so quickly.

"Fighting monsters, fang and claw." Katherine's voice takes on a sing-song tone.

"Uh, yeah." Caleb shifts uncomfortably. "Have you been doing okay?" He regrets the question immediately. Obviously, Katherine isn't doing well at all.

The woman doesn't answer him but shoves off the covers and swings her legs over the side of the bed. She's wearing a pale yellow nightgown and thick socks.

Caleb reaches toward her. "Are you supposed to be getting up?" He knows her mind is unwell, but he isn't certain just how much of a toll her illness is taking physically.

Katherine remains silent as she walks over to her dresser, opens the top drawer, and rifles through it. "I knew you would come. You had to, for this." She ambles back toward him and hands him a photograph.

Caleb takes the photo and studies it. He's never seen the tomb in the photo before and he looks up at Katherine with confusion. "What is this?"

"The answer." Katherine stares at him with an almost manic glaze in her eyes. "Or the question. Both, or neither."

He glances toward the door, regretting his decision to visit. "I'm sorry," he says. "But I don't understand."

"Can't you see? Can't you see?" Katherine taps the photo so hard it nearly falls from Caleb's hand. "She isn't dead. She lives."

Caleb angles his head to the side. "Who lives?"

"Kenna DeVoe is not dead." Katherine's stare sears onto Caleb's face. "She lives."

It's as if someone has dumped a bucket of ice over him. He breathes in sharply, freezing as his body goes cold. "No," he says. "She's not alive, Katherine." Has her mind gone so far that she doesn't remember her best friend's death? He reaches forward and takes her hand. Her fingers are ice cold. "Kenna died, remember?"

Katherine rips her hand from Caleb's grasp. "No! She lives."

She leans forward and clenches her fingers almost painfully onto Caleb's shoulders. She gives him a shake. "Do not believe the lies. Look! The answer and the question." She angles her face toward the photo.

Caleb studies the picture of the tomb again and his vampire eyes pick out details that he'd overlooked at first. The tomb is ancient, yet well-preserved. His heart jumps when he sees the mark of the infinity symbol scratched onto the stone surface.

Sirens wail in the background and he idly wonders if there was an accident. Still, he can't tear his gaze away from the photo. His mind races. What on earth could this mean? Could Kenna truly be alive, or is it merely the ramblings of a mentally ill woman?

Katherine suddenly grasps his face and tilts it up towards hers. "You will see," she whispers. "You will see." Then, she crawls back into bed and settles against the pillows. "It's coming for us all."

Caleb swallows. "What's coming for us?"

Stacy's mother doesn't answer him, however. She closes her eyes and rolls to the side, ending their visit. Caleb stares at the photo again and then his phone vibrates. He pulls it out, seeing Maddy is calling him. He quickly leaves Katherine's room and closes the door softly behind him, then pockets the photo before answering his phone.

"Hey, Maddy, what's up?"

"I need you." Maddy's voice shakes on the other end. "I need you now."

Caleb doesn't question her as he hurries down the hall. "I'm on my way." He barely remembers to give the nurse a goodbye wave as he rushes out the front door. Maddy isn't the kind of person who would call him on her girl's night unless it was important. The way her voice had been quaking is a huge red flag.

Something has happened, he could feel it in the pit of his stomach.

More than a few people honk angrily at him as he speeds down the streets of Creed. He rushes through one stop sign, eyes scanning for any sign of police, but he doesn't see any. As he pulls onto Nicole's street, he realizes most of them are already at the house...or what's left of it.

His heart flies to his throat as he jerks to a stop at the edge of the street. He slams his door shut and hurries toward Maddy. Behind her, her group of friends are talking to police while one girl is being checked out in the back of an ambulance. Maddy turns to face him just as he reaches her.

Throwing his arms around her, he holds her tight to his chest as he stares, wide-eyed, at the house that has been blown apart.

"God, Maddy." He eases her back, studying her stricken face. "Are you okay?"

She nods, though her heart sounds like it's about to beat right out of her chest. "I'm fine. Darbie got a bit of a scrape, but we'd just left the house when this massive fireball shot from the sky and blew up the house."

Caleb cups the back of Maddy's neck and presses his forehead to hers. Dammit. He'd almost lost her. Again.

"What happened?" he asks.

Maddy glances over her shoulder. "None of the others saw the fireball and I didn't see any sign of who had cast it down. I did find something, though." She tilts her head to peer up at him. "I went closer to the house to see if I could discover any hints of who may have attacked us or why. Caleb, I found the infinity symbol on the ground in front of Nicole's house."

Caleb's breath catches. "You're sure?"

"Yes, absolutely," Maddy says. "There was no mistaking it.

The symbol disappeared before anyone else had the chance to see it."

Caleb peers toward the house and rubs the back of his neck.

"What's the matter?" Maddy tugs on his shirt. "Caleb?"

He swings his gaze back to Maddy. "I visited Stacy's mother. Maddy, she told me Kenna is still alive. I know her mom is sick and could be rambling, but..." He pulls the photo of the tomb out of his pocket and points out the infinity symbol. "This can't be a coincidence."

Maddy studies it, her wide-eyed gaze rising to meet his. "Whose tomb is it?"

He shakes his head. "I have no idea. But...Maddy, what if Kenna really is alive?" His chest tightens at the thought.

She grabs his hand and laces their fingers together. "We'll find out the truth, Caleb. Together."

Caleb pulls Maddy in for another hug, thankful she's unharmed. And hoping that this isn't going to be the ultimate test of their relationship.

As he holds her tightly, he stares at the burning pile that was once a home. If Kenna's alive, what would she think of the cure?

Or his plans to make vampires stronger...

Ready for the next installment in the Keepers of the Chalice series? Check out VAMPIRE UNDEFEATED!
https://mybook.to/VampireUndefeated

VAMPIRE UNDEFEATED

To cure or not to cure, that is the question.

Maddy and Caleb have fallen for the enemy—each other. But their opposing allegiances are determined to tear them apart.

Caleb is the vampire king. He knows strengthening vampires will ensure they can fight for their survival. Except it may also make them invincible... Maddy is a hunter. Creating a cure will protect humans from violent, blood-thirsty vampires seeking to dominate the world. She just needs to stop the Order from using it to exterminate vampires altogether.

There is no right or wrong. Enemies are everywhere. And if they lose, humanity will pay the price. Maddy and Caleb are about to find out—is their love an abomination? Or are they the key to unite them all?

Click below to devour the next thrilling instalment of Keepers of the Chalice, Vampire Undefeated, today!

GRAB YOUR COPY HERE
https://mybook.to/VampireUndefeated

HAVE YOU READ THE KEEPER CHRONICLES PREQUEL?

As an exclusive for my subscribers,
you can download it for free!!

When Sierra sneaks out, determined to escape her over-protective family, she stumbles across a young man covered in blood. His last words are a plea. *Find the Grail Keepers. Warn them.*

Ryder is the young cop who was last seen with the murdered victim. Sierra doesn't trust him, no matter how drawn she is to him. Except it turns out they're both looking for the same thing—the Holy Grail.

They're quickly drawn into a dangerous hunt involving cryptic clues, a mysterious stone, and a Grail that hasn't been seen for centuries. One that leads to more questions than answers. Can Sierra trust her impulsive emotions? Should she believe Ryder's words or the truth she sees in his eyes? And ultimately, should she follow her heart?

Especially when every decision will decide the fate of countless lives.

CLICK HERE TO DOWNLOAD FOR FREE!
https://BookHip.com/TTBMTTV

THE KEEPERS-VERSE IS ALWAYS GROWING!

The Keeper Chronicles will continue to grow, with each new addition adding to its epicness. Each interlinked series will have you falling for unforgettable characters, being swept away by captivating romance and thrilling adventure, and re-visiting old friends (you'll discover all your favorites popping up when you least expect it!).

Check out what's coming your way!

Keepers of the Light
Angels and demons have battled for millennia. Their inevitable war has begun.
Check out Book 1, Hidden Angel, HERE.
http://mybook.to/HiddenAngel

Keepers of the Grail
Seven Gates of Hell. Seven deadly sins.
One impossible choice.
Check out Book 1, Gates of Demons, HERE.
http://mybook.to/GatesofDemons

ALSO BY TAMAR SLOAN

A supernatural war only they can stop.

DESTINED DEMIGODS
Love that defies the gods.
Powers that define destiny.

ELEMENTAL GAMES
Elemental powers. Deadly Games.
No escape.

THE SOVEREIGN CODE
Humans saved bees from extinction...and created the deadliest threat we've seen yet.

THE THAW CHRONICLES
Only the chosen shall breed.

ZODIAC GUARDIANS
Twelve teens. One task.
Save the Universe.

About the Author

Tamar hasn't decided whether she's primarily a psychologist who loves writing, or a writer with a lifelong drive to make a difference. She must have been someone pretty awesome in a previous life (past life regression indicates a Care Bear), because she gets to do both. She divides her time between helping families and writing emotion driven YA stories set in amazing imaginary worlds that surprise even her.

The driving force for all of Tamar's writing is sharing and connecting. In truth, connecting with others is why she writes. She loves to hear from readers. Find her on all the usual social media channels or her website, www.tamarsloan.com where can download one of her books for free.

(Seriously, I LOVE hearing from you guys!)